DEAD RECKONING

ALSO BY S.L. MENEAR

The Jettine Jorgensen Mystery Series

Dead Silent

Dropped Dead

Dead Ends

Dead Reckoning

The Samantha Starr Thriller Series

Flight to Redemption

Flight to Destiny

Triple Threat

Stranded

Vanished

Life, Love, & Laughter: 50 Short Stories

DEAD RECKONING

A JETTINE JORGENSEN MYSTERY
BOOK 4

S. L. MENEAR

All rights reserved. No part of this publication may be reproduced, stored in a retrieval system, or transmitted in any form or by any means (electronic, mechanical, photocopying, recording, or otherwise) without prior written permission from the publisher and copyright owner.

Disclaimer for Fictional Works

This is a work of fiction. Names, characters, places, and incidents are products of the author's imagination or are used fictitiously. Any resemblance to actual persons, living or dead, businesses, events, or locales is entirely coincidental.

AI Use Restriction

Without limiting the author's and publisher's exclusive rights under copyright, any use of this publication for training generative artificial intelligence (AI) technologies is prohibited. Unauthorized use for this purpose may result in legal action.

Piracy Warning

The scanning, uploading, or distribution of this book without permission is illegal and punishable by law. Please purchase only authorized editions and avoid participating in or encouraging piracy. Your support of the author's rights helps protect their work.

Copyright © 2025 by S.L. Menear. All rights reserved.

March 2025
ISBN: 978-1-64457-789-9

ePublishing Works!
644 Shrewsbury Commons Ave, Ste 249
Shrewsbury, PA 17361, USA
www.epublishingworks.com
Phone: 866-846-5123

*For Dorothy Metz Littlefield, mother and author extraordinaire.
My books would not be possible without her constant encouragement.*

R.I.P. Kevin (Kip) Edward Peterson

ONE

*They climb high and hide
while a hungry panther prowls,
eager for a kill.*

I agreed to replace my uncle, Hunter Vann, on a dual cross-country flight with a teenage student pilot who had a crush on him. My Harley rumbled to a stop inside the hangar, and I strolled out to the 1940 school-bus yellow airplane parked nearby.

He introduced us. "Kerri Lyons, meet my niece, Jett Jorgensen."

A blond beauty who radiated positive energy, Kerri offered me her perfectly manicured hand with pink nails and smiled. "Nice to meet you, and I love your long hair."

"Thank you." I smoothed my waist-length black hair. "Your pink top is pretty."

"Okay, girls." Hunter chuckled. "Jett's been flight instructing part-time for nine years. She was a Navy intelligence officer and now works as a private investigator." He thumbed at the plane. "I need a word with Jett while you finish the preflight inspection."

He took me aside. "Your P.I. mentor called while you were on your way here. Muffy Murdoch went missing from a nightclub last night. Her parents filed a police report, but they want you and Darcy to find her."

"I remember Muffy from my charity ball—a spunky blonde in her mid-twenties. Should I go now?"

"Not yet. Darcy said it might be nothing. She'll look into it while you help my student complete her 'old-school' cross-country flight."

Before we left, Hunter slipped a portable radio into the plane's front side pocket. "Just in case. You girls be careful, and I'll see you back here late this afternoon."

The engine roared, and the vintage airplane rattled as we flew southwest toward our first stop with Kerri seated behind me in the same tandem seat from which she soloed. Pilots were meant to fly alone from the back seat in the J-3 Cub to comply with aircraft weight and balance requirements.

My student landed the Piper Cub at our first stop, and we refueled. With no radios or navigation aids, not even GPS, the next leg of her dual cross-country flight would be even more challenging. We took off and navigated at 3,500 feet using a compass and dead reckoning, which meant we had a known starting point and factored in airspeed, wind, landmarks, and the airplane's heading—a skill used long ago.

It was a bright, clear day, and I had a panoramic view of South Florida through the windshield and side windows. We used battery-powered intercom headsets to overcome the loud engine. I keyed the mike and said, "Pay close attention to your heading, Kerri."

"The wind must be stronger than they said in the weather briefing." She made a small course correction using the control stick and rudder pedals.

Normally, I wouldn't fly over the open Everglades in a single-engine airplane, but no landmarks made that portion of the flight more challenging for my student. I allowed her to drift off course for learning purposes.

Big mistake.

A strong vibration shook the plane, followed by a loud bang. Black smoke billowed out of the engine compartment, oil splattered the windshield, and the propeller seized.

Kerri's yell blasted into my headset, "The engine's blown! What should I do?"

Except for the whisper of air rushing past, the cockpit was dead silent.

Adrenaline supercharged me as I pulled off my headset and glanced over my shoulder. "Remember your training. Check left and right, then make a gentle turn while maintaining best glide speed, and search for a place to land."

Seated behind me, she yanked off her headset, strands of long blond hair pulling out of her ponytail. Her lips quivered, and her voice shot up two octaves. "A place to land? There's nothing down there but a scary swamp with gators and snakes." She gripped the stick, her knuckles white but her gaze determined.

"Look out the side windows for a road or a clearing." I kept my voice steady.

I switched on the portable radio to call in a mayday, but before I could select the emergency frequency, we collided with a flock of pelicans. One smashed through the windshield, and its bloody carcass slammed into my chest, knocking the wind out of me. A sharp shard of Plexiglas pierced my left shoulder. I yanked it out and dropped it on the floor as blood soaked my blue T-shirt, and the coppery scent filled my nostrils.

Wispy white fragments swirled around the cockpit in a disorienting blizzard, and a second pelican smashed into my right hand, jarring the handheld radio loose and dragging it over my shoulder to the floor behind my seat. The big bundle of bloody feathers flopped around between Kerri's feet.

She screamed, opened the long, right-side door window, tossed out the bird, and realized her mistake. "Jett, I accidentally threw out the radio!"

"That's okay. Calm down." Wind whipped my long hair as I tossed the first pelican out the open window and yelled, "I've got the airplane." I took over the controls, which felt mushy. Looking out, I spotted damage to the leading edges of both wings.

"Kerri, pull your belts tight. The collision damage shortened our glide capability. We're going down fast."

I pulled out my cell phone and called for help. "No signal." Turning right, I spied a narrow opening in the trees and brush. "A white rectangle. Do you see it?"

"Looks super short," she cried. "Think we can make it?"

"It's maybe two hundred feet long, but the approach end is clear, and we're in a Cub." I scanned the area on the way down, searching for a road, but none existed. Alarm bells rang in my head as I realized the only access to that tiny strip was by air or water.

We descended through 500 feet in what had become a sluggish glider. A strong wind whistled through the cockpit, but at least I could see straight ahead after the pelicans destroyed the oil-splattered windshield. I nudged my sunglasses back up in place.

Her voice quavered, "Are we going to crash?"

"No, I've got this." I counted on the low landing speed as I willed the Cub to stretch its glide.

My main concern was who we might encounter while waiting to be rescued. As we neared what looked like an oversized helipad, I spotted a pier and a narrow path leading to the landing site. Scents of swampy water and green plants filled the cockpit.

Kerri kept calm, despite being only seventeen, and reacted like a pro. "I'm ready."

"Good. Brace yourself." My heart raced as I leveled off at a faster-than-normal speed above the marsh, our main wheels skimming the brush.

We were sixty feet from the edge of the hard surface. Would we make it?

As our wheels whizzed past the tall swamp grass, a stout bush speared the aft left side, ripping open the plane's fabric-covered fuselage.

Kerri gasped as we abruptly dropped onto the helipad, our landing cushioned by hot air rising from the crushed coral surface. We bounced once, I eased the brakes on, and we slid to a turning stop one foot from the end.

I glanced back at my wide-eyed student. "Reach back and switch on the Emergency Locator Transmitter."

She unbuckled her seat harness, turned, and cried, "It's gone!"

"What do you mean, gone?"

She pointed at a tear in the fabric on the left side where the ELT had been.

"Okay, is the emergency bag still back there?"

"Yep."

"Get it, and don't forget your handbag, rain jacket, and water bottle." I hopped out, slung my handbag over my shoulder, grabbed my water jug and jacket, and checked the small of my back where my Glock 26 was holstered under my shirt. The magazine only held six 9mm rounds, but I had another full magazine in my purse. I also had an eight-inch hunting knife in a sheath hooked to my belt.

Kerri joined me, stared at my shoulder, and shrieked, "You're bleeding."

"Oh, right, just a puncture wound. Hand me the first aid kit." I ripped my T-shirt a little at the collar to get a better view. Left over adrenaline masked the pain.

She helped me apply antibiotic ointment, a butterfly bandage, and tape gauze over it.

"Thanks. That should take care of it." I dropped the kit into the bag and zipped it shut.

Except for a few distant splashes, the jungle was eerily quiet.

She glanced around us, wide-eyed. "We're surrounded by dense plants and swamp. Think big snakes and gators will attack us?"

"Don't worry, I'm armed." I squeezed her shoulder. "I'll protect us.

I saw combat in the Navy." Scanning the brush, I said, "Keep a sharp lookout for panthers and black bears. Pythons and anacondas are eating all the prey and leaving the native wildlife desperate for food." I didn't mention I was just as worried about two-legged predators.

"Think we should push the airplane off this little airstrip?" Kerri asked.

"No, we want Search and Rescue to spot it easily."

"But nobody knows we crashed."

"We'll find a way to send a signal." I turned back to the Cub. "We should close the windows and door and plug the holes in the windshield and side with palm fronds so nothing unpleasant crawls in there."

Kerri helped me secure the plane, and then a loud engine echoed in the swamp.

She scanned the sky. "Sounds like an airplane, but I don't see it."

I grabbed her arm. "Don't wanna scare you, but this helipad probably belongs to drug smugglers, and that engine noise could be from their airboat."

"Where can we hide?" she asked, her voice rising in pitch.

After shoving our water bottles, purses, and jackets inside, I slung the emergency bag over my good shoulder. "Grab two long palm fronds and follow me. Hurry!"

It sounded like the airboat was approaching from the south side of the east-west airstrip where the dock was, so I led Kerri north. The crushed coral surface didn't show footprints. We laid a palm frond on the ground beyond the edge and walked over it to avoid leaving a trail as we carefully pushed through the jungle growth. We laid the second frond in front of us and picked up the first one, leapfrogging into the dense brush, careful not to break any branches or leave footprints on the soft ground beneath our palm leaves.

"Keep your head on a swivel. Predators might be out here." I drew my Glock.

We paused every few minutes and listened. It wasn't long before the airboat's engine shut down.

"The farther we go, the less likely they'll hear us." I urged her forward.

She glanced over her shoulder and whispered, "What if they came to rescue us?"

"Not a chance."

We kept moving through thick foliage and around tall cypress trees. I was fortunate my late mother, a Cherokee Shaman, had taught me much about plants and wildlife. That knowledge helped us avoid danger.

I stopped and whispered, "See that tree in front of us?" Mosquitoes buzzed around me.

Kerri slapped an insect on her arm and pointed. "That one?"

"It's a manchineel, also known as the tree of death. It's the most poisonous tree in the world. The sap oozing out of the trunk can cause nasty blisters, blindness if you get it in your eyes, and death if ingested. And if you eat the green, apple-like fruit on the branches, it'll kill you."

"Got it—don't touch anything on that tree."

We gave the manchineel a wide berth and continued away from the helipad. A half hour had passed, and I wondered what the occupants of the airboat were doing.

Ten minutes later, deep voices filtered through the marshy jungle, and we froze.

One yelled from a distance, "Come out and we won't hurt you."

Yeah, right.

I whispered, "Climb that cypress tree and hide in the upper branches. I'll give you a boost up." It helped that I was five-nine.

Kerri was only five-four, but she was an excellent climber. We found a good spot about thirty feet up where several branches spread from the main trunk, and we nestled in and waited. I pulled out my semi-automatic pistol and rechecked that it was cocked with a round in the chamber.

She peeked around the trunk. "They're getting closer. I can see the brush moving." Her hand trembled when she gripped my arm. "Will they kill us?"

"I'll protect you." I gripped my Glock and prayed I wouldn't need it.

A deep growl rumbled through the trees.

Kerri poked me and whispered, "Was that a panther?"

"Sounded like it." I looked down, searching for movement nearby. "Let's hope it goes after those men and not us."

TWO

"Where are they?" a hard-looking man said as he swung a machete at a branch blocking his way. "The plane over there looks empty."

"Maybe somebody already rescued them," the other man with a bushy mustache said.

"We didn't see anyone come for them on the remote camera feed." He strode to the Cub. "Need to switch off the ELT."

"What's an ELT?"

"Emergency Locator Transmitter. It sends out a signal so rescuers can locate the aircraft."

"Is it on the instrument panel?"

"No, it's supposed to be in the back so it'll survive a crash." He opened the door and looked inside the plane. "There's a big hole full of palm fronds where it probably was. If they took it with them, rescuers will come soon. We'd better find them fast and switch it off."

"Let's hide the plane first."

The guy with the machete said, "Okay, but hiding it won't help if those women rat us out."

The two men shoved the Cub into the brush and covered it with palm fronds.

One checked the remote video feed on his phone. "They went that way."

"They won't last long in this heat with only two bottles of water."

"Their duffel probably has survival stuff like flares, a first aid kit, and space blankets." He peered through the brush. "If they had GPS and a radio, they'd already be rescued."

"Why not leave them to feed the pythons?" His partner chuckled. "They'll never survive the night. If big snakes don't get them, something with teeth will."

"They looked hot on the video feed. Ron would pay major bucks for them. He traffics in high-end babes, mostly aspiring models. We're talking fifty K for the twenty-something brunette and double that for the blond teenager."

His partner glanced at his watch. "That's reason enough to keep searching, but if we don't find them in the next two hours, I want out of here. Every time I think about that twenty-footer that almost killed me last week—" He swatted a mosquito.

"Yeah, that Burmese python was a monster." The boat pilot pulled out a big knife. "Good thing I had my KA-BAR."

"Another minute and it would've killed me. Couldn't believe how fast it moved. Never saw it until it wrapped around me."

"Yeah, those girls won't stand a chance against the swamp monsters. We'll be doing them a favor taking them." He slashed another branch with his machete.

His partner broke off a low branch on a nearby tree and used it to swat away spider webs. Sap oozed from the broken end onto his hand. Seconds later, he dropped the branch and screamed, "My hand—feels like it's on fire!" His swollen hand was bright red and covered with blisters.

The boat pilot looked at him and then picked up the branch. "There's sap leaking out. You must be allergic."

"Getting dizzy." The guy with the injured hand collapsed onto the mushy ground.

"My hand's burning too." Machete guy reached down and pulled his friend up. "Forget the girls for now." He put an arm around his partner to steady him, and they stumbled back toward the dock.

Minutes Earlier

I nudged Kerri's arm, touched a finger to my lips, and pointed down. The men were approaching our tree.

Her eyes widened when she spotted them.

The men discussed kidnapping and selling us, and Kerri gripped my arm.

I aimed my Glock at the one wielding a machete and prayed they wouldn't look up.

Suddenly, the other guy screamed, dropped the branch he was holding, and yelled something about his hand. We watched them leave abruptly.

When they were out of earshot, I whispered, "Must've grabbed a branch from the manchineel tree. Too bad for them, but lucky for us."

"Are they going to die?" Kerri asked, sounding relieved they were gone.

"Not unless they lick the sap off their hands." I watched the twitching shrubbery as they blundered through it. "Good thing the pain made them leave."

"Think they'll come back?" Her lips quivered.

"Probably, but if we hear the airboat start up, that means they're leaving for now." I holstered my weapon.

A deep growl rumbled through the swamp. This time it sounded farther away.

"Ooh, think a panther is stalking those men?" Kerri scanned the jungle.

"Better them than us." I tilted my head. "I don't hear any screaming."

We waited in silence several minutes. No sounds of the men. Just insects buzzing.

She nudged me. "Waiting up here—it's scary. Can we talk about something fun?"

"Sure. What would you like to discuss?"

She looked at me. "Are you really Hunter's niece?"

"Yep, my mother was his older sister by eight years."

"So, you're a full-blood Cherokee too?"

"Half. My dad's family was from Denmark. That's where I got my blue eyes."

"Oh, right, Hunter's eyes are gold, but you have his black hair." She sighed. "He's sooo fine." She pursed her lips. "He passed me to you because he knows I have a thing for him, doesn't he?"

I smiled. "Yeah, but he also thought you'd enjoy flying with a female instructor."

"Nah, he's worried because I have a crush on him." She giggled.

"Kerri, my uncle is forty years old—probably older than your father."

She frowned. "Really? He looks a lot younger. My parents are thirty-eight."

"They must've been young when they had you."

"Yeah, they were in college. Their parents helped them raise me so they could stay in school and become doctors. My parents and grandparents are wonderful."

"Sounds like it. Hunter is the only close family I have left since my parents died."

"Sorry, Jett." She paused. "Do you have a boyfriend?"

"I did until last month. He left me to train for the FBI in Quantico."

"Won't he be back after he finishes the course?"

"Training takes five months. He'll return in late December for a few days. Then he'll be stationed at a remote FBI field office where senior agents don't want to work."

"That's a downer. Sorry, Jett."

I sighed. "He was the love of my life—left in August and not a word since."

"Not even a text or an email?" she asked.

"Nope. He totally ghosted me." I glanced at her. "Do you have a boyfriend?"

Kerri's expression turned dreamy-eyed. "There's this really hot guy—he's the field-goal kicker for the football team, but he's a senior, and I'm only a junior, so he doesn't know I exist."

"Do something to draw his attention."

"I'm the top of the pyramid on the cheerleading squad, but he never notices me."

The roar of the airboat's radial aircraft engine filled the jungle.

"Sounds like the smugglers are leaving." I listened as the engine noise became more and more distant. "Let's sneak back to the airstrip. I want to see if they did anything to our Cub. I doubt they left it in plain sight." I scanned the brush and then climbed down so I could help Kerri.

We followed the men's tracks back to where we left the plane. On the way there, I wondered how the bad guys knew about us so quickly. *Must have remote cameras.* Peering through the foliage, I scanned the helipad.

No Piper Cub.

Kerri gasped. "Where's our plane?"

"They must've hidden it, but first, we need to find the camera that sent our images to the bad guys. Look for one mounted on a tree—probably with a wide-angle lens near one end of the hard surface."

We searched the nearest end and got lucky.

"There it is!" Kerri led me to it.

The camera was in a cypress tree and aimed at the helipad. I climbed up, broke off the antenna, snatched the camera out of the mount, and smashed it on the hard coral.

"Think there's another one at the other end?" She glanced west.

"Maybe. We'll check after we find our airplane."

I hoped they hadn't chopped it up, and I looked for brush high enough to hide it.

"Over there." I pointed. "See the yellow peeking through the leaves."

We found the Cub unharmed, nestled under trees and a pile of palm fronds.

After pulling off all the branches, I said, "You lift the tailwheel and steer while I push on the prop and shove it back to the landing strip so Search and Rescue can spot us."

The little fabric-covered plane wasn't heavy, especially the tail. Kerri lifted the tailwheel, and I shoved hard on the prop hub. We struggled to overcome inertia, but once we got it moving, it was easy to push it back onto the crushed coral. We left it halfway from the west end on the centerline.

I peered west. "I guess we'd better check the other end for another spy camera."

We were well past the Cub when I sensed danger. "Stop. Do you hear anything in the brush?"

She paused and stared at the foliage. "Nope, nothing. Why?"

"I have a bad feeling." Primeval alarm bells rang in my head as I turned and studied the jungle on the other side of the hard surface. No movement, but now my spine tingled. What was I missing?

A huge snake burst from the brush behind me and sank its fangs into my wounded left shoulder. Startled, the sudden pain made me scream.

The reptile wrapped around me in seconds, coiling and tightening. Terror gripped me as I struggled to breathe.

THREE

It happened so fast. I tried to pull the monster off, but it was too strong, and my Glock was out of reach, covered by the giant green anaconda.

I gasped. "Kerri, quick, get the pistol from my back holster!"

She froze as the deadly creature encircled me. Its heavy weight made me fall, and we thrashed around in a life and death struggle. I kept my right arm free and reached for my hunting knife as the reptile coiled farther around me. I retrieved the blade just in time.

The curved fangs remained painfully clamped to my left shoulder.

I screamed, "Kerri, hurry, can't breathe!"

She snapped out of her trance and reached behind me. "Can't get the gun—the snake's in the way."

With less than a minute to live, I stabbed the snake again and again with no effect. My strength waned as I reached across and tried cutting through its neck. "Help me!"

She put her hand over mine and carved like a maniac. I took shallow breaths so I wouldn't trigger the anaconda to tighten its hold, but it was too late. My vision blurred.

Kerri sliced through its neck, and the reptile's severed body released its hold on me.

I blacked out momentarily inside the coiled heap, and then I was vaguely aware of her dragging me across the helipad, away from the quivering carcass. Its head was still clamped to my bleeding shoulder.

I gasped and took in a lungful of air. "Pry its jaws open and pull the head off me."

She steeled herself, grasped its jaws, and pried them apart. "Okay, pulling it off now."

The sharp fangs sliced through my flesh on the way out. Rivulets of blood ran down the left side of my chest. "Thank you. I think it missed any major vessels or arteries."

She unzipped the emergency bag and looked in the first aid kit. "This antibiotic ointment has a numbing agent. I'll put some on the puncture wounds after I clean them."

"While you do that, I'll sheathe my knife and check my pistol." My hand still clutched the knife in a death grip. I had to massage it with my other hand to relax the muscles and pry my fingers open. I concentrated on taking slow, deep breaths while she tended my wounds.

She rinsed my lacerations with bottled water before applying the ointment and bandages. When she finished, she glanced over at the twitching snake. "It's still moving. You sure it's dead?"

"Yep," I said, still out of breath. "Hard to live without a head." I studied the reptile. "Looks like a sixteen-footer. It'll make lots of meals for that hungry panther, and then maybe he'll leave us alone." I stood, my legs a bit wobbly, and looked around. "Let's find that other camera." My shoulder throbbed, but my vision had cleared.

Slowly recovering from the violent attack, I stayed on the centerline so we wouldn't be close to the thick foliage and another possible ambush. Near the end of the hard surface, I spotted a camera mounted high on a tree. "Think you can get that one?"

"Yeah, but keep your pistol ready in case something tries to get me." Kerri climbed up and destroyed the entire apparatus. She looked at her hands. "Darn, broke a nail." Before coming down, she scanned the area, searching for predators. "I don't see anything moving."

"Good, let's go back to the airplane." I paused and listened for predators before we returned to the Cub. "That remote camera probably sent everything it recorded back to the smugglers. That means they know about the snake attack and that I'm armed."

She hurried and stood beside the yellow airplane. "Think they'll come back for us?"

I watched the sun sink toward the western horizon. "If we aren't rescued today, they'll return tomorrow morning and hunt us."

"What can we do?" Her eyes radiated fear.

"The bad guys already know we're here, so it doesn't matter if we make a signal fire." I glanced at my dive watch. "The thing is, nobody will look for us until we fail to return. They'll wait maybe an hour after the arrival time we filed in our flight plan, which was four o'clock."

"If they don't start looking until after five, that doesn't leave much daylight." Kerri bit her lower lip and scanned the jungle.

"We'll make a big brush pile and save it until we spot an airplane or helicopter. The Cub has plenty of fuel in its tanks to help us make a bonfire."

The wind shifted from the west to the southeast. We didn't want to risk a spark igniting the plane's fabric-covered wings and fuselage, so we set to work piling dry brush in a heap near the west end of the strip downwind of the Cub.

When we finished, Kerri looked up. "Think that distant airliner will see the fire and call it in if we light it now?"

"It's worth a try."

I dumped the contents of my leather purse into the emergency bag so I could fill my handbag with aircraft fuel from the sump drain. After pouring gas all over the brush pile, I kept enough for a six-foot liquid fuse. My trusty butane lighter ignited it, and the flames followed the trail to our bonfire.

"I was hoping it would make thicker smoke," I said, gazing at the blaze.

"Cool lighter. I guess you're a smoker."

"No, I puff on a fine cigar occasionally with Hunter, but I never inhale."

Kerri thumbed at the southeastern sky. "Searchers had better spot our fire soon. We're about to be hit by a nasty thunderstorm."

The air freshened with a scent of ozone as a towering cloud with an anvil-shaped top rapidly approached. Dark clouds blanketed the horizon behind the storm.

She frowned. "Looks like the weather forecasted for late tonight arrived early."

Cool, powerful wind gusts lifted our long hair as the storm neared.

"We need to find something to chock the Cub's wheels. That little plane is the only shelter we have."

I grabbed some thick palm fronds and ran to the aircraft.

FOUR

Somewhere in South Florida

Caitlin feared her weird captor. He hadn't raped her—no violent behavior. Instead, they played board games. He preferred chess, but they also played backgammon, checkers, and many others. He always won.

The door lock rattled, and she gasped.

Her blue eyes widened as a man wearing a skeleton mask and a navy Armani suit entered carrying a white lace wedding gown. He dropped it on her lap. "Put this on." He tugged on his French cuffs and adjusted his ruby cuff links.

"W-why? Are we getting married?" She held the dress in trembling hands.

"No, it's for my photo gallery."

She slid off the bed and carried the gown to the bathroom, dragging her ankle chain behind her.

"Hurry."

A few minutes later, she returned wearing the white gown.

"Good, now stand next to the painting I hung on that wall and smile." He held up a Fujifilm instant camera.

Her heart pounded as she smoothed her blond hair and feigned a smile, terrified this would be her final act.

The masked man snapped a photo and waited for the picture to pop out. "Turned out great. Keep the dress on. I'll be back soon for another game." He turned and left.

The door lock clicked.

She glanced at her left ankle, sore from a metal cuff connected to a heavy chain anchored to the iron bedframe.

Caitlin blinked back tears.

"This might be my last day alive. I've got to get out of here," she muttered to herself.

She surveyed her prison—a ten-foot-square, sound-proof room with an adjoining bathroom, no windows, and one locked metal door leading into a hallway.

She prayed, "God, please help me."

Think. Maybe I can use the toothpicks I saved.

Caitlin took out two wooden toothpicks hidden under the tissue box. She stuck them inside the ankle lock and tried picking it. The lock started to move, but then one pick broke in half. Another attempt with a new toothpick resulted in a loud click, and the lock popped open.

"Yes!" she said to herself as she rubbed her free ankle. She grabbed the toothpicks and rushed to the locked door.

It took several careful attempts with the wood picks before the lock clicked open. When she reached for the handle, the door slammed into her, knocking her to the floor.

The man in the skeleton mask yanked her up and threw her onto the bed. He snatched up the ankle cuff.

"Clever girl! None of the others ever managed this." He clamped the cuff on her. "Sit still." He grabbed the toothpicks and shook a finger at her. "You don't want to make me angry."

The frightened young woman faced the menacing man, tears streaming down her pale cheeks. His sinister, ice-blue eyes, exposed through the skeleton mask, radiated a murderous lust.

She scooted back against the headboard and hugged herself, her body trembling.

The masked man said, "I'd better cool off." He stormed out of the room and locked the door.

Alone, Caitlin listened—nothing. *He'll probably kill me when he comes back.* She sat sobbing and trembling.

Two hours later, the door swung open, and the masked man entered.

He gestured to a chair. "Ready for another game?"

She nodded, fighting back tears, afraid she'd make him angry again.

He placed a checkerboard on a small table bordered by two chairs. "This should be easier for you. Chess isn't your game."

She sat in the chair and glanced at the round game pieces.

"Red or black?" He pointed at the checkers.

"Red." Her voice quavered.

"Good choice." He arranged the checkers on the board. "Remember, if you win this game, you get to go home, but if you lose, you're stuck here with me until you win one." He waved at the red checkers. "Your move."

"I'll d-do my best." She managed to take one of his black checkers on her first turn. As the game progressed, she continued to hold a small lead.

He made his moves quickly, sometimes making errors that benefitted her.

He never made mistakes before.

Unnerved by his creepy skeleton mask, she barely managed the courage to ask, "Will you really let me go if I win?" She took another black checker.

"My dear, I always keep my promises." His next move took one of her red checkers, leaving him behind by two. "Your turn."

Her final effort won the game, but was the win too easy, especially after losing every previous game?

He kissed her hand. "Well done, my dear. I knew you could do it." He glanced at his gold Patek Philippe watch. "We'll enjoy a celebratory dinner, and then I'll take you home." He stood. "I'll return with our meal. While you're waiting, why don't you fix your hair so you'll look nice for your homecoming?" He left the room and locked the door.

Am I really going home? I miss my family and friends.

Caitlin brushed her long blond hair and pulled it into a ponytail.

It wasn't long before her captor arrived with a dinner tray. She joined him at the table, eager to finish the meal and leave.

"I brought one of my favorite vintage wines." He poured red wine into her glass. "I hope you like Château Lafite Rothschild. It will pair nicely with this Châteaubriand Béarnaise for two." He paused. "Try the wine."

She took a generous sip, set the glass down, and smiled. "It tastes wonderful."

"I'm glad you like it." He motioned toward her glass. "Drink your fill. We have plenty."

She took a deep drink, savoring the smooth wine with a hint of almond. Then she leaned back against the chair and closed her eyes.

Forever.

He smiled at the corpse, her cheeks and lips cherry red with a bit of foaming at her nose and mouth. The killer left the room and sauntered down the narrow basement corridor to a small office at the end of the hallway. He pulled off his mask and hung it on a hook, then sat in a leather executive chair and leaned back, smiling.

Every time another blonde dies, I feel almost as good as I did when my mother and sister died. Blondes are so evil.

FIVE

Jett and Kerri

Wind whipped around us while we crammed whatever we could find against either side of the main wheels and tailwheel. Then we shut ourselves inside the Piper Cub. Seconds later, the storm hit. Heavy rain drenched our bonfire, smothering the flames.

The tiny airplane rocked in the noisy downpour as rain and light debris pelted it.

"At least we're dry in here," Kerri said, gripping her seat.

"Almost." Water droplets worked through the palm fronds crammed into the broken windshield and dripped onto my knees, soaking the lower legs of my jeans. "Let's hope this is a brief, isolated storm, and the searchers will find us soon." My wounded shoulder throbbed.

Luck wasn't with us. Turned out the violent thunderstorm was part of a big weather front moving up from the southeast that arrived several hours early and kept us in heavy rain. Our little training plane rocked and buffeted as the storm raged around us.

I glanced back at Kerri. "Buckle yourself in and pull the belts snug in case the storm flips us upside down." I did the same and then gripped our emergency bag on my lap.

We didn't attempt further conversation amidst booming thunder with deafening rain pounding the Cub's wings and cabin.

When the deluge finally stopped hours later, we cracked open the windows for fresh air. It was dead calm outside and pitch black with low clouds blocking the stars.

My intrepid young student pilot pressed her nose against the window. "I guess everything's too wet out there to make a signal fire."

"Doesn't matter. It's too dangerous outside in the dark, and Search and Rescue won't come looking until daylight." I unfastened my seat harness and checked my Glock.

Her stomach rumbled. "It's two a.m., and we haven't eaten since lunch. Any food in the bag?"

"Several granola bars, but we should wait until sunrise. If you eat now, you might need to relieve yourself outside." I scanned the darkness for movement.

"Oh, right, we don't want to leave the safety of our plane." She sighed. "Think we'll live through this?"

"You can survive almost anything if you don't panic. I wouldn't have survived the python attack if you hadn't helped me." I gripped my pistol. *A big snake could shove its way through the palm fronds blocking the holes.*

A deep growl resonated nearby.

My heart pounded, but I kept my voice calm. "A panther is claiming the dead python. He'll want to eat as much as he can before gators drag it into the swamp." I closed the windows so our scent wouldn't be easy to pick up.

Kerri squeezed my good shoulder. "There it is!"

I whispered, "Keep still and don't make a sound."

The big cat slowly circled our plane. We froze when it put its front paws on a window and sniffed as it looked at us with its perfect night vision.

I held my breath and prayed it wouldn't shred our fabric-covered aircraft with its powerful claws.

It hesitated, then dropped down and faded into the darkness.

"Is it gone?" she whispered.

"Yeah, I think it went for the dead snake, but keep still. It can see us in here, and movement will attract its attention."

"What'll we do in the morning? Think the cat will still be here?"

"No, it'll climb somewhere up high to sleep."

Her voice sounded anxious. "Everything will be too wet in the morning to make a signal fire."

"No worries, I'll cut some fabric off the tail and pour avgas on it."

She chuckled. "That'll work."

"Let's get some sleep. It'll be dawn in a few hours." I tried to sleep, but my aching shoulder and fear of a python pushing in through our palm-frond patches kept me awake.

Earlier

Darcy walked into the living room where her dad, the Garnet Chief of Police, was watching television. Her cell phone rang, and she made a quick retreat into the hall and answered it.

A deep masculine voice said, "Is this Darcy McKay of the Sniffers Agency?"

"Yes, and who are you?" Her dogs crowded around her.

"I'm Jett's uncle, Hunter Vann of Vann's Flight School over in Aerodrome Estates."

"Of course. We spoke earlier today. How may I help?"

"Jett and her teenage student went missing on a training flight in a vintage aircraft. They never made it to the second airport on their flight plan, which means they might've gone down in the Everglades somewhere northwest of Miami."

"Oh no. Did they call Air Traffic Control?" She smoothed her long, auburn hair.

"They have a handheld radio, but no one's heard from them."

"If they went down in that huge area, how will we know where to look?" she asked.

"Once the weather clears, we're hoping they'll make a signal fire."

He paused. "The thing is, there could be lots of reasons they might not remain close to the fire."

"Want me to use my dogs to help find them?"

"We'll only have room in the helicopter for you and one dog so we can take the girls onboard. We have clothing with their scents and forward-looking infrared radar. Do you have a dog that's good in water?"

"My Labrador retriever, Laddie, is trained for water searches, but I'll need you guys to shoot any predators that threaten us. I'll be packing too."

"Tim and I will be heavily armed." He hesitated. "It's only fair to warn you there could be two-legged predators in the mix. All sorts of smugglers and bad people hide out in the Everglades."

Darcy didn't hesitate. "I'm in. When do we leave?"

"Tonight, as soon as possible. We'll spend the night in Fort Lauderdale, north of a big weather front that's coming in from the southeast. I was told you have an empty field behind your house. Shine some headlights on it, and we'll pick up you and your dog in thirty minutes. Bring one small overnight bag."

"Okay, Hunter, we'll be ready. See you in thirty."

She pocketed her phone and rushed in to tell her dad the news.

After she filled him in, he said, "Pack your bag and bring extra ammo. I'll position both cars to light a landing area. Meet me out there."

Time flew as she raced around, gathering everything she needed for her dog and the rescue mission. When she tied an orange bandanna on Laddie's neck, the other dogs slumped down, disappointed they weren't chosen.

"Sorry, guys, I can only take one this time. Mind Dad and take care of the ranch." She kissed all their noses, clipped on Laddie's leash, slung the bag over her shoulder, and ran out the back door.

Thundering rotor blades assaulted the peaceful night, a bright floodlight shined down on them, and the helicopter touched down on the field.

Darcy hugged her dad. "I'll be careful and call when I can. Love you."

She hopped into the idling chopper before he could reply, and her yellow Lab joined her. She waved and shut the side door.

In seconds, they were airborne, the ranch fading into the distance. She pulled on a headset with a voice-activated microphone so she could communicate with the men in the noisy chopper.

Tim and Hunter turned and smiled at her. Darcy had met them at Jett's ball.

Tim was a good looking, fortyish, super-fit guy who looked like a soldier. He said, "Thanks for coming and trusting us with your search dog."

Hunter's black hair, golden eyes, and chiseled features accented his handsome face. He said, "Don't worry. I'm a trained tracker, and Tim was a SEAL."

Yep—a Cherokee god with a SEAL sidekick. I'm not worried.

"This is Laddie. You can count on him to find the girls if you brought something with their scents."

Hunter held up a Ziplock bag with the girls' recently worn underwear in it.

SIX

Jett and Kerri

I slept restlessly and woke in the dim, pre-dawn light. Kerri was sound asleep. I cracked open the windows enough to freshen the air and looked out in every direction, hoping not to spot any predators

None were in sight.

She woke and yawned. "Is it time for a granola bar breakfast?"

"Yep." Wary, I opened the Cub's door and climbed out. "Stay close while I slice fabric off the tail for a fire."

"Wait, is your shoulder okay?" She hopped out and checked the bandage.

"Feels a little stiff, but there's no fresh blood. I'm good. Let's check the snake."

Warm, humid air flowed over us as we sneaked up to the ravaged carcass. It looked like the panther had ripped into it and eaten his fill. He was probably sleeping it off in a nearby tree.

"Keep a sharp lookout." I paused and listened for predators. "Alrighty, let's hurry back to the plane." *Don't know if I'd survive another snake attack.*

We trotted back, looking left and right. So far, nothing scary emerged from the brush, but I wasn't reassured because the attack yesterday came without warning.

"Fill my purse with fuel from the sump drain like I did yesterday, and I'll cut off fabric from the rudder." I pulled out my knife.

After I sliced off all the rudder and elevator covering, I cut into the horizontal stabilizer. When I finished, the entire tail section was stripped to its framing. There was a strong wind out of the southeast, so I piled the crumpled fabric pieces well downwind of the Cub.

Kerri poured fuel over my neat little pile of aircraft skin, and I let it soak for a minute while I nibbled on a granola bar.

When I lit the fire, the fuel provided a big blaze, especially with the dope-treated aircraft fabric. "I'll put a small palm frond on the fire to make smoke. It'll dry out pretty fast. Then we can add another frond." I grabbed a damp branch from nearby.

Kerri finished her snack and glanced around. "Think the smugglers will return soon?"

I nodded. "We need a plan. Let's search their dock area. Maybe we'll find something that can help us."

She tossed another palm frond onto the fire.

"Let's go." I pulled out my pistol and slung the emergency bag over my good shoulder. "Move slowly and quietly in case a predator is nearby."

We entered the narrow path to the pier. My heart pounded as I kept looking left and right, hoping we wouldn't encounter the panther or another giant snake. Gators would probably be in the water, but one could be hiding in the brush.

Kerri whispered, "There's the pier, and that looks like a storage shed under the trees."

"Good. Let's see what's inside."

There wasn't a lock on the door. I yanked it open and found two full five-gallon gas cans, a machete, a coil of rope, and six one-gallon jugs of spring water. I ripped off the seal on a gallon of water and took a long drink.

"Here, Kerri, open this water and drink all you want. We'll refill our smaller bottles in the duffel too." I unzipped our bag, shoved the rope inside, and pulled out the bottles.

We hydrated ourselves and replenished our personal water supply. Then I carried out the water jugs and gas cans.

She grabbed the machete. "Now I'm armed too."

"Douse the shed with gas, while I pour some on the pier, and then I'll light everything on fire." I carried a can to the thirty-foot pier and started pouring gas on the far end.

I was halfway back to shore when a ten-foot gator reared up and snapped his toothy jaws at me. Startled, I yelped and spilled fuel on his snout. He slid into the water as I rushed past and continued dousing the dock.

"Search and Rescue has to spot the big fires this will make." She splashed gas on the wooden walls of the storage shack and then poured a fuse trail.

I lit the pier first. "Whoa, that'll get their attention." Bright flames rose high above it.

A twelve-foot python slithered around the shed toward us just as I lit the fuse. In two seconds, the shed and snake were engulfed in a massive blaze.

"Let's get back to the plane. The fires should scare away predators." I followed Kerri on the path to the airstrip. This time we ran.

When we reached the Cub, she nudged me. "Do you hear that? It's not an airboat, is it?"

I cocked my head. "Yep, the bad guys are coming back. This time we'll run to the far end of the strip and head west. Use palm fronds again to hide our tracks, and run your hands over the low brush we pass through so a search dog can find us."

We reached the west end of the helipad and carefully made our way into the jungle. I prayed somebody in law enforcement would reach us in time.

The airboat driver slowed. "Dammit! They lit the dock and shed on fire."

The wood pier burned fiercely, and smoke and flames from the burning shed rose high into the early-morning sky.

His buddy said, "We should turn around. Search and Rescue is bound to spot the fires."

Heat from the fire blasted his face as the driver said, "We're not leaving without the girls. They're worth at least a hundred and fifty grand." He had an MP7 submachine gun strapped across his chest and a handgun in a thigh holster.

"They're probably waiting by their plane, but remember the brunette is armed." The sidekick checked his bandaged hand and the strap on his MP7, then drew a pistol.

The driver ran the airboat up onto the edge of the island upwind of the fire. "Don't worry about snakes or gators near these fires." He shut down the engine and hopped ashore.

The guy with the bandaged hand hesitated and studied the jungle.

"Hurry, before they have time to hide." The driver drew his handgun and pushed through the foliage to the path.

His accomplice jumped off the boat and followed him. When they reached the Cub, no one was there.

"Dammit! They ran away again." The driver scanned the trees.

"Maybe they were already picked up by a rescue chopper." He looked around.

"We would've seen the helicopter. Besides, those fires haven't been burning long. The SAR crews don't start looking until dawn, which was less than an hour ago. They have a lot of ground to cover, especially if there's no ELT signal."

"Looks like the girls used part of the plane to make a signal fire before they found our storage shed and burned it."

The driver frowned. "We don't have much time, so you check the north side, and I'll look west. There's nothing east but water, and they probably aren't hiding near the fires on the south side."

He rubbed his bandaged left hand. "You sure you want to split up? The black-haired chick is armed."

"We have automatic weapons. Start searching. I'm going that way." The boat pilot paused. "Wait, I hear a chopper." He scanned the eastern horizon. "It's coming this way—looks like a civilian bird. Hide and shoot them down if they get too close."

SEVEN

"Big fire near a tiny strip with the Cub on it, dead ahead about five miles." Hunter pointed.

"Got it." Tim began a descent and turned to Darcy. "Hold the dog. We're landing."

She nodded from the rear center seat, pulled Laddie between her legs, and wrapped her arms around him.

When they were close to the enlarged helipad, Hunter said, "We've got company. Airboat at eleven o'clock."

"The FLIR is picking up two people on foot nearby, two farther away, and what looks like a panther near them," Tim said.

Before they had time to react, bullets peppered the helicopter. Some went through the glass on the side door and barely missed Darcy and her dog. A bullet grazed Tim's right shoulder, and he turned their bird away so the shooters would be behind them. The barrage of bullets continued, and their right engine caught fire.

Hunter keyed the radio microphone. "Mayday, Mayday, Mayday. Miami Center, this is helicopter Two Tango Sierra calling Mayday. Do you copy?"

"Miami Center copies. Go ahead helicopter Two Tango Sierra."

"Helicopter Two Tango Sierra is under attack by armed assailants, our right engine is on fire, and we have three adults and a search dog on board." He gave the controller his GPS coordinates and asked for armed assistance. "We came to rescue two women who made a forced landing here in a Piper Cub yesterday. Tell whoever you send to look for them too. We're landing now."

Tim avoided the open hard surface where they'd be easy targets. Instead, he aimed for a marshy area fifty yards to the south of the airstrip, downwind of the fires. He yelled, "Brace for impact!"

As the helicopter descended into the jungle, the rotor blades sliced into cedar trees and sent broken metal and shredded wood flying in every direction. When the blades broke off, the chopper dropped the last fifteen feet and slammed into the marsh. Mud splattered the windshield during the sudden stop.

"Sorry for the hard landing, but the smoke from the dock and our engine fire might keep the shooters and wildlife away from us." Tim glanced around. "Everyone okay?"

Darcy nodded, and Hunter said, "We're good, but your shoulder's bleeding."

"Just a graze. Make sure the ELT is on, grab the weapons, and get the heck out."

Darcy said, "I've got the first aid kit and my pistol." She looked around. "Where's that bag with the women's panties?"

"Over there." Hunter pointed at a small compartment.

They hurried off the burning helicopter with Laddie on his leash. Darcy shoved the plastic bag with Jett's and Kerri's scents down the front of her shirt so her hands would be free, then she slung the first-aid kit's carry strap over her shoulder.

"I'm hoping the smoke from the fires will mask the smoke from our chopper, so it won't be easy for the shooters to find us." Hunter scanned the area. "Let's move downwind fifty yards and then angle back toward the Cub." He led the way.

Darcy leaned down and gave Laddie a command. "Quiet."

He understood and nudged her with his nose.

Jett and Kerri

We stopped when a helicopter with Tim's tail number approached the helipad. The smugglers fired automatic weapons at the chopper, and one of the engines burst into flames. The wounded bird disappeared into the smoke-filled jungle on the south side of the hard surface. Terrible sounds of sheared metal and shredded trees thundered through the jungle.

"That was Tim's new helicopter! His company handles my home security." My gut churned.

"Think Hunter is with him?" Kerri bit her lip.

"Yeah, probably. Hope they survived the crash." I glanced around. "Climb that tree so we can spot where they went down."

I boosted her to a low branch and then followed as she climbed higher. When I reached a good vantage point, I scanned the jungle, searching for movement. "There's a fire in the trees fifty yards downwind of the dock."

"Yeah, over there." She pointed at it.

"I'll go help them. You stay hidden here."

She grabbed my arm. "Don't leave me! A snake or a panther could kill me." She sucked in a breath. "And … and don't forget about the guys with automatic weapons. My machete won't stand a chance against them."

"The fires and loud weapons probably scared away predators, but you're right, the bad guys could be hunting us instead of looking for the downed chopper. They'll want to grab us quick and escape before help arrives."

Her voice rose to a high-pitched squeak. "What should we do?"

"Our best chance is to spot them before they find us. Be very quiet." I pulled out my pistol.

The guy with the bandaged hand said, "That crash sounded bad, and they probably called it in before they went down. Let's forget about them and grab those girls before cops arrive."

"Yeah, I promised we'd snatch them," the airboat driver said. "I'll go back to the helipad and enter the jungle at the west end, and you continue searching here." He glanced at his watch. "We'll meet at the boat in thirty minutes, girls or no girls."

"We should stay together in case a big python attacks one of us," the accomplice said.

"All the fires and noise scared away the wildlife. You'll be fine." As the airboat pilot pushed through the foliage, he yelled over his shoulder, "See you in thirty minutes."

The guy who'd been wounded by the manchineel tree the previous day checked his bandage. "This place—nothing but bugs and critters that want to kill me," he grumbled.

He clutched his submachinegun with both hands and trudged ahead, taking slow, tentative steps. The brush rustled, and he caught a glimpse of tan fur.

A panther!

He spun around, scanning every direction. A branch moved, and he opened fire, emptying his magazine in a wide spray pattern.

EIGHT

Hunter paused when loud staccato gunfire echoed through the jungle. "One weapon firing." He coughed and peered through the smoky air.

"There were two shooters on FLIR." Tim glanced around. "Maybe they split up."

"Maybe one's looking for us, and the other one's hunting the girls." Darcy leaned down and whispered into Laddie's ear, "Where is the bad man?"

The Lab sniffed the air, cocked his head, and pointed his nose toward the helipad.

She nudged Hunter. "Laddie says one of them is that way. I think he hears him."

"He probably entered the jungle from the west end of the helipad." Hunter pointed at a nearby tree. "That's a manchineel, the deadliest tree in the world. Don't touch any part of it." He pulled metal arrows out of his crossbow's quiver and jammed the tips into the trunk. "This sap will kill my target no matter where the arrow hits him."

"Maybe you should sneak around while I stick with Darcy and her dog," Tim suggested. "Think you can maneuver behind him if he targets us?"

Hunter nodded. "I'll give it my best shot. Continue downwind five minutes and then cut over to the Cub. I'll work my way around and silently nail him with the crossbow." He hesitated. "Don't forget about gators, snakes, and panthers." He faded into the brush.

Kerri grabbed my arm and whispered, "What's he shooting at?"

"Not sure, but he sounds close. Is there any movement?" I scanned the brush from on high.

"Down there on the back side—some plants moved." Kerri pointed at a bush.

A panther emerged from the thick foliage and slowly circled the tree, never taking his eyes off us.

"Oh, crap, he sees us. If he climbs up here, I'll have to shoot him, and then the killers will find us." I aimed my Glock.

"Maybe I can spear him with the machete if he climbs close." Kerri clutched the weapon with the curved blade pointing downward.

The big cat growled and slowly clawed his way up the tree. A relative of the mountain lion, he was just as deadly.

Kerri gripped my arm. "You said he wouldn't be hungry after eating the snake last night." On the edge of panic, her voice turned high and squeaky again.

"Might be a different panther." I stared into his murderous eyes when he stopped five feet below us and snarled. Goosebumps crawled over my arms as my body shuddered with a burst of adrenaline.

I nudged my brave student pilot. "Spear his head with the machete. Now!"

She threw it down at him, and it brushed past his left ear.

He sprang at us, and she let loose with a terrified scream that reverberated throughout the marsh. The big cat's fangs snapped at me just as I shot him in the head. The loud gunshot echoed through the trees, and my ears rang.

The dead predator fell to the ground in a heap of tan fur, landing beside the machete.

After exhaling a big breath, I holstered my pistol and put an arm around Kerri. Her body trembled, and her breath came in short spurts. My heart rate was at maximum.

"We're safe now." I hugged her side against me and felt our bodies vibrating from the aftermath of such an intense attack.

She was still panicked when she glanced downward, and her eyes widened.

A deep voice said, "Hello, girls. You weren't easy to find." He chuckled. "Good job killing the big cat. Drop the handgun and come down, or I'll shred you with my MP7."

Tim and Darcy made the scheduled turn and paused when a single gunshot rang out. It was hard to determine the direction because the swamp magnified the sound.

"Sounded like a nine-mil. handgun. Jett carries a Glock 26. Maybe she shot one of the smugglers." Tim paused and scanned the nearby foliage.

"Or she could've been protecting the teenage girl and herself from a predator. This area is loaded with lethal wildlife." Darcy reached down and petted Laddie.

The dog stiffened and rammed his nose into Darcy. Before she could react, a man sprang from the bushes and pointed an MP7 submachinegun at them.

"Drop your weapons or I'll shoot you." He glared at Tim, then looked at Darcy and grinned. "I just won the trifecta—a blonde, a brunette, and now a redhead. My luck has finally changed."

Tim slowly lowered his rifle. "We have no interest in your smuggling business. We just want to rescue the girls and go home. If you leave now, you can get away before law enforcement arrives."

"The three women are worth at least two hundred grand. We're not walking away from that kind of payday. Besides, they destroyed our operation here." He waved the weapon. "Hurry up and drop your guns."

Darcy stepped in front of Laddie and dropped her pistol in the mud. "Don't hurt my dog. He only does search and rescue—no attack training. He won't bother you." She glanced back at her yellow Lab. "Show the man how nice you are, Laddie."

The dog wagged his tail. He didn't bark or growl.

"It's your call, dearie, but shooting him would be more humane than leaving him to be eaten by gators. Now drop his leash and come over to me." He kept his weapon trained on Tim.

"If I come to you, you'll shoot my friend." Darcy moved in front of Tim, and her dog crouched in the brush.

"Lady, I don't have time for this crap. If you don't come here right now, I'll kill you both and be done with it." He pointed his weapon at her chest.

Darcy's dog sprang forward and clamped his jaws onto the man's right wrist, pushing the MP7 to the side. A few bullets sprayed out, missing everyone.

Then the man went limp and fell facedown into the muck with a metal arrow buried in his back.

Laddie sniffed the dead man as Hunter emerged from the brush. "Everyone okay?"

Tim nodded. "You cut that a little close, buddy."

A high-pitched scream pierced the jungle.

The three listened, and the dog's nose pointed northwest.

Silence.

Tim gathered his weapons, Darcy retrieved her pistol, and Hunter picked up the dead smuggler's MP7 and handgun.

She held the open Ziploc bag under Laddie's nose. "Find the girls."

NINE

Earlier

I reluctantly dropped my Glock at the gunman's feet. "Why can't you just let us go? We won't tell anyone about your smuggling operation."

He glared at us. "You girls destroyed everything, and the Feds will find our base. Selling you will cover our losses." He waved the MP7. "This is your fault. If you hadn't landed here, none of this would be happening. Come down now or I'll shoot you."

I climbed down to a lower branch and stopped. Pointing behind him, I yelled, "Look out!"

"Nice try. I'm not falling for that." Those were his last coherent words.

A fifteen-foot python bit the back of his head and wrapped around him from behind, trapping his arms, and making him drop his MP7. He shrieked and gasped for breath.

My mind and body instantly relived the attack I suffered the previous day, and I froze. Kerri's scream jolted me, and I reached up and squeezed her leg. "Stay up there."

She nodded, her eyes transfixed on the horrifying attack below us.

47

I climbed down to the ground and grabbed my Glock. The huge snake was seconds away from swallowing the smuggler's head when I jammed my pistol's barrel into its gaping mouth and pulled the trigger twice, just to be sure.

The hollow-point bullets left very large exit wounds in the snake's head, and it released its hold. The coiled reptile slid down his body to the ground, but it was too late.

The man's lips were blue, and blood ran out of his mouth as he collapsed onto the pile of snake flesh. His bulging eyes were frozen in a blank stare.

I was so pumped full of adrenaline, my breath came in short spurts as I spun around, searching for more predators. None were apparent.

My hands trembled as I slung the dead man's MP7 over my shoulder, shoved his handgun into my waistband, and holstered my Glock. After taking another careful look around, I stepped over the panther carcass, picked up the machete, and climbed back up the tree.

Kerri waited at our highest perch where we stashed the emergency bag. When I reached her, I handed her the long, bladed weapon.

"Are you okay?" I patted her hand.

"Yeah." She sighed. "Just really shaky." She looked down. "Think the other guy will come?"

"If he does, I'll shoot him with his buddy's gun." I brandished the MP7.

Kerri squeezed my arm. "Jett, I don't know if I can handle any more scary stuff."

I wasn't sure I could either, but I said, "Sweetheart, you're the bravest teenager I've ever met, and you've been amazing throughout this whole nightmare." I hugged her. "Don't worry. I have a feeling Tim or my uncle will rescue us soon."

Right on cue, Hunter emerged from the jungle, looking like a Cherokee warrior god with a bandanna tied around his thick black hair and holding a crossbow.

Kerri poked me and whispered, "Does my hair look okay?"

I grinned. "Yep, perfect." It was almost impossible for a teenage girl to look bad.

Hunter said to someone behind him, "Come out. It's just the girls."

Tim and Darcy, along with her yellow Lab, pushed through the brush and stopped a few feet from the carnage. Decked out in combat gear, Tim looked hot and heroic, and Darcy still looked perfect.

I glanced down at myself. My shirt was torn and soaked in my blood, snake blood, and snake slime. My hair was a mess, my body was splattered with mud, and I reeked.

Hunter inspected the smuggler's body, the snake carcass, and the dead panther. He looked up at me and grinned. "I'm definitely taking you on my next hunting trip, Jett."

"Is the other gunman dead too?" I asked.

"Yeah. Come down, ladies. I'd like us to be on the helipad when the rescue chopper arrives." He helped me down and reached for Kerri.

She wrapped her arms around his neck and hugged him hard. "Thanks for saving us."

I smiled at Tim and Darcy. "Thanks for coming. I'd hug somebody, but I'm all slimy and smelly."

Tim pulled me in for a bear hug. "Glad we got here before it was too late."

I noticed his wound. "Your shoulder is bleeding."

"So is yours. We'll deal with it when we get back to the helipad."

Laddie wagged his tail and kissed my hands and Kerri's. He found us—job done. We petted and fussed over him, and Darcy gave him his reward, a big dog biscuit.

―――

Everyone trudged back to the Cub, our bodies still pumped full of adrenaline from all the life-threatening incidents we'd endured.

When we arrived at the hard surface, Darcy said, "I'll dress the wounds, starting with him." Darcy pulled off Tim's green camouflage T-shirt.

As she cleaned and bandaged his shoulder, I covertly admired his muscular chest and said, "I can't thank you three enough for risking your necks to rescue us."

"And we're really sorry you guys were shot down because of us," Kerri said.

Hunter squeezed her shoulder. "No worries. The birds are insured."

"Jett has been hell on my helicopter insurance." Tim grinned at me.

"Oh, geez, that's right. Thanks to me, you've lost two choppers in little more than a month." I kissed his cheek. "Sorry. I'll pay for everything."

"The helicopter is replaceable, but the vintage Cub isn't. How will we get it out of here?" Kerri asked, as Darcy taped a fresh bandage on my shoulder.

Hunter ran his hands over the airplane. "No sweat. I'll take the wings off, hire a big airboat, and ferry it out of here, while Jett and Tim ride shotgun and shoot anything that moves."

Tim gave a nod. "We can do that, and I'll help dismantle the wings."

"And I'll re-cover the plane when we get it back to your hangar," I volunteered.

Thundering rotor blades heralded the arrival of a big Coast Guard rescue chopper and two heavily armed helicopters from the Miami-Dade Sheriff's Department.

We put the weapons on the ground, stepped several paces back, and put our hands on our heads. A police chopper landed first and secured us and the area.

The cops signaled the rescue bird it was safe to land.

Once it was established that we were the victims, Hunter said, "Jett, wait in the Coast Guard helicopter with the others, while Tim and I take the cops on a tour of the carnage."

"Gladly." I climbed aboard, relieved to be out of reach of the swamp monsters.

TEN

The Coast Guard dropped us off at the Fort Lauderdale International Airport, and Hunter rented a stretch limo with a catered lunch for our ride home. Everyone ate and drank their fill, then Laddie took a nap.

I checked Tim's bloodstained bandage. "You need an antibiotic shot and a few stitches."

"Nah, it was just a graze, but you should go." He took a sip of coffee.

"I'll go if you go," I said. "Banyan Isle has a small ER that's never crowded."

Tim smiled. "Deal."

Kerri told the guys about the giant snake that attacked me and the panther that stalked us. "I had no idea the Everglades was such a terrifying place."

Hunter patted her back. "I'm relieved you and Jett made it out alive."

"Heck, yeah," Tim agreed. "You girls did all right—totally badass."

I looked at my P.I. mentor. "I forgot to ask if you found Muffy Murdoch."

"No one's heard from her, and no ransom demands have been

made," Darcy said. "The nightclub claims they don't have security cameras, but I don't believe them."

"I'll join you on the case after a hot bath and a nap."

"Do you know the owner of Club Bacchus?" she asked.

"No, but Sophia's son, Dominic, might be able to help us. I'll call him later."

It wasn't long before the limo pulled into Aerodrome Estates and stopped in front of Hunter's hangar home. We said our thanks and goodbyes to Darcy and Laddie, then Kerri and I exited with Tim and Hunter. The limo would take Darcy ten miles west to her father's ranch where she and her pets lived temporarily while waiting for her inherited mansion to be redecorated.

We waved at the limo, and then I hugged Tim and Hunter. "I can't ever thank you guys enough for saving us from that hellhole."

"Yeah, thanks a ton." Kerri hugged them. "I hope I never see another snake as long as I live."

"I'm guessing you won't fly near the Everglades any time soon." Hunter chuckled.

"More like never ever." Kerri looked at me. "Jett, will that flight still count as my dual cross-country?"

I laughed. "I doubt it. What do you think, Hunter?"

He shook his head. "Sorry, we can't fudge your logbook after all the news coverage your Everglades adventure will generate. You still need a three-leg dual cross-country flight. I just hope your parents will let you fly again."

Her jaw dropped. "You think they might pull the plug?" She frowned. "I want to earn my private pilot license, and I only need about twenty more flight hours."

"In that case, you might not want to tell your parents everything that happened," I suggested.

On cue, Doctors Riley and Kat Lyons drove up in their white Range Rover. They jumped out and took turns hugging their daughter.

They checked Kerri for injuries, and her mother said, "You aren't hurt, but you're a muddy mess and covered with bug bites."

"Tell us all about it," her father said.

She glanced at us and grinned. "Piece of cake. We landed without a scratch, spent the night inside the plane, and then Darcy and the guys rescued us this morning."

Her father shook hands with Tim and Hunter. "Thanks for saving our daughter." He noticed Tim's and my bandaged shoulders. "What happened?"

"Just a deep scratch from a sharp tree branch in the jungle. No big deal." Tim smiled at Kerri.

"Same here," I said. "Your daughter is an excellent pilot. You should be proud."

"We are," Kat said, "but we'd prefer it if she flew a modern airplane next time." She patted her daughter's back. "No more of that dead reckoning nonsense, and no flying over the Everglades."

Hunter grinned. "That can be arranged." He winked at Kerri.

We waved goodbye as they drove away.

"Let me know when everything is organized to rescue the Cub," I said. "I hate leaving it there."

"I'll make some calls and get the ball rolling." Hunter gently put his arm around my shoulders. "Even though you're safe now, Karin is eager to see you." He wrinkled his nose. "Time to go home and take a bath. Your Harley is in the hangar."

Tim nudged me. "Don't forget we're both stopping at the Banyan Isle ER first."

ELEVEN

I cranked up my teal and cream Harley Davidson custom classic with white-walled tires and pulled on the helmet with winged Valkyries that matched the ones on my gas tank.

Thirty minutes later, I rode over the Intracoastal Waterway on the tall Banyan Isle Bridge. Majestic banyan trees shaded upscale middle-class homes, condos, and quaint shops, all in pastel colors and four stories or less to preserve the small-town atmosphere.

I stopped at the Banyan Isle Medical Center's Emergency Room, and Tim walked in behind me. No one was waiting, and they took us in right away.

"A snake bite and a gunshot wound? You two must have an exciting story," Doctor Norma McRae said. "Sorry, but I'll have to report the bullet wound to the police."

"Tell them the Miami-Dade Sheriff's Office already knows about it." Tim shrugged. "We crashed in the Everglades and encountered smugglers."

Doctor McRae glanced at me and raised her eyebrows.

"Yep, and a huge green anaconda almost killed me—very scary."

"Those fang wounds need treatment and a shot of antibiotics." She turned to Tim. "Same goes for your bullet graze."

When Doctor McRae finished with us, Tim and I hugged and parted ways. He climbed into his Hummer, and I hopped on my Harley.

The brief ride to the ocean side of the island took me past the Banyan Harbor Inn and Marina on the southern curve. Wide inlets to the Atlantic Ocean separated the island from Singer Island to the south and Juno Beach to the north. I turned left onto Ocean Drive and passed a beachfront hotel, a public beach, a pastel condominium building, and the six southernmost mansions that had been converted to luxury condos.

Continuing north, I rode past several magnificent mansions built over a century ago by industrialists from New York and Boston. At the northernmost end, I clicked my remote gate control and turned east between tall stone pillars onto a tree-lined drive.

Valhalla Castle, the Viking fortress my great-great-grandfather built over a hundred years ago, stood tall with turret towers rising from the corners of the four-story stone mansion. Parapets and battlements adorned what had been my home since I was twelve, and where I enjoyed living except for six years in the U.S. Navy after graduating college.

My parents kept the home fires burning in the castle until they died tragically almost three years ago when their sabotaged jet crashed into the Atlantic Ocean. A strong desire to catch their killer spurred me to leave the Navy and become a private investigator.

I entered a circular drive that curved around a fifteen-foot statue of Odin standing with his sword held high in the center of a fountain surrounded by four wolves spouting water from their fanged mouths. Veering right, I headed for the remodeled ten-car garage that stabled ten horses a century ago. After parking my Harley in a rear corner, I closed the big door, left through a side door, and strolled to the castle's front entrance, grateful to be home safe.

Karin and my Timber-shepherd pups must've heard my motorcycle. They greeted me in the foyer where ten-foot winged Valkyries guarded twin staircases curving twenty feet up to the second floor and continuing to the top floor.

Karin Kekoa was a lovely blend of her Hawaiian father and British mother. My extraordinary chef had also become a good friend. A U.S. Navy veteran and taekwondo black belt, she would assist me once my Valkyrie Private Detective Agency was up and running early next year.

She hugged me. "I'm glad Hunter found you, and you made it home safe and sound."

"Actually, it was a group effort." I grinned.

I glanced to my left where my late mother, a beautiful Cherokee Shaman with waist-length black hair, gold eyes, and golden skin peered down at me from a life-size painting on the south staircase wall. I was fortunate to resemble her, but I inherited my late Danish father's blue eyes. Tall, blond, and ruggedly handsome, he had been the image of a Viking.

Karin checked me over. "Any injuries?"

"Just puncture wounds and bruises from a giant anaconda." I pointed at my shoulder. "I'm okay. The ER doc cleaned me up and gave me antibiotics."

She gasped. "Sounds almost as scary as that king cobra you survived in March."

"My sentiments exactly."

She looked into my bloodshot eyes. "You need a hot bath and a long nap."

"Yeah, it'll really hit me once the adrenaline wears off. It was quite a harrowing experience."

"Before you bed down, better call Gwen. She's been worried sick about you."

"Okay, I'll plug in my cell so the battery can charge while I bathe." I headed up the south staircase to the top floor. My bedroom suite was on the end of the southern wing and had windows and balconies facing east, south, and west. Rose colored draperies covered the windows and French doors.

The south balcony faced a next-door mansion a hundred yards away. My best friend since childhood, Gwen Pendragon, lived there, and her bedroom faced mine. Ten years ago, Gwen lost her parents during a deadly carjacking. Her uncle and late aunt, the Duke and

Duchess of Colchester, took care of her in England until she started college back in the States. The sole heir of wealthy parents, Gwen earned an advanced degree in criminology. Hellbent on catching her parents' killer, she eventually became a detective with the Palm Beach Police.

After enjoying a soothing bath, I blow-dried my hair and donned a nightgown. I left my phone plugged-in when I called Gwen. "Hey, girlfriend, I survived the Everglades."

"I was worried when your plane went missing, especially since Hunter thought you probably landed in that horrid swamp."

"Horrid is putting it mildly. I'll probably have nightmares about giant snakes, gators, panthers, and bad guys."

"Bad guys?"

"Yeah, we landed on an oversized helipad for smugglers, and we overheard two of them say they intended to sell us to traffickers."

"Were they there when you landed?"

"No." I filled her in and ended saying, "They're both dead, and I hope they didn't tell their buddies about us. We don't want to be targeted for revenge now that the DEA knows about their secret spot."

"Your episode in the 'glades has been all over the news, and the smugglers' deaths will be reported by the police. You can bet the dead guys were part of a much larger operation, and their associates will know your names and where you live."

"I'm guessing they'll do what's best for their drug business and lay low while the heat is on. It wouldn't make sense for them to come after us—too risky."

"I hope you're right, but just in case, I'll check with my DEA contact."

"Any news on Muffy Murdoch?"

"Nothing. Muffy's parents hired you and Darcy's Sniffers Agency to find her. They also asked for Sophia and me. They want the same women who solved the Body-Drop Murders." She paused. "I explained Sophia is in Italy with her boyfriend."

"Muffy disappeared in Club Bacchus?" I asked.

"Yes, that trendy new dance club for wine connoisseurs over on

Clematis Street in downtown West Palm Beach," Gwen said. "Very exclusive."

"What are the police saying about her disappearance?"

"They think she met a guy and went home with him." Gwen blew out a sigh. "The police opened an investigation, but they haven't found any evidence she was abducted."

"What about surveillance cameras? Did they show Muffy with someone?" I asked.

"It's an elite club, and the owner claims the customers don't want cameras recording them. I think he's lying, but there's not much I can do about it. The case belongs to the West Palm Beach Police."

"I bet Sophia's family has Mafia connections that could get us a look at the club's security tapes. Too bad she's in Italy enjoying the high life. I really miss her, but maybe her oldest son, Dominic, will help."

"Good idea. Let me know what he says, and don't forget to keep a sharp eye out for bad guys. Drug smugglers are known for being vengeful."

I signed off and called Dominic DeLuca, who was *don* of the most powerful New York Mafia family.

"Jett, good to hear from ya. I heard about your Everglades adventure. Ya okay?"

"Yeah, just a few bites and bruises." Hearing his voice made me think of Sophia and miss her more. "How's your mom doing?"

"She's having the time of her life with Count Medici. The guy's got a palace in Tuscany and a huge villa in Sicily. Ma said Aldo has people waiting on her hand and foot. She's loving it." He paused. "Between you and me, I think wedding bells are in her future."

"I want her to be happy, but I really miss her and wish she were here."

"Is that why ya called?"

"No, I need a favor if it won't be too much trouble."

"Anything, Jett. How can I help ya?"

I filled him in on our missing friend and the need for cooperation from the club manager.

"Let me make a few calls. I'll get right back to ya."

I paced in front of my nine-month-old puppies, Pratt and Whitney, named after my favorite aircraft engine manufacturer. They seemed confused by my behavior.

Dominic called ten minutes later. "Hey, Jett, turns out I know the club's owner. Expect a call soon from a guy named Vic Montana. He'll help ya."

"Thanks a million, Dom, and give my best to your brother." I hung up and waited for the call.

Five minutes later, Vic Montana called and said, "You're welcome to look at our security tapes, and if you come an hour before we open at eight, you can bring your search dogs and see if they pick up her scent."

I thanked him and called Darcy. "Hey, have you talked to Gwen?"

"Yep. Muffy's parents don't want to wait until the police come up with something. That might be too late."

"Sophia's older son hooked us up with the owner of Club Bacchus." I filled her in on what Vic Montana said.

"Sounds good. I'll bring Max and Dobie. Bad guys automatically fear German shepherds and Dobermans."

"Plan to meet us there at seven tonight. We'll finish before they open at eight."

Next, I called Gwen and looped her in on our plan. After a brief chat, I slid under the covers for a much-needed nap.

TWELVE

I woke an hour before Gwen and I were due to leave. After dressing, I slowly walked downstairs for a light meal on the back terrace. My body ached from my Everglades adventure, and my shoulder throbbed. Karin kindly served me a yummy salad with grilled chicken on top.

"Feeling better?" she asked.

I nodded. "It's wonderful to be clean and dry and safe from snakes."

My cell rang. It was Uncle Hunter. "Hey, Jett, how are you?"

"Much better. Thanks again for the rescue. I feel bad about the Cub."

"No worries. It's already back in my hangar. We're stripping it now."

"What? How did you get it so fast?"

"Jeff Rowlin and Kelly Mahone helped me retrieve it. Shot a big snake in the process."

"I have to help find Muffy tonight, but I can probably work on the Cub tomorrow."

"No need. We've got it handled. Work with Darcy, save the girl, and nail the perp."

"Thanks, Uncle Hunter." My doorbell boomed Wagner's "Ride of the Valkyries."

Karin jumped up and said, "I'll get it."

As I swallowed a bite of chicken, she returned with Banyan Isle's replacement for Detective Mike Miller, the former love of my life. The new guy, Detective Blake Collins, looked like a tall, blond Adonis. He was thirty-two and a widower with a seven-year-old son, a German shepherd puppy, a British nanny, and a Hispanic cook and housekeeper. Two years ago, Blake's son inherited his late mother's enormous trust fund, and Blake was appointed trustee until his son's twenty-fifth birthday. He assured me the huge new income didn't stop him from wanting to fight crime and protect the public.

My dogs sniffed his pant legs, probably smelling his puppy and son.

Blake patted their heads and smiled at me. "Glad to see you survived the swamp."

"Thank you. What brings you by?" I asked.

He stood by an empty chair at the round glass-top table where I sat. "I was worried about you when I heard what happened. May I sit?"

"Please do. Would you like a drink?"

"That iced tea looks good." He paused. "I feel like we might have gotten off on the wrong foot the first time we met."

I grinned. "You mean when you referred to my home as Murder Central?"

He winced. "Yeah, sorry about that. I'm sure you'd like nothing more than to have a nice, peaceful life. Sometimes stuff just happens."

"I'm hoping things will calm down now."

"Please allow me to take you out to a fancy dinner as a peace offering. Are you free Friday night?" His face held a friendly, sincere expression.

"Yes, is seven o'clock good?"

He smiled. "Seven is perfect. See you then." Blake stood, nodded to Karin, and said, "I'll see myself out."

After he left, Karin said, "Congratulations. You have a date with a major hottie."

"I admit he's good looking, but I'm not sure if I like him. Maybe my opinion was clouded by all the negative stuff that preceded him, none of which was his fault."

Darcy met Gwen and me at Club Bacchus and brought her honey-colored German Shepherd, Max, and her black and brown Doberman, Dobie. The dogs had helped us take down the Body-Drop Killer, and we trusted them.

Darcy pulled Muffy's shirt out of a large Zip-loc bag and held it under the dogs' noses. "Take scent and find."

The dogs spread out and sniffed the carpeted floor, chairs, and leather-covered barstools. They avoided the wood dance floor that had been mopped with a strong cleaning agent, stopped at a barstool by the rear bar, and barked. When we joined them, they sniffed the carpeted floor and led us to the rear exit and into the parking lot. The dogs sat beside an empty parking space and barked once.

I pulled out my phone and snapped pictures of the lot and the parking spot in question. Then I texted the photos to Muffy's friend, Bunty, and asked if that was where they parked.

In minutes, she texted: *We valet parked in front.*

I showed my friends the text. "Looks like someone took Muffy in his car."

Gwen took photos of the parking lot. "Let's go inside and review the security tapes." She found the manager. "We'd like to look at the indoor videos first."

"Sorry, I only have cameras outside the building." He led us to a small room. "Which night do you want to see?"

"Night before last, please." Gwen stood beside him, and we gathered behind his chair.

We spotted Muffy on video, struggling to walk beside a dark-haired man about six feet tall wearing a custom-fitted navy suit. She seemed drugged, and they could only be seen from behind. He laid her across the back seat of a black Bentley sedan. The license plate wasn't readable on the video because an electronic device was obscuring it.

"I can't run the plate," Gwen said.

"You have the make, model, and color. Can you follow it on traffic cams and see where he took her?" I asked Gwen.

"Good idea. My police laptop is in the car." She turned to Darcy. "Take your dogs for a brief walk while Jett helps me scan the traffic cams."

"We'll circle the block and check back with you." Darcy clipped on their leashes and strolled out with Max and Dobie.

We climbed into the front seats of Gwen's white Lincoln SUV.

"Let's hope he took a major road, like Okeechobee Boulevard." She tapped the keys on her laptop.

"Some of the traffic lights on Clematis Street have cameras. Check those first and see which way he turned." I slid closer beside her and stared at the computer screen.

Gwen keyed in the same date and time that the club's security video showed Muffy being helped into the car.

"There." I pointed. A traffic camera showed the black Bentley with the obscured plate turn left onto Quadrille. The driver wore a ballcap that hid his face.

"Give me a sec." She typed in commands, and another camera showed the car turn right onto Okeechobee Boulevard, heading west.

We followed the stolen car on sporadic traffic cams for twenty miles to where it turned right and disappeared into Equestrian Estates, a new housing development.

"No cameras inside the neighborhood, unless we find new homeowners that have them," Gwen said. "We'll have to canvass every street and ask if anyone has seen the car or Muffy."

"It's been two days since she went missing. We'd better go now." I spotted Darcy walking toward Gwen's car with her dogs.

We filled her in and took both cars west on Okeechobee Boulevard to the subdivision's entrance.

THIRTEEN

The housing development was so new the guard house was still under construction. A main road ran down the center with cross streets along every oversized block.

We pulled over, and I hopped out and tapped on Darcy's window. She opened it, and I said, "We'll take the first cross street while you search the second one, and so on."

"I'll call if I find anything." Darcy drove down the street.

I hopped back into Gwen's car, and we turned onto Eventer Lane. Halfway down the block, we found an occupied house with the lights on and pulled into the driveway.

"I'll flash my badge and put the homeowner at ease." Gwen clutched her Palm Beach Police credentials as we approached the front door.

A gray-haired man in his sixties answered our knock. He seemed wary until she held up her badge. "Ah, Officer, how may I help?"

She showed him screen shots of the man with Muffy in the black Bentley. "Have you seen this car, man, or woman? They entered this neighborhood two nights ago."

He studied the photos. "Yeah, real late the night before last. The car pulled into that garage across the street. Must've been after two in the morning. I figured it was the new homeowner seeing as how they used the garage door opener."

"Did you see them get out of the car?" Gwen asked, trying to hide her excitement.

"Nope—closed the garage door before they got out."

"What about the next day? See anyone?" I asked.

"I walked over the next morning around ten—wanted to introduce myself to the new neighbors, but no one was home, and the car was gone."

"How did you know the car was gone?" Gwen asked.

"Peeked through the garage windows." He shrugged. "Hasn't been back since."

"Thanks for your help. We'll check the home and ensure everything is okay." Gwen turned, and I followed her across the street.

The front door was unlocked.

She said, "We're going in—exigent circumstances."

I followed her in and helped her search every room and the garage. No Muffy.

"Well, darn it, why would he bring her here and then leave with her?" Gwen sighed.

My phone rang. Darcy was calling.

"Hey, any luck on your end?" I asked.

"Yeah, meet me at twelve-ninety Friesian Lane. Hurry." Darcy hung up.

I nudged Gwen. "Darcy needs us right away."

We hopped in Gwen's car, and I gave her the address. It was the street behind the one we were on.

"Looks like this house is directly behind the one we searched." I found Darcy waiting for us at the open front door.

"A neighbor walking her dog in the middle of the night saw someone park the Bentley in the garage. It was gone when she checked at eight in the morning." Darcy turned and led us through to a screened-in porch with a pool. "My dogs confirmed Muffy was in the garage and in the house. I wanted you both here before we search the backyard."

"A guy on the street behind us saw a black Bentley sedan drive into the garage of the house behind this one. He left before morning," I said.

Darcy shook her head. "Maybe Max and Dobie can make sense of this." She let them into the backyard.

The dogs sniffed the grass and went straight to a spot along the back fence, which was four feet high and made of cedar. They barked once and sat.

"What's behind the fence?" Gwen asked, pointing at the dogs.

We peeked over it and recognized the house we searched.

I switched on my cell phone flashlight and shined it on the grass behind the fence. "It looks like fresh dirt and sod. What does that little red flag mean?"

"New construction. A septic tank was recently installed there," Darcy answered.

"Oh, no, you don't think—" I stared at the flag.

"Only one way to know," Darcy said. "Meet me back there and my dogs will check."

As we headed for the cars, Gwen said, "He came here first and dropped her body behind the fence. Then he drove to the other house, went to the backyard, and buried her."

We hurried to our vehicles and drove around the block. The helpful neighbor was probably surprised to see us park across the street again.

I followed my friends and the dogs around to the backyard. Max and Dobie went straight to the red marker, sat, and barked once.

Gwen gasped and her shoulders slumped.

Darcy bit her lower lip and looked at me. "Sorry."

"Any chance the dogs are wrong?" I asked, holding on to hope, even though my Cherokee Wolf Clan intuition told me otherwise.

"They've never been wrong before, but I suppose there's always a chance."

"Hate to say it—he killed Muffy and buried her in or under that new septic tank." Gwen sighed. "But with no hard evidence, I can't get a court order to dig it up."

Darcy shrugged. "As you know, I inherited millions from a serial killer. I'll buy this house and arrange for an expedited closing. Should take about a week."

"That's a big step. Are you sure you want to do that?" I asked.

"Yeah. After we close the case, I'll donate the house to a military veteran's family." Darcy narrowed her eyes. "I want to nail the bastard who killed Muffy."

"We'd better hurry in case she isn't in the septic tank," Gwen said.

"The dogs and my *Aniwaya* intuition say she's there." I bit my lower lip. "Wish we could've saved her."

"I bet this is the only time detectives with dogs showed up right after he killed somebody." Darcy petted her dogs.

"Any chance he'll move her before Darcy can buy this property?" Gwen asked.

"I hope he does. That'll prove he killed her, and we'll find out who he is," I said.

"We'd better take turns watching the backyard," Gwen said.

I glanced at my friends. "I can arrange for Tim's security guards to watch the property for us." I pulled out my phone and called Tim.

After I explained what we needed, he said, "Working for you is never boring."

"Tim has it covered," I said to my friends. "But we need to narrow down the suspect list by finding out who owns a new black 4-door Bentley sedan."

"There can't be too many local owners who match the killer's description," Gwen said. "I'll run a search through the DMV tomorrow and weed out any owners who aren't men between the ages of 25 and 45."

"Good. Let us know who you find and we'll interview them. Maybe Jett's Wolf Clan intuition will kick in during the meeting." Darcy patted my back. "We'll need all the help we can get on this case."

"I don't have any control over it, but it usually warns me in dangerous situations. Let's hope not many young men drive that Bentley model."

"Guys that age usually drive sports cars," Gwen said.

"Unless they need a back seat or a big trunk for their victims," Darcy said.

FOURTEEN

Somewhere in South Florida

He finished his breakfast, adjusted the ruby cufflinks on his crisp white dress shirt, and asked the man seated across from him, "Where's the young blonde you promised me?"

Ron handed him the front section of the *Miami Herald*. "As you can see in the headlines, things didn't go as planned."

The man in the navy Armani suit read the front-page article. "It says both women were rescued, and the smugglers were killed." He shook his head. "A pity, but I still want the blonde."

"Our cyanide source deals mostly in drugs, not women. The money for the girls was supposed to be a bonus for them." He wiped sweat off his forehead. "We should stick to your usual procurement method. That's why we've never been caught."

"Relax, the article said both girls come from wealthy families. Drive down to Miami and meet with the smugglers' boss. Tell him he can get a million dollars each for," he scanned the article, "Kerri Lyons and Jett Jorgensen." He stared at the photos. "Jorgensen? That last name sounds familiar. Too bad Jett isn't a blonde."

"What should I say about her?"

"They can sell the brunette in Europe after the ransom is paid, and remind him you'll pay a hundred K for the young blonde after he collects the million from her parents."

Ron wrung his hands. "What if his men get caught?"

"We have no provable connection to their operation. They only know your first name, and you always pay in cash. No worries." He stood. "Meet with him today."

Arrangements were made using burner phones, and a few hours later, the bossman sat across from Ron at an outdoor table at Bayside Marketplace on the Miami waterfront.

The mobster sipped a margarita. "Your plan sounds lucrative. I'll have my people look into it and get back to you."

Ron nodded, left the table, and vanished into the throng of shoppers and tourists.

After finishing his drink, the boss strolled down a long pier and pulled out an encrypted satellite phone. He had already checked the backgrounds of the two young women who landed on his organization's secret helipad.

He called his military connection overseas. When a man answered, he said, "Do you know a former Navy lieutenant named Jettine Jorgensen?"

"Yeah, we were stationed at the same base until she left the Navy earlier this year. Why?"

He watched a bright-colored cigarette boat race past on Biscayne Bay, its deep, throaty engine reverberating across the water. "She destroyed a secret delivery base we used for years. How well do you know her?"

"We dated a while, nothing serious."

"Good. I hope she's not more important to you than the millions you're adding to your retirement account in the Caymans." He stopped walking and stood on the end of the pier.

The military man hesitated. "We parted ways last year."

"Find a reason to come to South Florida and take her out to dinner. If you require a death in the family, we can arrange one."

The man paused, probably taken aback, but then he must've remembered someone he'd like to be rid of. He said, "I have a grandfather in Miami, Arnold Amherst, who's a nasty bugger. He's old and sickly. Make it look like natural causes, and you'll be doing the family a favor." He spelled the name and gave him the address.

"We'll take care of it today. How soon can you be here?"

"Once I'm notified of his death, I can ask for bereavement leave and fly to Florida for the Jewish funeral, which will be the next day." He hesitated. "What is it you want me to do?"

"Help us kidnap Miss Jorgensen."

Three hours later, a home healthcare nurse visited Arnold Amherst. He was sitting in a wheelchair on his screened-in porch, watching his great-grandchildren swim in his massive pool.

"Hello, Mr. Amherst. I'm nurse Laura, subbing for nurse Kristin today. I'll just wheel you in out of the heat for a few minutes and check your vitals."

He snapped, "Now, see here, Nurse. You're not taking me anywhere. I'm in charge, understand?"

Nurse Laura smiled and waved when his relatives glanced in her direction from across the pool. "Whatever you say, Mr. Amherst." She unlocked his wheelchair and pushed him into a quiet room where they were alone.

No one noticed them leave.

"What do you think you're doing? Kristin never does this," he said. "I'll have you fired."

"Relax, Mr. Amherst. I'll get more accurate readings if you're isolated. You'll be back outside in a jiffy." She checked his blood pressure and oxygen levels, then handed him a novel she pulled off a nearby shelf. "Have you ever read this one?"

"I'm chairman of the board. I don't have time for stupid books."

He threw the novel across the room and broke a crystal vase filled with fresh flowers. "Clean that up!"

When he pointed at the mess, she pulled a hypodermic syringe out of her pocket, removed the needle cap, and plunged a lethal dose of insulin into the back of his neck above the hairline where a needle mark wouldn't be noticed.

"Hey! What did you—"

Laura packed up her nursing tools, said, "Have a nice day," and slipped away.

In a few minutes, seventy-five-year-old Arnold Amherst was dead. An autopsy would show natural causes from a heart attack because everyone has insulin in their bodies.

Jett

One day after my Everglades rescue, Kerri called.

"Hey, Jett, how's your shoulder?"

"Much better since the antibiotics kicked in. How are you doing?"

"Better than ever. That hottie I like on the football team saw a television news story about us. He found me today in school and asked me out. We have a date this weekend."

"Congratulations! I'm glad something good came out of our swamp nightmare." We chatted a little longer and promised to keep in touch.

Then an old boyfriend called. "Hey, Jett, it's Carl Amherst. Having fun in sunny Florida?"

"Most of the time." It took a moment to picture him. "I'm surprised to hear from you, Carl."

"Well, I kinda have bad news and good news."

"What's up?" I hoped none of our Navy friends had been killed.

"My grandfather died, but he's been sick a long time, so this was expected and might even be considered a blessing. I'll be in Miami for the funeral tomorrow."

"Oh, Carl, I'm so sorry for your loss. Is there anything I can do?"

"Yeah, I'd like to escape the relatives and take you out for a nice dinner tomorrow night. Make a reservation wherever you want, and I'll pick you up at seven-thirty."

"Okay, I'll reserve a waterfront table at the Banyan Isle Bistro. You can catch me up on what our friends have been up to."

"Sounds good. What's your address?"

"My home is at One Ocean Drive. It's on the north end of Banyan Isle on the east side. It's a very small island, so everything is easy to find. I'll look forward to seeing you."

"I'll knock on your door at seven-thirty. See you then."

I pocketed my cell phone and reminisced about Navy Lieutenant Carl Amherst. We only dated a few times, and he wasn't what I'd call a keeper, but we parted on amicable terms last year. It might be fun to see him again."

Hope he wears his white officers' uniform.

FIFTEEN

The next day, Gwen called me with a list of local Bentley owners that matched our suspect. It was a short list: three men.

I joined Darcy and Gwen for a meeting with the first man on the list, Matt Hanson. He was a wealthy realtor and real estate investor with a fancy office in a high-rise building on Flagler Drive along the Intracoastal Waterway. A lovely blond receptionist ushered us into his office on the twentieth floor where floor-to-ceiling windows showcased a spectacular view of the waterfront, Palm Beach on the far side of the Intracoastal, and the Atlantic Ocean beyond the famous town.

A handsome dark-haired man in his early-thirties wearing a navy Armani suit stood and greeted us. He smiled, introduced himself, and asked, "How may I help you lovely ladies?"

Gwen flashed her police badge, and Darcy and I showed him our P.I. credentials.

"Do you know a young Palm Beach socialite named Muffy Murdoch?"

"I might, but I'm better with faces than names. Do you have a photo?"

I showed him a head shot of her on my phone. "Recognize her?"

"Yeah, we go to a lot of the same clubs. Why do you ask?"

"Muffy is missing, and she was last seen leaving Club Bacchus three nights ago with a man who looked like you," Gwen said.

He smiled. "I danced with her that night, but she didn't leave with me."

"She might've been murdered," I said, my senses tingling.

"Sorry to hear that." He didn't look sorry.

Gwen asked, "Do you drive a new black Bentley Flying Spur Milliner?"

"Yep, it's the fastest 4-door sedan in the world. Want a ride?" His blue eyes twinkled.

"Did you drive to Equestrian Estates when you left the club Monday night?"

"No, I went home to my condo on Flagler drive. I had an early morning meeting."

"Witnesses saw a man with a black Bentley like yours enter two different homes in Equestrian Estates late that night. Sure that wasn't you?" Darcy asked.

"Must've been some other handsome guy with the same kind of car." He paused. "My friend, Greyson Prescott, drives a car like mine, and he was at the club that night."

"Did he dance with Muffy?" Gwen asked.

He ran his hand through his dark-brown hair. "He might have. I wasn't watching him. Too busy dancing with lots of beautiful women."

"Is Mr. Prescott a close friend?" I asked.

"Yeah, we have our own rat pack," he said. "Four of us drive identical cars—I got us a fleet rate."

I looked into his blue eyes and spotted an evil glint. His smug grin made me want to slap him. Instead, I asked, "Matt, did you kill Muffy?"

He smirked. "I wouldn't confess if I did. Sorry to disappoint, ladies, but good luck to you." He glanced at his watch. "I hate to cut short the fun, but I have an appointment in Palm Beach." He stood and ushered us out the door.

While we waited for the elevator, Gwen said, "Interesting he mentioned Greyson Prescott. He's on our list. I called for an appointment, but he flew to New York today for a business meeting. We'll have to catch him when he returns."

"Alarm bells rang in my head during our conversation with Matt," I said.

"What about the third guy, Nate Briscoe?" Darcy asked.

"We have an appointment with him in fifteen minutes. His office is in this building on the fifteenth floor, and get this," Gwen raised her eyebrows, "he was the developer for Equestrian Estates, *and* he owns a company that builds and installs septic tanks."

"Ding, ding, we have a winner!" I said, grinning.

"But Matt said there were four guys with the same car," Darcy said. "We only found three."

"Maybe the fourth guy has his car registered in his company's name," I suggested.

"First, let's see if your internal alarms go off when you meet Nate Briscoe." Gwen stepped into the elevator and punched the button for fifteen.

Another blond receptionist in her twenties ushered us into a comfortable waiting area and offered us Pellegrino water. As we sat and waited, I hoped Nate would be our killer so we could stop the murders. A wealthy, successful man like him probably wouldn't make it easy for us. My *Aniwaya* intuition had never let me down. What would it tell me about him?

Apparently, navy Armani suits were the uniform of elite men, because Nate wore one too. Like Matt, he was six feet tall and fit with dark hair and blue eyes. We flashed our credentials, introduced ourselves, and sat across from him at his massive desk.

Gwen started by handing him a photo of Muffy. "Mr. Briscoe, have you ever met this woman? Maybe you danced with her at Club Bacchus Monday night?"

He studied the picture. "I've seen her at all the trendy clubs—danced with her at Club Bacchus and elsewhere. Why?"

"Miss Murdoch was seen leaving the club with a man matching your description in a black Bentley like yours. Was that you?" Gwen asked.

"Monday night?" he asked.

She nodded.

"I left alone at eleven thirty, I think. Had an early morning meeting with one of my builders."

"The thing is," I said, "she was last seen with a man matching your description driving a Bentley like yours at an unoccupied home in Equestrian Estates, your new development." I paused. "Did you take her there?"

He glared at me as alarm bells rang in my head. "I told you I went home alone. Is Miss Murdoch accusing me of something?"

"She's missing, possibly murdered," Gwen said.

"You're not pinning this on me just because I drive a black Bentley sedan. There were three other cars like mine there Monday night. Talk to their owners."

"Do you know them? Are they your buddies?" I asked.

"Sorry, ladies. We're done here. Questions can be directed to my lawyer." He stood and handed Gwen his lawyer's card, then walked us to the door.

After we entered the elevator, I said, "Geez, I had major alarm bells with Nate too. He and Matt can't both be guilty, can they?"

Darcy shrugged. "Could be they both did bad things, but chances are only one of them killed Muffy."

"Ah, but which one?" I asked.

"Maybe neither," Gwen said. "We still have to question Jett's neighbor, Greyson Prescott, and a fourth guy."

"Yeah, who's the fourth Bentley owner, and why didn't he show up in the DMW search?" Darcy asked.

I headed home, wondering if we had interviewed a killer. My former coworker and brief boyfriend, Carl, would be picking me up in a few hours for a nice dinner, so my thoughts turned to getting ready for my date.

My watch showed seven-thirty as I descended the stairs and reached the foyer when the doorbell boomed "Ride of the Valkyries." My father had always loved that crazy doorbell.

I opened the door, and Carl greeted me with a bouquet of red roses. "Jett, you look beautiful in that blue dress." His jaw dropped when he spotted the tall Valkyrie statues guarding the twin staircases behind me. "You failed to mention you live in a Nordic castle, and that doorbell was something else."

He chuckled, but it was a nervous laugh, and he avoided looking into my eyes. When he took my hand and kissed it, tingles ran down my spine, but maybe not the good kind. Something seemed off, or I might've been overreacting after the Everglades trauma and meeting creepy Matt Hanson and Nate Briscoe.

I glanced back at the winged statues. "My great-great-grandfather from Denmark built this castle as a tribute to his Viking heritage. It's a bit over the top, but I've lived here since I was twelve, so I'm used to it."

Tan with a square jaw and sandy hair, Carl looked fit and handsome in his short-sleeved white Navy officer uniform. "This must've been quite a culture shock for your late mother. Didn't you tell me she was a Cherokee Shaman?"

I nodded. "That's a life-size painting of her on the south staircase wall." She was pictured in buckskin, flanked by timber wolves, and holding flames in her palms. "Her name was Atsila, which means fire in the Cherokee language, and she was Shaman of the *Aniwaya* Clan."

"*Aniwaya?*"

"It means wolf in Cherokee."

"Interesting. Wish I could've met her and your father."

"I lost them almost three years ago in a plane crash near the Bahamas."

"Yeah, I remember reading about it, and then earlier this year, I heard through the grapevine that their crash wasn't an accident."

"Their murderer almost killed me too. Turned out he was a serial killer."

"Sorry to dredge up bad memories. Let's go to the restaurant and you can fill me in on what you've been doing since you left the Navy."

"Give me a sec to stick these roses in water." I hurried to the kitchen, and Carl followed me.

The scent of roasting lamb filled the room. Karin was there with Pratt and Whitney. When I laid the roses on the counter, my half-wolf dogs planted themselves in front of me and snarled at Carl.

That was unexpected.

"Sorry for their unfriendly behavior. They're very protective of me around strangers." I reached down and petted them. "Carl, this is my dear friend, Chef Karin Kekoa. She's originally from Hawaii." I glanced at her. "Karin, this is Lieutenant Carl Amherst." I had filled her in on him before he arrived.

She looked into Carl's hazel eyes. "Nice to meet you, and I'm sorry for your loss."

He gazed around the spacious kitchen. "My grandfather's passing was a blessing. He had terminal cancer." He glanced at me. "I wanted to escape my relatives for a while, and it was worth the drive from Miami just to see you in this dress."

I smiled at Karin, handed her my flowers, and noticed a look in her eyes that worried me. The dogs snarled softly, and my intuition, inherited from my mother, made me tingle all over. I first felt it when Carl walked in, but I mistook it as the pleasure of seeing a Navy colleague.

Karin set the roses in the sink. "I won't keep you from your dinner reservation." She eased beside me and grabbed the dogs' collars. "I'll hold them while you leave."

I waved goodbye, wondering why Carl worried Karin, my dogs, and me. He didn't seem dangerous as I followed him down the front steps to his rental car. And I had enjoyed a few dates with him when I was in the Navy—no scary vibes back then.

Carl's custom white uniform hugged his body—no room to hide a firearm—but his intentions must be bad, or my internal alarm system wouldn't be jolting me. What should I do? I decided I'd figure it out over dinner.

On the way to the restaurant, my cell phone chimed. I pulled it out of my small shoulder bag and read a text from Karin:

He's hiding something.

SIXTEEN

The Banyan Isle Bistro had waterfront tables overlooking the Intracoastal Waterway, and their outdoor deck was shaded by a huge banyan tree. Tiny blue lights strung across the branches and around the seating area created a romantic ambiance, and my blue silk dress shimmered under the sparkling lights. Scents of grilled meat mixed with the salt air.

Our table was at the water's edge and overlooked a long pier where boaters docked while dining at the restaurant. I noticed a dark-blue Cigarette boat tied up near us. Four hard-looking men sat in the spacious cockpit, drinking beer and laughing. They didn't look or behave like the usual clientele for gourmet dining.

Seated across from Carl, I noticed he glanced at the men and shifted his gaze.

He pointed down at the water. "I can't believe how clear it is. Even in this dim twilight, I can see fish swimming around."

A lovely young waitress took our meal orders, and Carl ordered a bottle of Meiomi Pinot Noir. Before the wine was poured, I noticed my glass was wet inside. Had it not been properly dried before it was brought out, or was there a more sinister reason? A waiter poured the wine, and when I lifted my glass, internal alarm bells clanged again.

Carl raised his glass. "Let's toast to our brief reunion in South Florida." He tapped his glass against mine and took a drink.

A warm wind from the west caressed me as I swirled my wine and inhaled the aroma. Nothing smelled off, but my hand tingled as I held the glass, so I lied. "My wine smells funny. Taste it and see what you think."

Carl knitted his brow. "Mine is fine and it came out of the same bottle. You haven't tried it yet."

"Since you're so sure there's nothing wrong with it, you won't mind tasting it for me." I held my glass out to him.

"Jett, why are you acting so weird? The wine is fine. See?" He took another drink from his glass.

My phone dinged with a text message from Karin. I put down my glass and read: *Are you okay?*

I texted back: *Send help ASAP.*

It was a five-minute drive from my home to the restaurant.

Carl glanced at my cell phone. "Everything all right?"

"Yep, that was Karin asking if it's okay to give my dogs leftovers from the rack of lamb. She always asks first because some people foods don't agree with them."

I put my phone away and reached for my wine glass, deliberately knocking it onto the hardwood deck and feigning an accident. "Sorry." I looked around and noticed a fit man with a buzzcut sitting alone and staring at me.

A waiter rushed over and cleaned up the broken glass and spilled drink. Meanwhile, another server brought me a fresh wine glass and filled it from our bottle.

I took a sip. "You're right. The pinot noir is superb. I was being silly." I glanced at the dock area and noticed the men in the Cigarette boat staring at me. "It's just that so many bad things have happened recently, I've become a bit paranoid."

Carl's gaze darted to the men in the boat then back to me. His nerves seemed on edge. "That's okay, Jett. Tell me about your life as a civilian while we wait for our meal."

I filled him in on my successful hunt for my parents' killer, my new career as a private investigator, including catching the body-drop killer and solving the Mystery Fest murders, and then wrapped it up with an account of my ordeal in the Everglades.

"Wow, you really have been through the ringer. No wonder you're paranoid."

A server arrived with our plates of prime rib with asparagus tips and red potatoes.

As I cut into the tender beef, I asked, "Anything new with your unit in the Navy?"

"Yeah, we've been assigned to a carrier group in the Med keeping watch on that explosive situation with Israel and the neighboring countries. I think your SEAL friends rescued some hostages."

"Good. I just hope everyone stays safe. A lot of crazy stuff's going on."

A huge yacht cruised down the Intracoastal Waterway nearby, and it looked like the passengers were having a fancy party. A soft breeze carried mellow live music from the open upper deck as they motored past.

Carl thumbed at the luxury yacht. "They're having fun. Know who owns it?"

He was trying to distract me, so I played along. Out of the corner of my eye, I saw him pour a tiny vial of liquid into my wine.

I pointed and said, "There's another yacht behind them that's even bigger." When he looked away, I poured half my drink into a nearby potted plant.

His gaze returned to me as I swirled the wine in my glass.

"Looks like you took a big drink."

"I did. It's really quite good." I swallowed a bite of prime rib.

For the first time since Carl arrived at my doorstep, he looked into my eyes and studied me.

I acted woozy and slurred my speech. "Thissh meal is delisshus."

He gave a brief nod at the men in the Cigarette boat, then said, "You look like you need a walk in the fresh air on the dock. Let me help you."

I slung my small purse around my neck and across my chest as he moved to help me stand. A deep rumbling from the Cigarette boat signaled it was on the move. The big speedboat pulled out of the dock space and idled around to the end of the pier.

Carl helped me down the steps. "We'll take a nice walk to the end and back. It'll make you feel better." He gripped my waist and walked me down the pier.

I didn't want to fight five men on my own, so I stomped my four-inch stiletto heel into Carl's instep and shoved him into the water. He made a loud splash.

Three of the men on the sleek speedboat jumped onto the pier and sprinted toward me. I turned and ran toward the steps.

The beefy man that had been eating alone blocked me and pulled out a switchblade. He waved the knife and said with a Russian accent, "Be good girl and come with us."

I took a step back and executed a spinning heel kick into his jaw that knocked him sideways into the water. Several diners were on their cell phones, hopefully calling 9-1-1.

I spun around as the three men from the boat reached me. Before I had a chance to make a defensive move, two men held my arms while the third one pulled out a syringe. I tried to kick it out of his hand, but he was too quick. He sidestepped my foot and plunged the needle into my neck.

My vision blurred as a fist smashed into the face of the man with the syringe. He went down, and the men holding me jerked, released their grips, and fell onto the dock.

I barely recognized Karin as she zip-tied their hands behind them. Then I collapsed and looked up at the blurry face of retired SEAL Tim Goldy as he scooped me into his arms. After that, everything went black.

SEVENTEEN

Earlier

Ron waited until he received a call on his burner phone while outside the shops at City Place in West Palm Beach. "You're about to snatch the brunette? What about the blonde teenager?" He paused, listening. "Okay, grab her tomorrow."

He sauntered to the parking garage, climbed into a white Ford F-150 pickup truck, and drove home. Ron pulled into an eight-car garage and parked in the empty space. His boss waited for him inside the study.

"Well? Did they take her yet?" the man in the Armani suit asked.

"They'll take the Jorgensen woman within the hour. The teenager will require a little more time."

"Let me know the moment they have the blonde." He glanced at his gold watch and grinned. "Time for another photo shoot." He picked up a bridal gown and left.

A petite blonde in her early twenties trembled when the door lock rattled. *Oh no, he's coming back.*

A tall, well-dressed man entered the ten-foot-square room. His tailored navy silk suit and crisp white shirt with French cuffs would've made him look attractive had it not been for the skeleton mask he wore. His ruby cuff links contrasted with the white-lace wedding dress draped over his left arm.

He handed her the gown. "Put this on. I need a picture for my bridal gallery."

Her hands shook so much she almost dropped the gown as she limped to the bathroom, dragging her ankle chain.

"And fix your hair." He pulled out his instant camera.

When she returned, he pointed at the picture he'd hung on the wall by the game table. "Stand beside that and smile."

She stared at *The Face of War*, a macabre painting by Salvador Dali depicting a skeleton head with the eye sockets and mouth filled with more skeleton heads. Trembling, she thought this was the end. She tried to smile, but tears streamed down her face. "Sorry."

"What's wrong? Why are you crying?" He handed her some tissues.

"You're going to kill me," she sobbed.

"No, my dear, I just need a nice photo before we play another game. Give me a smile, and then we'll play."

She dried her tears and feigned a smile.

"Good, that turned out fine," he said after checking the picture. "Now, have a seat." He pulled out her armchair.

She sat opposite him and set up the backgammon game he'd placed on the table. Her trembling hands dropped several game pieces. She leaned down and picked them up.

"Let's get started. You roll first," he said.

Her dice stopped on double sixes. His roll landed on snake eyes.

"You won the roll, and don't forget—if you win this game, you get to go home." His creepy smile showed through the mouth opening on the skeleton mask.

She rolled double sixes again and was off to a good start, but it was hard to concentrate on the game. His scary mask and the creepy painting hanging nearby added fuel to her living nightmare. She dabbed her eyes with a tissue.

Despite her fear, she maintained a small lead as the game progressed.

"This could be your lucky day." He paused. "What's it been—three months?"

"I'm not sure. It's hard to keep track of time here." She took four more of her pieces off the board.

Two to go. Would she finally win a game?

He rolled a three. "Uh oh, I'm four behind you." He smiled, unconcerned. "Your turn."

She threw double twos. "I win." Her eyes brightened as she moved her last two pieces off the board, but she worried it had been too easy. "Will you let me go now?"

"Of course. We'll have one final dinner together, and then I'll take you home. Sit tight while I bring our meal." He closed the game board and left.

The door lock clicked, and she exhaled a relieved sigh. *I miss my family. Will he keep his promise?*

An hour later, the masked man returned with a large meal tray and a bottle of cabernet sauvignon.

"This is a special wine from California that was aged in casks lined with almonds. It'll pair nicely with the steak Diane and steamed asparagus." He pulled out the cork and filled her glass. "Try it. It's quite tasty."

She reached out with a shaky hand and lifted the glass to her lips. After a deep sip, she said, "It's good." She took another drink and leaned back against the tall armchair.

A sharp intake of breath preceded her eyes widening as she gasped for breath and stiffened.

———

The man in the mask watched her lips turn cherry as foam bubbled out of her mouth and nose. *Hair and eyes just like my evil mother.*

"This one's for you, Mommie Dearest. I can only imagine your surprise when our yacht blew up with you, my spoiled sister, and me on board. While I slept under the stars on a mattress on the bow, you two were in your aft staterooms above where my friend planted explosives under the stern. It was such a pleasure to swim the hundred yards to shore while flames devoured you both, leaving me the sole heir to billions. Checkmate, you sadistic bitch."

He stared at the dead girl in the chair. *Getting away with these murders has been too easy, and I only have two girls left to play with. Time to buy that teenager and watch the cops fail to catch me—such a fun game!*

EIGHTEEN

Kerri

Cheerleading practice had gone well. Kerri looked forward to performing their new cheer at the Friday night game. She was the only junior on the varsity squad and held the coveted position at the top of the pyramid formation. Warm wind caressed her as she drove with the top down.

A Taylor swift song played on the radio, and she sang along with the lyrics, happy to have her life back to normal after that brief but awful ordeal in the Everglades. It was twilight on the two-lane state road, and traffic was sparse as she headed home to Jupiter Island.

A large black SUV pulled up alongside and swerved into her little Mazda Miata sports car, forcing her off the road on the right where the road curved left.

She screamed, and an airbag slammed into her face when the car came to an abrupt stop in a muddy drainage ditch filled with three feet of murky water. "My car!" She released her seatbelt as the airbag deflated. Tepid water covered her feet and ankles.

She didn't realize she was in danger and assumed the driver had been texting and hit her accidentally. The SUV stopped and backed up beside her. Kerri turned and reached for the cell phone in her purse on the passenger seat. Before she could grab it, someone yanked her door open, and beefy hands dragged her from the car.

Her abductors wore ski masks, and one held her arms while the other injected something into her neck. She tried to memorize their faces, eyes, clothes, and size, but her vision blurred, and seconds later, everything went black.

The kidnappers hid Kerri under a blanket in the cargo compartment of their Suburban and drove south. One called their boss.

"We have her—she's unconscious in the back. Drug worked like a charm."

"Plans have changed. A ransom pickup is too risky after the mess up with the other girl last night. Feds are looking for us."

"Want us to ice her?" He glanced over his shoulder toward the back of the SUV.

"Call Ron on his burner. Tell him the price is a hundred and fifty K tonight or we slit her throat and dump her."

Jett

I woke in my bed with my dogs snuggled against me. The room seemed to spin a little when I sat up, but after a moment everything looked normal. I petted my precious pups and wondered what went down after I blacked out on the pier.

Karin knocked on my door and peeked inside. "You're awake. How do you feel?"

"A little unsteady but okay. What happened?" I rubbed my aching head.

She sat beside me. "Carl must've set you up to be kidnapped. We think the guys in the boat are connected to that smuggling base you burned down in the Everglades."

"Well, I hope this is the end of their vendetta. Did Carl say how he got involved with them or why he set me up?"

"The cops couldn't find him. The boat driver escaped and left the thugs we caught, but they aren't talking."

My thoughts jumped to the worst-case scenario. "I shoved Carl into the water. Any chance he drowned?"

"Navy officers know how to swim. Besides, his rental car was gone. He must've slipped away while we were busy with the kidnappers."

"What about the Russian I knocked into the water?"

"Banyan Isle's new detective, Blake Collins, caught him when he climbed onto the pier. That bad guy isn't talking either, but the handsome detective wants a word with you when you're able."

I rolled my eyes. "He'll probably blame the entire incident on me."

"What makes you think that?" Karin petted the dogs.

"Remember when he stopped by to meet me a couple weeks ago? He referred to my home as Murder Central and implied my former police detective boyfriend allowed me certain liberties because I'm a crime magnet."

"Detective Collins called you a crime magnet?"

"Not in those exact words, but that's what he thinks. He said he runs a tight ship, and he'll be keeping a close eye on me."

Karin gazed at me. "You already admitted you might've misjudged him, and don't forget you agreed to go out with him Friday night."

"Yeah, but you know that bad feeling we picked up from Carl? Banyan Isle's new detective gives off negative vibes too."

"I didn't notice, probably because I got lost in his sexy blue eyes." She patted my hand. "I'll pay closer attention next time I see him."

Tim tapped on the door jamb. "How's the patient?"

"Better now. Come in." I glanced at my digital alarm clock. It was 8:00 p.m.

He stood beside my king-size bed, and my dogs wagged their tails. He reached over and ruffled their fur.

"Any news on the whereabouts of Carl Amherst?" I asked.

"Detective Collins said he checked with the relatives in Miami. No one has seen him since he left yesterday to take you to dinner. The security guard at your gate recorded the plates on his rental car. It was turned in late last night in Jacksonville."

"He probably drove up there to catch a military transport back to where he's based in the Mediterranean." I balled my fists. "No way he's getting away with this."

"Are you certain he was involved in the kidnapping attempt?" Tim asked.

"Positive. I saw him pour something into my wine, and he gave subtle signals to the men in the boat. He's up to his eyeballs in this."

"That means he's connected to the drug smugglers." Tim frowned. "I thought you said you dated him overseas."

"I did, briefly. He must've covered his tracks well. There was never a hint of wrongdoing."

"Better notify NCIS," Karin, a former Navy officer, said.

"Want me to loop in my active-duty SEAL buddies?" Tim asked.

"Good idea," I said. "I don't want that slime ball weaseling out of this."

"What about your SEAL friend, Snake Sanchez? Should we call him?" Karin asked me.

"I'd hate to interrupt his romantic vacation with Mona, but I should ask him to contact his team so they can be on the lookout for Carl." I grabbed my cell phone off the nightstand and made the call. When Snake answered, I filled him in on everything.

"What about your teenage student pilot? Did anyone try to take her?" Snake asked.

"Oh, crap! Let me make some calls and get back to you." I ended the call and tapped Kerri's number. It went straight to voice mail, so I called her mother.

"Jett? Kerri's missing! I'm worried sick. We can't find her anywhere," Doctor Kat Lyons said, her voice tense.

"Several men tried to kidnap me last night. I'm recovering from a drug they injected." I heard her gasp. "When did Kerri go missing?"

"She was last seen driving away from cheerleader practice three hours ago." She sobbed.

"If the smugglers took her, this might not be for ransom. Call the FBI and I'll see what I can dig up." I glanced at Tim and Karin.

"Are you saying the men connected to that Everglades base did it?" Kat asked.

"It's a strong possibility. Let me know if you get a ransom call, and I'll keep you informed on my end."

"I already called the police. All they can do for now is tell all units to be on the lookout for her car." She gasped. "Hold a minute. The police are calling my other line."

A few minutes later, Kat came back on, sounding breathless. "The cops found Kerri's car—said it had been run off the road. No witnesses. Her cell phone and purse were on the front seat."

"Any traffic cameras nearby?"

"No. I told them about the drug smugglers, and they said they'd call the Miami-Dade Sheriff's Office and coordinate with them." She choked on her next words. "Jett, please, find my daughter."

"We might have a lead in the US Navy. Stay positive. I'll get back to you."

I called Snake and put him on SPEAKER. "Kerri is missing, and I'm pretty sure the smugglers took her. Carl could be the key to finding her. Should I call NCIS, or would it be better to ask your team to find him and covertly drag his butt back here?"

"If he's on the aircraft carrier, my team can't take him anywhere, but they can make him talk, unless NCIS locks him up first. Hold off calling the Navy until you hear from me."

"Okay, we'll look for Kerri while I wait for your call. Thanks, Snake."

"Anytime, Jett."

I looked up at Karin and Tim. "My mind is still a bit muddled from the drug. You're both former Navy. How do you think I should handle this thing with Carl?"

"He'll lawyer up and say nothing to NCIS. Better wait like Snake said, then Carl will think he got away with it." Tim paused. "He won't have his guard up when the SEALs come for him."

"I agree," Karin said.

"Hey, girlfriend." Gwen stood in my doorway. "I'm ready to kick some bad-guy butt. Who attacked you?"

We brought her up to speed on everything, including recent developments with Kerri.

"No witnesses or traffic cams?" Gwen shook her head. "I don't suppose it happened in a neighborhood with doorbell cams, did it?"

"Nope, and if anyone saw it happen, they didn't stop or call it in," I said.

Tim joined in. "Jett's date might be our only chance for a quick recovery."

"Then let's hope the SEALs find him fast and make him talk." Gwen looked at me. "Afterward, they should beat him to a pulp for what he did to you."

I smiled. "Amen to that."

My cell rang. Darcy was calling. I answered and filled her in.

"That's terrible. I hope they find her soon." Darcy paused. "I called because that property I'm buying in Equestrian Estates is scheduled to close four days from now. Then we can dig up the septic tank and search for Muffy."

"I'm not looking forward to that, but we need to give her family closure. In the meantime, if you get any ideas that might help us find Kerri, let me know." I set my phone back on the nightstand.

NINETEEN

The USS *Lawrence Lee* cruised the eastern Mediterranean Sea under a dark, moonless sky while intrepid fighter pilots practiced night launches and landings on the carrier deck.

A few levels below the action, Lieutenant Carl Amherst lay in his bunk, ignoring the loud catapult noise and heavy vibrations. He had the cabin to himself while his fighter-pilot roommate participated in night ops. It had been twenty-four hours since the fiasco in Florida. No calls from the smugglers and no visit from NCIS. Had he gotten away clean?

Four muscular men slipped into his quarters, seized him, and bound his wrists and ankles before he had a chance to react. They yanked him off the bunk and pinned him to the floor. One of them switched on a desk light.

Carl recognized the men as SEALs Jett worked with during her service in Navy Intelligence. The angry looks in their eyes told him they knew what he had done.

One said, "Thought you got away with it, didn't you, Carl?" He didn't wait for a response. "Here's how this will go: Answer our questions truthfully. Lie, and we break your bones. Refuse to answer, you become fish food. Understood?"

Carl nodded. He knew no one would hear him scream in this noisy environment.

The interrogator leaned closer. "Did you help drug smugglers kidnap Jett?"

Carl swallowed hard. "Yes. They aren't the kind of people I can say no to."

"Neither are we." He punched Carl's gut. "Have you been assisting them with their smuggling operations?"

He choked out, "Yeah, I'm their middleman—I conceal the drugs in military shipments back to the States."

"Who's your contact in shipping?" He pressed his knee on Carl's left elbow.

Carl hesitated.

A SEAL broke his left index finger. No one outside the cabin heard him scream.

"Okay, okay—Master Chief Jordan Briggs—been with me six years. He handles all the carrier's cargo shipments." He paused and sucked in a deep breath. "He facilitated the same arrangements in Afghanistan before they transferred us to this ship."

The interrogator cracked his knuckles. "The day after the kidnap attempt on Jett, the same group kidnapped Jett's teenage student pilot, Kerri Lyons. Where did they take her?"

Terror gripped Carl. He knew nothing about the girl, but he feared Jett's deadly friends would never believe him.

"Guys, I'm a coward. Don't break more bones, or feed the fish. The smugglers never mentioned a teenage girl. They only asked about Jett. I swear to God I know nothing about her. You can torture me, but I can't tell you what I don't know."

One of the men started to bend back another finger. "You sure about that?"

"Yes! Ask me something else. If I know the answer, I'll tell you."

"Why did they want to kidnap Jett?" He bent the finger a little farther back.

"Payback. She destroyed their hidden base in the Everglades."

He eased up on the finger. "Was the girl with Jett when she destroyed their base?"

Carl's eyes widened when he remembered their conversation over dinner. "Yes, she told me a teenage girl was with her when they made a forced landing at that secret base. Must've been who the smugglers took."

"How do you contact them?"

"I don't. They contact me using an encrypted SAT phone."

"Who pays you?" he asked as the ship shuddered from a catapult launch.

"Money is direct deposited into my offshore account."

"Have you met any of the smugglers based in Florida?"

"No, just phone conversations."

"Any idea where they live or hang out?" His gaze bored into Carl.

"Probably somewhere in Miami. They have a dark blue Cigarette boat named *Miss Behavin*. Cops could check the marinas, but it might be docked at a private home."

The men stepped back and conferred. Then the interrogator leaned over Carl. "We decided you can confess everything to the ship's NCIS officer or you can take a dive off the fantail after we cut you up enough to attract the sharks tailing the ship."

"Call NCIS."

TWENTY

I took a refreshing shower and enjoyed a relaxing dinner on the back terrace with Karin. A gentle sea breeze washed over me as I contemplated recent events and sipped a glass of spring water.

My Viking doorbell boomed out Wagner's tune, and Karin trotted inside. She returned with Banyan Isle Police Detective Blake Collins.

The blond Adonis smiled at me. "How are you feeling?"

"Much better, thank you. Any progress on catching my kidnappers?"

"None of the men we caught are talking. Seems they're more afraid of their employer than doing major jailtime." He hesitated. "That Navy officer who took you to dinner could be the linchpin to this case. How well do you know him?"

"We dated a few times when I was in the Navy, nothing serious." I paused. "His family is wealthy, and there were no red flags when I knew him overseas. He must be good at covering his tracks."

He sat back and crossed his arms. "Why did he set you up to be kidnapped?"

"The only explanation I can think of is that he's connected to the drug smugglers whose secret base in the Everglades was destroyed." I sipped my water.

"Destroyed by you. Looks like you put a target on your back ... again."

"Listen, Blake, the plane's engine failed, and I had to make a forced landing. I did what was necessary to survive and save the teenage girl who was with me."

"The same teenage girl who's been kidnapped?" He arched a brow.

"It wasn't my fault." I glared at him, and my dogs snarled.

He held up his hands. "Of course, it wasn't your fault. Simmer down. I'm not accusing you of anything, and I apologize again for any misunderstandings earlier. I'll make it up to you Friday night with a fancy dinner at The Breakers." He gave me a warm smile and seemed sincere.

I calmed down, and my dogs stopped snarling.

"Right. Tomorrow night, seven o'clock?" I raised my eyebrows.

He nodded, pushed back his chair, and stood. "If I learn anything about this case, I'll keep you informed. Please do the same for me." He strode to the door.

Karin stood. "Relax, Jett. I'll take the plates inside."

A gentle breeze ruffled the calm water as Carlos slung the rifle across his back and slipped into the inflatable dinghy. He looked up at the cigarette boat's driver. "Wait here, and keep the engine idling. This no take long."

"*Ten cuidado*. Remember, there's an armed guard out front and another in the backyard," the boat driver said.

"*No te preoccupe*. I can handle two rent-a-cops. Probably never shot nobody." Carlos started the silent electric motor and turned away from the speedboat.

Clad in black, Carlos was almost invisible in the darkness as he silently motored toward Jett's pier at the north end of Banyan Isle on the inlet to the Atlantic Ocean. Outside lights on her distant terrace helped guide him. Drone surveillance after her attack on their Everglades base revealed his target spent a lot of time outside on the oceanfront terrace at Valhalla Castle.

After the recent kidnap failure, his boss decided on swift retribution, rather than another attempt at grabbing her for ransom and a later sale. They had already sold the blonde. He wanted to make Jett Jorgensen a graphic public example of what happens to someone who messes with his business.

Carlos cut the dinghy's silent motor and glided up to the dock. He paused and listened. Gently lapping water and chirping crickets implied he had arrived unnoticed. Scanning the shoreline, he was satisfied nothing moved nearby—no guards, people, or dogs. He snugged a line to a cleat and hurried off the floating pier to a huge banyan tree.

Drone footage had shown the tree offered a clear line of sight to the terrace. He climbed to a branch facing the castle. Leaning against a stout trunk, he straddled a thick branch. Then he swung the rifle to his right shoulder and rested the barrel on a branch in front of him.

He scanned the castle with his scope and spotted two women on the terrace. One matched his target's photo. The other woman stood and walked inside. This looked easier than he expected. The guards would come running after he eliminated the target, but he'd shoot them and escape. He adjusted the scope and took aim.

———

Seconds after Karin went inside, my dogs, who were lounging at my feet, jumped up, pointed their noses toward the boat docks, and snarled. I sensed danger, but I couldn't see anything unusual out there in the dark. I glanced at my dogs, who'd never been wrong. Were they growling at a raccoon, and was I becoming paranoid after all the recent bad stuff that had happened to me?

Pratt and Whitney gently grabbed my wrists and tried to pull me off the terrace. Tim burst through the French doors in a full sprint and dived on top of me, pinning me to the tiled floor. A gunshot pierced the silence as a bullet pinged off the castle wall in line with where I'd been standing. My dogs crouched over us as gunfire erupted from the direction of my boat docks. The shots ended moments later, and a male voice from the radio clipped to Tim's hip said, "All clear."

It had happened so fast I didn't have time to react. My breath came in short spurts as my heart hammered my chest.

My dogs sniffed the air and climbed off us. They were unharmed, thank God.

Tim looked into my eyes. "You okay? Hope I didn't hurt you." He lifted his weight off me and rested on his forearms.

"I'm good," I said, out of breath. "You all right?"

He smiled. "Yeah, I landed on something soft."

"Who was shooting at us?"

"A sniper docked at your pier and climbed a nearby banyan tree. He was taking aim at you when one of my men shot him and made him miss." He stood and pulled me to my feet.

"Or you tackling me made him miss." I kissed his cheek. "Thank you, and now I need a huge hug." I wrapped my arms around him and held tight for several seconds.

When I backed off, I asked, "Do we know who he was?"

"My money is on somebody from that smuggling operation you burned down."

Karin rushed out. "Was that gunfire I heard?"

I nodded and hung my head.

"A sniper took a shot at Jett," Tim said. He glanced from her to me. "Don't worry. I'll beef up security, but you two should be extra vigilant and remain indoors for a while."

Detective Blake Collins and two uniformed officers jogged around the corner of my home.

Blake ran up to me. "What happened? We heard gunfire."

Tim stepped forward. "My men shot a sniper. He fell under the tree by the boat docks, and his dinghy is tied to Jett's pier. Soon after, a big powerboat raced away."

"A sniper?" Blake asked Tim, "Who was he shooting at?"

Tim and Karin turned and looked at me.

"Jett? Are you all right?" Blake asked, checking me over. "Who did it?"

"I'm okay." I shrugged. "No idea who shot at me. Maybe those smugglers from the Everglades want revenge."

He pulled out his cell phone. "I'll call in a county CSU and medical examiner." After he made the call, he walked me to the French doors. "Stay inside away from windows until we get this sorted out." He turned to Tim. "Show me the body."

I strode inside, leaned down, and hugged Pratt and Whitney. "Good dogs." Only nine months old, they were already good protectors.

When I straightened, Karin hugged me. "I can't believe he tried to shoot you."

"It all happened so fast, I haven't even had time to feel frightened." I sighed. "Good thing Tim got there in time. He saved me."

I called Gwen and filled her in. "Will you please contact the Miami/Dade cops and see if they can do something to make this stop?"

"Darn right I will. It must be those smugglers wanting revenge. Meanwhile, stay inside and give Tim time to ramp up security at your place."

"Okay and thanks. Let me know what the cops in Dade County say." I hung up and wondered what to do next.

My body started shaking—a delayed reaction.

TWENTY-ONE

Snake called me the next day while I was doing research on the computer in my study. "Hey, Jett, expect a visit from NCIS soon. Carl confessed everything about the smuggling operation and your attempted kidnapping, but he knew nothing about Kerri."

My stomach churned as I stood and paced. "Does that mean they have no leads?"

"They know how and when the drugs are smuggled into Jacksonville. After the shipment is offloaded, they'll follow it to Miami and nab the smugglers. Once they're captured, they can lean on them to locate Kerri."

"How long will that take?" I didn't want to think about what the smugglers might be doing to her or how many things could go wrong with following the delivery guy.

"The plane is arriving tonight. Hopefully, they'll know something by tomorrow morning. Keep the faith."

"Thanks, Snake. I'll let you know how it turns out." I pocketed my phone and stared at my dogs. They wagged their tails and looked at me like they wanted to go outside and play. "Sorry, my darlings, we'll have to play frisbee in the ballroom until the bad men are caught."

Karin joined me. "Two NCIS agents are here to talk to you. Do you want to see them here in your study or in the great hall?"

"Let's offer them lunch in the dining room. They probably had a long drive from NAS JAX." I strode to the foyer. "Welcome, Agents. I'm Jettine Jorgensen. Please call me Jett."

They flashed their IDs, and a lovely blonde in her late twenties said, "We're NCIS Agents Pam Herndon and Nick Profitt."

The handsome guy with the brown hair said, "Thanks for seeing us, Jett. Let's keep this simple. Call us Nick and Pam."

"Good to meet you." I led them to the dining room. "Pam, Nick, please, join me for lunch." I took a chair opposite them at the long, mahogany table. Viking ancestors stared down at us from portraits on the teal silk walls.

Nick pulled out an electronic tablet. "We're here to discuss Lieutenant Carl Amherst, the drug smugglers you encountered, and their attempted kidnapping of you."

"Mind if we tape this?" Pam placed a recorder on the table.

"Whatever you two need to put away Carl and his criminal associates." I waved my hand around the room. "We're eating in here instead of on my oceanside terrace because a sniper tried to shoot me last night." I gave them the details.

A few minutes later, Karin wheeled in a cart with pitchers of iced tea and lemonade and a tray of assorted finger sandwiches. She set everything on the table, along with glasses and place settings. "Please, help yourselves."

I passed the sandwich platter as Nick asked, "What happened in the Everglades?"

They weren't in a hurry and wanted to know everything from the forced landing in the swamp up to my attempted kidnapping and Kerri's disappearance. When I finished my testimony, I said, "Please do everything you can to bring Kerri home safe."

"We understand a teenage girl's life is at stake." Pam looked into my eyes with determination. "We'll do our best to get her back."

The NCIS agents finished their lunch and stood.

"Thank you, Pam and Nick." I shook their hands and walked them out.

Karin joined me in the foyer. "Well? Are they going to find Kerri?"

"I doubt it. Kidnapping usually carries a life sentence. Those smugglers aren't going to admit to anything." I sighed.

"Maybe they still have her, and the Feds will rescue her when they raid them."

"I wouldn't count on that. We need to think of another way to find her." I was about to walk back to my study when my doorbell boomed.

A broad-shouldered man over six feet with auburn hair and hazel eyes greeted me when I opened the door. He held out a NYPD ID and badge. "Good afternoon, ladies. I'm New York City Homicide Detective Sean Sullivan. May I have a few moments of your time?"

"Of course. Please come in. I'm Jett Jorgensen, and this is Karin Kekoa. Come through to the dining room." I led him there.

Karin put a clean place setting in front of him and said, "Help yourself."

"Thank you, Miss Kekoa." He poured a glass of iced tea and chose a ham and cheese sandwich.

"Please, call us Karin and Jett."

"Thanks, and call me Sean. I'm here on my own time—took a leave from work, and was impressed that your guard ran a check on me before he let me in."

"The guards are very thorough, especially after the kidnap attempt and the sniper attack," I said.

"Who was almost kidnapped and shot?" he asked.

I thumbed at myself and gave him the short version.

"So, Karin here, who's a black belt in taekwondo and a Navy veteran, and another friend who's a retired SEAL, rescued you?"

"Yep. They kicked butt and saved me. I was too drugged to defend myself from the kidnappers, and the retired SEAL tackled me an instant before the sniper fired at me."

Sean smiled. "Impressive."

I had to ask, "What brings a NYPD homicide detective to my home on tiny Banyan Isle?"

"I Googled you. You're a private detective and a socialite who holds and attends charity balls. I'm hoping you'll be sympathetic to my cause." He pulled a photo from his sport-coat pocket and slid it across to us. "I'm looking for my daughter, Alannah. She's nineteen and disappeared two weeks ago after she interviewed for a modeling job with the Worldwide Modeling Agency in New York City."

I studied the photo. His daughter was a blond beauty with expressive green eyes. "I'm sorry she's missing, but why look for her here?"

"The CEO of the modeling agency, Greyson Prescott, lives six doors south of you, and I suspect he took her." The detective took a sip of iced tea. "Two hours after her interview with him, he flew to Florida in his private jet. I checked his flight history. Every time a modeling applicant disappeared he returned to Florida that same day."

"How many missing girls are you talking about?" Karin asked.

"At least ten, probably more, over the past five years. Those are just the ones I'm aware of. There could be plenty of young women who traveled from other states to New York for an interview and never made it home. I only know of the city girls who vanished."

"How's your wife holding up? Losing her daughter has to be hard," Karin said.

"She passed five years ago—cancer. Alannah is all I have left, and I know she's counting on me to save her." His tone determined and his eyes filled with heartache, he said, "It's been two weeks of hell."

My heart broke for him. "I'm guessing you don't have any hard evidence, or you would've arrested him." I handed him the picture. "How can I help you?"

"Prescott is holding a charity ball at his home in two days. Any chance you can get me in as your plus one?" He searched my eyes. "I need to meet him face to face—get a read on him, but he's never available for an interview."

I glanced at Karin. "Sophia usually handles my mail. Did you notice anything that looked like an invitation?"

"Maybe. Let me check." She jumped up and trotted away.

I reached across and patted Sean's hand. "I know how you feel. A seventeen-year-old flight student of mine was kidnapped recently, and I'm desperate to find her."

Before he had a chance to respond, Karin rushed in waving a cream-colored envelope with gold lettering. "I think this might be it." She handed it to me.

I opened it and read the invitation aloud: "The pleasure of your company is requested for the Greyson Prescott Annual Charity Ball benefitting homeless shelters. A single ticket, tickets for two, or tables for four or six are available." The date and RSVP info was listed after that.

I pulled out my cell phone and called the contact number. "This is Jett Jorgensen. Mr. Prescott is my neighbor, but I was late opening my mail. I'd like to book a table for four if one is available." I waited while the secretary checked and said she could fit us in. "Great. Book the table." I gave her my credit card number.

Sean raised his eyebrows. "Four?"

"The more opinions the better. I'll ask my Palm Beach Police Detective friend and her detective boyfriend to come with us. We can all give Greyson Prescott the once over and sniff around for clues. It might be fun, and one of us is bound to discover something useful."

"Thank you, Jett. This is my last hope of finding my daughter."

"I'll introduce you as a close family friend from New York, and I'll set you up with a James Bond style tuxedo from my designer friend, Cam Altman. He keeps several sizes on hand to loan for tuxedo emergencies." I dialed Cam's number.

Sean squeezed my arm. "I can rent one."

"Cam's loaner will make you look like you can buy and sell Greyson Prescott." I grinned and said, "Cam, it's Jett with a tuxedo emergency. Can you help?" I put the phone on SPEAKER.

"Anything for you, my darling. What's his size?"

I glanced at Sean and held my phone close to him.

"Forty-four jacket, thirty-four waist, thirty-two inseam, six-one, and one-eighty," Sean said.

"Shoe size?"

"Eleven, medium width."

"When do you need this?" Cam asked.

I answered, "Don't kill me—charity ball in two days. It might be a matter of life and death."

He chuckled. "It always is with you, literally. I'll pop over today at five for a fitting. Toodle pip." He laughed. "I'm trying out British goodbyes." He hung up.

I called Gwen. She agreed to attend the ball with Clint and help Detective Sullivan.

"We're all set," I said. "In the meantime, would you like to stay here? We have plenty of guest rooms, and maybe you can give me some pointers on how to find my teenage friend."

"That's very generous," Sean said. "I'd love to accept your offer if you're sure it wouldn't be too much trouble."

"My pleasure, Sean. Would you prefer a room facing the ocean or the island side and Intracoastal Waterway?" I asked.

"A soothing ocean view. This ordeal has been the worst thing I've ever faced."

I patted his back. "Let's get you settled. If you need to use your laptop, WIFI works everywhere in the castle. The code is Valkyrie28. Grab your stuff and I'll show you your room." I waited while he retrieved his luggage and then led him to the elevator and took him to a room midway on the fourth floor. It had a huge four-poster bed, adjoining bathroom, and a balcony that overlooked the ocean.

"Relax now, Sean. You need some time to decompress. Feel free to explore the castle or take a dip in the pool. We'll come and find you for your fitting at five, and dinner with Karin will be around six. I have a dinner date." I gently closed his door.

Maybe I could help find Sean's daughter, and he could help find Kerri. It sounded like nobody else had any luck tracking down those ten missing models. Detective Sean Sullivan might be an answer to my prayers. I hoped so for Kerri's sake.

TWENTY-TWO

Clothing and jewelry designer Cam Altman rang my doorbell at 5:00 p.m. When I let him in, he kissed my cheeks and said, "Jett, darling, you look exhausted. Still recovering from your ordeal in the Everglades?"

"I guess you're referring to my bloodshot eyes." I sighed. "I'm recovering from being drugged, almost kidnapped, and shot at by a sniper." I filled him in.

He stared at me, hands on hips. "Well, dearie, you can't say your life is boring." He glanced around. "Where's my James Bond?"

Just then, Karin and Sean strolled into the foyer.

"Cam, you remember my chef, Karin, and this is your Bond, NYPD Detective Sean Sullivan."

Sean shook Cam's hand. "Thank you for coming."

"My pleasure." Cam had a suit bag slung over his left arm and handed it to Sean, along with a sack containing shoes, socks, cuff links, and studs. "This was for a client your size. Give it a go. With luck, it may not need altering."

I directed Sean to a nearby powder room. "We'll wait for you in the great hall."

We sat in leather armchairs and chatted with Cam while Sean changed.

Cam glanced around and leaned forward. "All right, spill. Tell me all about the life and death situation that involves wearing that tux." He arched an eyebrow.

Trust was never an issue with Cam, who was a confidant to many friends and high-end clients, but with lives on the line I didn't want to risk sharing too much. "One of Greyson Prescott's friends might be involved in a missing person case. What do you know about him?"

"Greyson Prescott? He's been on Banyan Isle intermittently for the past five years, most of which time you weren't here. He had that home built on top of truckloads of dirt—claimed it was to prevent flooding during hurricanes, but I think he just wanted to tower over the nearby mansions."

"How do you know so much about him?" Karin asked.

He chuckled. "Darling, I keep tabs on all the rich, single men in the tri-county area. I have them added to guest lists for all the balls—men are always needed to dance with the single women—and I end up with new clients for my formal wear."

"Why wasn't he at my charity ball?" I asked.

"He was with a bunch of friends on a dive trip at his estate in the Maldives."

"If you're going to his ball, would you introduce us to him?" I asked.

"I'll be there—Roger is taking me. I'm happy to help."

"Thanks, but don't let on to anyone that we're looking for a suspect." I turned my head when Sean walked in looking like a movie star.

Cam jumped up. "I can't believe it—a perfect fit." He grinned and bowed. "My work here is done."

"Would you like to stay for dinner?" I asked. "I have a date, but Karin and Sean will be here."

"Must dash—hot date with Jeremy. See you at the ball."

"My, you do get around, Cam. Wish I had your social life."

"Say the word and I'll fix you up." He rolled his eyes when he caught my confused look. "Relax, Jett, I know loads of straight single guys. All the hot ones want my tuxedoes."

"I'll let you know after I see how my date goes tonight. See you at the ball." I waved.

Sean waved at Cam and said, "Toodle pip."

Cam looked over his shoulder at him, said, "Don't tease me," and sailed out the door, humming the tune for "YMCA." He was such a jokester.

Karin straightened Sean's collar. "You look fabulous."

"And he's my handsome escort to the ball." I smiled at him. "Dinner is on the back terrace at six, so wear something casual and relax. We have lots of extra guards patrolling, and I won't be there, so you should be safe from snipers."

An hour before my date, we gathered in the great hall with the draperies drawn. My dogs curled up beside Sean's feet and took a nap. They liked him—a good sign, especially after their surprising but appropriate reaction to Carl.

"Tell me about the men you think kidnapped your teenage friend." Sean took a sip of cold beer.

"I don't think human trafficking or kidnapping for ransom is their usual gig. They're drug smugglers and distributors." I poured a smooth cabernet into my glass.

"What makes you so sure?" he asked.

"I overheard them when they were hunting us in the Everglades. They discussed selling us to a drug customer to recoup their losses." I took a sip. "Judging by the way they botched my kidnapping it wasn't their area of expertise."

Karin joined in. "I agree. They complicated things and aroused suspicion by bringing in Navy Lieutenant Carl Amherst."

"Yeah, Carl could've gone years without being caught if they hadn't included him in my kidnapping just because I knew him from my time in the Navy." I shook my head. "That was a rookie move. If they were experts at snatching women, they wouldn't have needed his help."

Karin put down her wine. "You know what else? I bet Carl's grandfather didn't die of natural causes. Carl needed a death in the family to get leave and fly to Florida for the funeral. Someone should look into that."

Sean smiled. "You're catching on. I bet they sent a fake nurse to his house the day he died. Ask your police detective friend to call whoever is handling the Miami end of this investigation. Odds are the grandfather died shortly after a so-called home nurse visit."

My dogs leaped up and wagged their tails when my best friend joined us.

"Hey, girlfriends, who's your handsome guest?" Gwen asked.

Sean stood as I said, "This is the NYPD Homicide Detective I told you about, Sean Sullivan, and Sean, this is my friend and neighbor Gwen Pendragon, a detective with the Palm Beach Police. She and her detective boyfriend will join us at the ball.

He smiled and took her hand. "We were just talking about how you can assist us in another matter."

We explained our theory about Carl's grandfather.

"Sounds plausible—I'll make the call. They already know me from when I reported the sniper attempt on your life." She glanced at us. "Any leads on finding Kerri?"

"The kidnappers know the heat is on. If the family hasn't received a ransom call," Sean said, "that means they decided not to risk a money pickup so soon after their men were caught trying to take Jett."

I almost choked on my wine. "Are you suggesting they killed her?"

"That or they sold her to someone local." He paused. "What color is her hair?"

"Golden blond. Why?" I asked.

"It's a long shot, but so far, every woman who went missing after interviewing with Greyson Prescott was a blonde." He shrugged. "He's local, he's rich, and he likes young blondes."

"Right," Gwen said. "He's the guy you want us to check out at the ball—you suspect he took your daughter."

He nodded. "The trail leads to him. I'm good at reading people. When I meet him, I'll know if he's hiding something."

Gwen smiled. "Jett's good at that too. She inherited her Cherokee Mom's almost mystical intuition. Prescott won't know what hit him when he meets you two."

"And two days after the ball, we'll know whether we found Muffy Murdoch." I took another sip of wine. "Darcy will own the house by then, and we can dig up the septic tank."

Sean sat back and looked at us. "Tell me about it."

We filled him in, and I explained, "Our search for Muffy was a separate case before Kerri was grabbed."

He nursed his beer. "What if they aren't separate cases? Was Muffy a blonde?"

My jaw dropped. "Yes, she had long blond hair."

"Got a description of the perp?" he asked.

Gwen answered, "Six feet tall, dark brown hair, wears navy Armani suits and white dress shirts with French cuffs."

He sat up straighter and leaned forward. "Age?"

"Early-thirties," I said.

"After he left the club, we tracked his black Bentley sedan on traffic cams." Gwen poured herself a glass of wine.

Sean's eyes brightened. "Greyson Prescott is six feet tall, has dark brown hair, wears navy Armani suits with French-cuffed shirts, and drives a black Bentley sedan."

This time Gwen, Karin, and I shared a collective jaw drop.

"We've never met him. Could he be involved in crimes with different MOs?" I asked.

"Anything's possible. I'm hoping we'll solve this at his ball." Sean drained his beer.

Just then, my doorbell boomed. I assumed Blake had arrived to take me to dinner.

Tim had suggested we go in his bulletproof Humvee, but Blake didn't think that would be necessary.

TWENTY-THREE

I answered the door and smiled at Blake. "Are you sure you want to take me out? I might still be a target for snipers, and just so you know, I'm armed."

"Yes, and I'm always armed." He helped me into his new midnight-blue BMW M8 sportscar. The light-blue leather seat hugged me as I belted in.

"This is a beautiful car, Blake. Does it handle well?" We headed south on Ocean Drive then west over the tall Banyan Isle Bridge to the mainland.

"Zero to sixty in three seconds, corners like it's on rails, and stops on a dime," he said, grinning. "Wanna drive?"

I put up a hand. "Not now, thanks. Are you into other things, like motorcycles, boats, or airplanes?"

He nodded. "Used to do offshore racing before my wife died. Now that I'm a single parent, I try to reduce the risk factors. I still drive my cigarette boat, just not flat out."

"I heard about your wife. Sorry. That must've been really hard on you and your son."

A quick sigh. "It was, but the pain has diminished over time. We lost Kim the same year you lost your parents." He took Flagler Drive south along the Intracoastal Waterway past homes and open waterfront to the northernmost bridge to Palm Beach.

"I still miss my parents every day," I said with a sigh. "At least catching their killer gave me some closure."

"How did you know their plane crash wasn't an accident?" he asked as he turned left onto the bridge over the Intracoastal Waterway.

"Experts did a deep dive with me on the underwater crash site, and we found evidence of explosives."

"Interesting, but how did that help you catch him?" He drove east a few blocks and turned right onto South County Road.

"Long story. Initially, I didn't have much to go on." I sighed, remembering the ordeal. "Probably wouldn't have caught him if he hadn't kept trying to kill me."

"As I recall from the police report, your old boyfriend, Mike Miller, helped you shoot him."

"Turned out the bad guy was a serial killer and decided I was getting too close. He sneaked into my home late one night."

"That must've been before you hired all those retired SEALs as guards."

"Yeah, the previous security company was incompetent."

Blake turned left onto Breakers Row, lined with royal palm trees, and split by a huge fountain. He pulled under the porte cochere, and valets swarmed the car. One helped me out.

We strolled through the magnificent lobby under a twenty-foot ornate ceiling and turned down a long hallway lined with fabulous ballrooms, each an example of Old-World elegance. A short stairway and hall led us up to The Seafood Bar where the glass bar held an aquarium stocked with colorful fish. The restaurant had floor-to-ceiling windows showcasing the ocean, which was so close it was as if we were on a cruise ship. The hostess seated us at a window table overlooking a rising full moon glinting on the sea.

"Wine?" Blake asked as he perused the voluminous wine list.

"Whatever you think will complement the lobster, that is, if you're having seafood too."

He glanced over at me, smiled. "You read my mind, and I found the perfect bottle, Wine of the Sea, 2017 *Soave Superiore*." He grinned. "Italians age it one hundred feet below the surface of the Adriatic Sea for one year, and the extreme pressure combined with wave action speeds the aging process. Clever, huh?" He ordered the wine and lobster for two.

I watched a cruise ship heading south in the distance, probably one that departed from Port Canaveral. The ocean sparkled like a trillion diamonds aided by the brilliant moon as Blake's blue eyes seemed to reflect the sea. So far, he hadn't said anything to offend me. It was like he was a different person from the one I'd met soon after Mike left. Maybe my first impression of him had been clouded by my dark mood at the time. I decided to keep an open mind.

We sipped chilled white wine while we chatted and waited for our meal.

He asked, "Will I see you at Greyson Prescott's ball?"

"Yes, a friend of my parents' from New York is visiting and thought it would be fun to attend. Do you know Prescott?"

"He's a longtime friend. I knew him in Boston before he moved to Banyan Isle." He took a sip. "We play chess once a week."

"I've never met him. What's he like?"

"I guess you'd call him a confirmed bachelor. He's thirty-five and has never been in a serious relationship. Don't get me wrong. He's a nice guy, a majority share-holder in several multi-national corporations, and the CEO of Worldwide Modeling in New York City."

"Does he date a lot?" I asked.

Blake chuckled. "He has a thing for blondes—always has one on his arm."

"That rules me out." I laughed. "I heard he's super rich. Where did his wealth come from?"

"The family fortune was created by his late father. When Grey's mother and sister died in a yacht explosion, he inherited the entire estate worth billions."

"So, you guys are buddies?" I took another sip of the smooth white wine.

"Yeah, we have a lot in common. We love fine automobiles, boating, and polo. We play on the same team in Wellington—he helped me get accepted when I moved here."

"That was nice of him. What about his house? I love architecture. Have you noticed anything noteworthy about his mansion?"

"You mean apart from the hill it sits on?" He paused. "He's a security fanatic. All the windows are barred, and he has electronic locks on all the doors and windows."

"Isn't he worried about getting trapped inside if there's a fire or hurricane?"

"He has a manual override for the locks and bars."

I sipped the delicious wine. "But what does the interior look like?"

"Typical lavish mansion—elegant and breath-taking, like this hotel."

"I'll look forward to seeing it at the ball."

"Save a few dances for me." He sat back as the waiter served our meals.

The lobster was delicious, and we laughed and joked while we ate.

Halfway through the meal, I asked, "Do you still enjoy being a detective, even though your son's inheritance can provide you with a carefree life?"

He chuckled. "Concerned Banyan Isle crimes might be too boring for me?"

"Yeah." I smiled. "I mean, the only thing of note that's happened since you moved here was my attempted kidnapping, followed by the sniper attack, right?"

"Actually, Marjorie Wentworth reported the theft of a one-hundred-thousand-dollar diamond necklace." He grinned and cracked open a lobster claw.

"No kidding? Did you catch the thief?" I washed down a bite of lobster with wine.

"Turned out she forgot she dropped it off at her jewelers to have the clasp replaced."

I laughed. "You just proved my point."

"The thing is I like protecting the public and catching bad guys, and Banyan Isle is the ideal place to do it without undue risk to me as a single parent." He arched an eyebrow. "You don't have to work either, yet you chose to be a private investigator."

"True, but that's not going well since Muffy disappeared and Kerri was kidnapped." I pushed my food around with my fork.

"Can I help?" He sounded sincere.

"Maybe. Any chance you were at Club Bacchus Monday night?"

"Yeah, I was there with my rat-pack buddies."

I almost choked on my wine. "Matt Hanson mentioned the rat pack—Greyson, Nate, and him. You're in it?"

"Yeah. We're the only single guys on the polo team, and we all bought identical Bentleys—Matt got us a fleet rate. It's a good size family car, and it's fun to drive."

"You didn't appear on our list of local Bentley owners. Is the car registered in your name?"

"No, I put it in the name of Ryan's trust fund for tax reasons. Why?"

"Muffy was seen leaving the club in a black Bentley."

I pulled out my phone and showed him a photo of Muffy. "Did you see her there?"

He nodded. "We danced a couple times. I think she said she lives in Palm Beach."

It never occurred to me that Blake had been there or that he was a member of the rat pack. "Did you drive your BMW to the club that night?"

"The Bimmer was in the shop, so I took my Bentley."

Holy cow! "Did you see who Muffy left with?"

"Sorry. I left early, around eleven. I think she was still there, but I'm not sure."

I shrugged. "Too bad so many black Bentleys were there that night." I turned to the side and leaned down to drop my phone into my purse. My spine tingled with a warning jolt a second before a bullet zipped past my ear, followed by a shower of broken glass.

I dived under the table, and so did Blake. Then he tilted the table on its side against the broken window.

"Get behind the table, Jett." He dragged me close to him, pulled out his phone, and called for help as a barrage of bullets slammed into the table.

Can't believe this is happening again. This is scary. If I hadn't bent down...

"Think he's firing from a boat?" I asked, my voice quavering.

"Has to be, but don't peek out or he'll kill you." Blake clutched my arm.

It was difficult to hear him with so many people screaming.

When the firing stopped, he said, "Follow me on your hands and knees."

We crawled past terrified guests into the hallway and sat on a bench against the wall. I reached out and squeezed his hand.

"Sorry—thought the threat was over." I trembled as I leaned my head against his shoulder.

"No worries, Jett. I really like you, despite the gunfire."

I squeezed his hand. "I like you too."

"Good. Do you ride? My polo ponies need regular exercise."

It took a moment for my brain to switch gears. "Yes, I love horses."

"Assuming the sniper threat is over by then, let's plan to ride next week in the early evening when it's cooler." He glanced up. "Palm Beach Police are here." He helped me up.

I was happy and surprised to see Gwen's boyfriend, Clint Reynolds, who looked like a young version of Pierce Brosnan. He was also a very competent police detective.

"Hey, Jett, I heard about the sniper attack at your place. Think this was more of the same?"

"I'm afraid so. A bullet barely missed me when I bent over to put away my phone." I nodded at my date. "This is Banyan Isle Police Detective Blake Collins."

Blake showed Clint his ID. "Lots of broken glass in there, but no one was hit. The sniper had to be offshore on a boat."

"Thanks. We'll take it from here, and please send me whatever you have on the other sniper attack."

I grabbed Clint's arm. "Please don't tell the Breakers' manager I was the target. I'd hate to be banned."

He nodded. "I can honestly say we have no proof of who was targeted." He glanced at Blake. "Get her home safe now."

"Will do, and I'll keep you posted if I learn anything about the shooters." Blake took my hand and led me back to the lobby.

The valet area was mobbed, but Blake flashed his badge and got fast service. In minutes, I was seated beside him in his BMW. He drove past the row of tall palms and turned north on County Road. A few blocks later, we were headed west to the bridge. The drive home seemed a blur as I replayed the sniper attack in my mind. Blake was quiet, probably trying to think of a way to catch the shooter and whoever hired him.

He parked and walked me to my door, pausing on the threshold and blocking me with his body to give me a light kiss. "Better hurry inside. I'll see you at the ball." He smiled and returned to his Bimmer as I closed the door behind me.

My doggies greeted me inside, and I wondered if Detective Blake Collins was the perfect gentleman he seemed. Maybe losing Mike wouldn't be so bad after all.

I called Tim.

"Jett, I heard about the shooting at the Breakers. Were you the target?"

"Yep. The shooter must've fired from an unlighted boat near shore."

"I'm glad he missed. Was anyone hurt?"

"No. I hope the Feds catch those smugglers later tonight or tomorrow morning and end this."

"Keep me posted and hold off on dating for a while."

TWENTY-FOUR

The next day after breakfast, Jacksonville FBI SAC Jean Short called me. She said, "A joint task force caught the drug smugglers at their warehouse in Miami. They're being held without bail, so you might be safe from sniper attacks now."

"What about Kerri Lyons? Did you find her?"

Agent Short hesitated. "Sorry. There was no evidence she'd ever been there, and they denied taking her."

"Has anyone tried offering them a good deal to rat out who took her?"

"Yeah, we offered immunity, but no dice. Sorry."

"I hope you'll keep looking for her." My voice quavered as I fought back tears.

"Of course, we will. Like I told her parents, don't give up hope."

I pocketed my phone and decided to do something useful. I found Sean in the hallway and said, "I'd like to take a stroll with you past Prescott's mansion and maybe spot something. And in case there's a sniper lurking around who didn't get the memo, I'll stay extra vigilant and disguise myself with these." I held a ballcap and sunglasses.

We headed for the terrace.

Tim intercepted us. "Where are you going?"

"We're taking a walk on the beach to check out the back of Prescott's house and maybe spot a significant clue."

He frowned. "You should stay inside. Don't forget the snipers."

"The Feds called and said they caught the smugglers, but just in case, I'll stuff my hair inside this ballcap and wear sunglasses." I showed him the cap.

He shook his head. "Not good enough. Got a wig?"

"Yeah, I wore it to a masquerade party. Give me a minute." I ran upstairs and put on a long blond wig.

When I returned, Tim handed me a bulletproof vest. "Wear this under a big shirt." He grinned. "You look really different as a blonde."

Sean spotted the Kevlar vest. "Good idea wearing a wig and vest, Jett. You can't be too careful in case snipers are still hunting you."

"Got a shirt I can borrow to wear over this, Sean? None of mine are big enough."

"Sure. How about a touristy-looking Hawaiian shirt?" he said.

"Sounds perfect. I'll put on the vest while you go get it." I pulled the body armor over my head and secured the Velcro straps. "Thanks, Tim."

"I'd rather you didn't go outside until we're sure all the men behind the attacks are locked up. Are you armed?"

I pulled a Glock 26 out of my waistband holster behind my back as my dogs danced around me, wanting to go with me.

Tim ruffled their fur and looked at me. "Sorry, Jett, you'd better leave them here so no one will suspect you're the blonde."

"Aww, sorry, my darlings. We'll have a fun game of frisbee in the ballroom when I return." I turned to Karin, who had just joined us. "Don't let them out until I get back or they'll follow me."

She looked at the dogs. "Who wants a biskie?"

They wagged their tails, and she led them to the kitchen so I could slip out while they were gone. Sean brought me a cotton floral shirt that easily fit over the Kevlar vest.

Tim walked us to the terrace door. "I'd go with you, but too many people will draw attention, and I'm pretty sure the bad guys know what I look like. Be careful."

I scanned the trees in my backyard. No snipers that I could see. We strode across the back lawn to the beach and turned right. No one was on the beach, and no boats were on the water. Unless a sniper popped out of the water in scuba gear, I was safe so far.

Prescott's mansion was six doors south of my property. It was easy to spot because his two-story home stood tall atop a twenty-foot hill made from trucked-in dirt. A small beach building bordered his ocean-front fence.

"Looks like there's plenty of room under the house for a concrete basement to imprison young women." I stared at the imposing stone structure. "The only entrance to underneath the building must be from inside the house."

Sean frowned. "And it's probably a hidden entrance in case police search."

I nudged him. "He can hide from people, but he can't fool Darcy's dogs. If we can get them inside, they'll sniff out the secret door like they have in other buildings."

He looked at me. "Thanks to you and your friends, we might find my daughter alive. Kerri too, I hope."

We turned and headed back up the beach to my place. The sand felt warm on my bare feet, and a steady east wind carried the scent of the sea over us. Hard to think that on such a lovely day two women might be nearby, fighting for their lives.

Somewhere in South Florida

"That's right." The man wearing a skeleton mask waved to one side. "Stand closer to the painting. You look lovely in that wedding gown."

The young woman trembled and fought back tears, not wanting to make her captor angry. So far, he hadn't harmed her, but this might be her day to die.

He snapped her picture with his instant camera and checked it. "Turned out great. You're a perfect addition to my bridal gallery." He pulled out a chair. "Have a seat and we'll play our game. You're a better chess player than my last guest. I should be careful, or you might win this one. Then I'd have to let you go."

The beautiful blonde, only twenty years old, lifted a shaky hand and moved her pawn across the chessboard. "Will you really let me go if I win?"

"Of course. I'm a man of my word." His sinister eyes gleamed from inside his macabre mask as he blocked her knight.

She fought back tears and glanced at the disturbing painting she'd posed beside. It was on the wall by their table, and she noted the faint signature. "Is that a real Salvador Dali?"

He nodded. "The Face of War." He grinned through his frightening mask. "Appropriate, don't you agree?"

"You mean because it's a skeleton face, kind of like your mask?"

"I find the similarities interesting." He waved his hand at the board. "Your turn."

The game seemed easier for her this time. Maybe a little too easy. She bit her lip and made her move. *Why is he making mistakes?*

He did what she hoped and took her rook.

She sucked in her breath and made the decisive move. "Checkmate."

He sat back and studied the board. "Well done, my dear. I didn't see that coming. Looks like your stay here has come to an end. We'll enjoy one last dinner together, and then I'll take you home."

"How far is it from here?" she asked, hoping he was telling the truth.

"About a three-hour flight in my private jet. I'll call my pilots and have them get the plane ready."

He left and locked the door.

Am I really going home? She stared at herself in the bathroom mirror and prayed her captor would keep his word.

An hour later, he returned with a dinner tray. He pulled the cork on a bottle of French Chardonnay. "This delightful wine will complement the chicken cordon bleu we're having." He filled her glass. "Try it."

She lifted the wine glass and took a deep drink. "It's delicious." She set down the glass, leaned her head against the chair, and gasped.

Her eyes widened, and her lips turned cherry. Foam bubbled around her mouth and nose. She stared at the masked man with her soft brown eyes permanently locked open in terror.

He leaned back in the wingback chair and adjusted his ruby cuff links. Smiling at the blond corpse, he said, "This one's dedicated to you, sister dear. Unlike my endless losses with you, here I never lose until it's time for you to die again. I consider that a win too." He took in a deep breath and exhaled. "Ah, Sybil, it gives me great pleasure to imagine I'm killing you over and over. I also take great comfort in knowing you'll never rest in peace with pieces of your blown-up body charred and rotting in the vast sea."

The man in the mask stood. Still two blondes to play with now that the new one was here. He strode to the door, opened it, turned, and took one last look at the dead girl.

Blondes truly are evil—every one of them.

TWENTY-FIVE

The night of the ball had arrived. "Ready?" I asked.

Sean nodded

We made an attractive couple with my date in his classy tux and me in a sultry red gown that hugged my curves. Tim pulled up to drive us in his bulletproof Hummer.

I patted my dogs' heads and told them, "Be good and guard Karin and the house while we're gone." I didn't want to walk to the ball in five-inch stilettos, even though Prescott's mansion was only a two-minute drive down the street, and Tim didn't want me exposed to snipers. All had been quiet since the drug smugglers' arrests. Hopefully, things would stay that way.

Tim dropped us under the porte cochere. I took Sean's arm as we strolled up the entry steps to where a butler opened the massive oak door and welcomed us inside.

A lovely, long-legged blond hostess in her early twenties led us to our table in the ballroom. Gwen and Clint were already seated and had an open bottle of champagne and four glasses on the table. Clint stood when we arrived, and I introduced him to Sean. Clint wore a classic Bond tuxedo, and Gwen wore a green silk gown that matched her eyes.

"Have you met our host yet?" I asked her.

"No, we just arrived." She glanced around. "The room is filling up fast. Looks like a good turnout for the homeless charity."

The ballroom was as big as a basketball gymnasium with a twenty-foot ceiling, crystal chandeliers, tall windows, and life-sized marble statues of mythical gods and goddesses standing along the perimeter. Round tables covered with red linen bordered the polished oak dance floor.

Cam glided over, fashionable in a black silk tux accented with a red bowtie and matching pocket square. He leaned in and lowered his voice, "I just met our host—quite the hottie." He touched his hand to his lips. "He's mid-thirties, and he doesn't appear to have a date with him." He winked.

"Pick up any negative vibes?" I asked.

He shook his head. "Greyson is quite the charmer. You ladies might fall under his spell."

Gwen rolled her eyes. "There's no danger of that happening, Cam."

I squeezed his arm. "Where is he now?"

"Ocean end of the ballroom. I'll take you and Sean to meet him, explain you're his neighbor, and Sean is a family friend here on vacation."

"Sounds good. Let's go." Sean pulled out my chair.

We followed Cam across the crowded room to the east end where tall, barred windows and French doors showcased the sea, and the orchestra played a waltz.

Our host wasn't there.

Cam glanced around. "Sorry, he was here a minute ago."

"No worries, we'll meet him eventually." I took Sean's arm, and we strolled back to our table.

"What was he like?" Gwen asked.

I shrugged. "Didn't meet him. Seems to have vanished."

"He's probably circulating through the crowd," Clint said.

"I'll pretend I'm looking for a bathroom and search the mansion." I stood and headed for a door on the side wall. I spotted bathrooms along the back, but my plan was to slip away and explore the huge home.

I entered a deserted hallway and turned a corner at the far end. My heart pounded as a strong sense of malevolence enveloped me like a heavy fog. The passage led to a spacious room with a vaulted ceiling, velvet-covered furnishings, a black-lacquered grand piano, and tall windows with decorative bars on the outside.

The ballroom windows were barred too. Is he afraid of something, or is this house meant to be a prison?

The sound of a door closing made me freeze. I scanned the lavish room. Nothing moved.

I entered the hallway, still sensing dark energy, which had probably been masked earlier by all the guests in the ballroom. The passage was lined with beautiful oil paintings of ocean scenes. Somewhere ahead the floor creaked.

My sense of danger grew stronger, and goosebumps erupted on my arms. Just as I rounded a corner, I bumped into a dark-haired man in a black Armani tuxedo. Alarm bells rang in my head, and my heart raced.

His piercing, ice-blue eyes seemed to penetrate my soul. I half expected to see satanic horns on his head, but instead he looked remarkably like real estate investor Matt Hanson and similar to property developer Nate Briscoe.

He smiled. "Ah, you must be Jett Jorgensen. I'm Greyson Prescott." He kissed my hand. "Welcome to my home."

"Thank you, but how did you know my name?" I asked, my heart pounding. "We've never met."

"You look like your mother. I met her a few years before your parents' fatal plane crash. So sorry for your loss."

"Thank you. I love your home—so unusual—built on a manmade hill. Does it have a basement?" I hoped he couldn't see how tense I felt.

"In coastal Florida? Too risky—just a wine cellar. The underground temperature is perfect for wine storage."

Greyson seemed charming, but my *Aniwaya* senses picked up a scary undercurrent. I squeezed his hand and felt powerful jolts of electricity as alarm bells rang louder in my head. "So nice to finally meet you."

"My pleasure, Jett, but you seem to have wandered away from the ballroom. Can I help you find something?"

"I was looking for you." I smiled. "I've been meaning to meet you for months, but circumstances kept getting in the way."

"I'm flattered." He gave me a million-dollar smile. "Sorry about all the murders and mayhem at your ancestral home." He shook his head. "Word travels fast on this small island, and if the human element wasn't bad enough, I heard a crocodile invaded a private party in your ballroom."

"A neighbor's pet." I sighed. "It's been one disaster after another since I returned home in January. An old family friend from New York is visiting me now, and I'm hoping everything will go smoothly." I glanced at my watch. "I brought him to your ball, and he'll be wondering what happened to me."

Greyson offered his arm. "Allow me to guide you back, and you can introduce us."

As we strolled, my inner senses zapped me with alarms. When we reached my table, the men stood, and I introduced everyone to Greyson. Sean looked into his eyes, and they shared an intense moment during their handshake.

Greyson broke the tension by saying, "Nice meeting you all. I hope the ladies will save a dance for me."

I smiled. "Yes, of course, and thank you for holding this event for the homeless."

Sean pulled out my chair after Greyson walked away and said, "He took Alannah. I saw it in his eyes and felt it in my bones."

I said, "He gives me strong negative vibes too, and his eyes are scary. Sean could be right about him, but how do we prove it?"

"I suggest we dance with as many guests as possible and casually ask them about Greyson and his buddies," Clint said. "Maybe we'll pick up helpful info."

"Good idea," Gwen agreed. "You men might get good gossip from some of the older ladies, and we'll chat with the male guests."

I weighed in, "My Wolf Clan senses picked up dark energy here. We need to search this house."

"Any chance we could sneak in while he's on one of his trips to New York?" Gwen asked.

Sean frowned. "I doubt it. My research indicated he has a high-tech, automated security system. Did you notice all the windows are barred, even in the ballroom?"

Clint nodded. "And there are security cameras everywhere. I'm guessing all the outer doors and windows are connected to an electronic locking system. I've seen setups like this at some of the newer mansions on Palm Beach."

"Any chance a first-rate hacker like Mona could disarm the system?" Gwen asked.

I shrugged. "Possibly, but she's visiting Snake in Texas."

"True, but she might not need to be on site," Gwen said.

"There might be another way in," I said. "Maybe Greyson likes dogs. What if Darcy and I show up with two of her search dogs? We could say we're collecting for a no-kill shelter and ask to come in for a moment."

Gwen's eyes brightened. "Right. The dogs could be primed with Kerri's and Alannah's scents beforehand. Then they could suddenly bound off and search the place before Greyson had a chance to stop them."

Sean furrowed his brows. "That sounds like a long shot, and if the dogs don't find Alannah and Kerri, he'll know we're onto him and kill them."

"If the girls are there, Darcy's dogs will find them," I said. "Their noses never fail."

"We need to move fast. Know any skilled hackers?" Sean asked.

"Ask Tim," Gwen said. "His Trident Security Company is very high-end. He probably has every base covered, and his retired SEALs know how to do all sorts of things."

I agreed. "Tim has helped us with lots of tricky situations. I'll ask him when we get home. While we're here, let's learn what we can about Greyson and his security system."

Blake strode to our table in a custom tux, looking like Ryan

Gosling at the Academy Awards. "Good evening, everyone." He smiled at me.

I made the introductions and noted he seemed a bit jealous of Sean. He asked me to dance and pulled out my chair.

"You look beautiful, Jett," he said as we hit the dance floor. "Are you enjoying the ball?"

"I am." I glanced around. "Greyson has a lovely home."

He pulled me closer. "Have you met him?"

"Yes, he's quite charming. I was surprised he was alone—no blonde on his arm like you said."

"He's probably busy playing host. Believe me, he has plenty of women on speed dial who would jump at the chance to spend time with him."

"Hope springs eternal. They're probably vying for a chance at matrimony."

"What about you, Jett? Would you like to be married some day?"

I hesitated. "I thought things were headed that way with Mike, but he took a major detour and left me for the FBI."

"I was surprised they offered him a spot after he humiliated the Feds by proving they arrested the wrong people in the Mystery Fest murders."

I sucked in my breath, remembering how I solved the murders and gave Mike the credit. Never dreamed that would backfire. At least I had the consolation of knowing the two Feds from Miami, who wrongly accused my friends, were transferred to a field office in Alaska. Good riddance to them.

The dance ended, and I explained, "I hope you don't mind, but I intend to dance with as many guests as possible so they remember me the next time I host a ball."

"Of course. We all have ulterior motives at these events." He glanced around. "I dance with all the wealthy Banyan Isle widows, so they'll approve of my appointment as detective and second-in-command under the police chief—you know, politics—I have to play the game, especially since the police chief will retire soon." He squeezed my hand. "Would you like me to bring you a red wine from the bar in, say, forty-five minutes?"

"That would be perfect." I kissed his cheek. "And give me a call next week when you want to go riding, that is, assuming I'm not still dodging bullets."

"I heard that ended when the FBI arrested that smuggling ring."

"Yeah, probably."

TWENTY-SIX

Blake and I parted ways, and Matt appeared beside me. "May I have this dance?"

I smiled. "Of course." I offered my hand, and he whirled me into the middle of the floor with a flourish. "Wow, Matt, you've got some impressive moves."

"I learned ballroom dancing in prep school and then taught it in college. My parents weren't wrong when they said it was a skill that would prove useful throughout my life."

I gazed into his handsome face. "Has anyone ever told you how much you resemble Greyson Prescott?"

He grinned. "Yeah. Sometimes we pretend to be twins who were adopted by different parents."

"Nate could pass for your brother, just not a twin. Are you guys all close friends?"

"Yeah, we play on the same polo team, hang out at the same nightclubs, even drive the same Bentleys. Sometimes our real estate deals overlap, and everyone benefits." He gave a smug smile. "And you, Jett, did you solve your missing person case?"

"I wish. Any suggestions?" I asked, hoping he'd slip up.

"Have you considered the possibility you're looking in the wrong place? I mean, did you see Muffy's face on the security video of the woman leaving in a black Bentley? Maybe she walked out the front door with someone else."

"Anything's possible. I'll keep looking."

The waltz ended, and I excused myself and wandered toward the oceanfront windows. Nate intercepted me and asked for a dance.

As we started around the floor, I asked, "Aren't you here with a date?"

"I loaned her to an old geezer who owns a property I'm trying to purchase." He winked. "What about you? Are you here with someone?"

"A family friend from New York. Poor guy is being mobbed by aging cougars."

Nate laughed. "The things we do to network at these events." He pulled me a little closer. "Any progress on your missing person case?"

"Not yet. I don't suppose you've heard anything about a guy using your new Equestrian Estates development to dispose of his victims?" I felt his muscles tense up.

"No, and I can assure you that no bodies have been found there. Look elsewhere. Maybe she ran off with some guy her daddy didn't like."

Just then, we found ourselves beside two angry women fighting over Clint. Mimsy Farnsworth and Marjorie Wentworth, wealthy Banyan Isle widows in their fifties and sixties, each gripped one of his muscular arms and wouldn't let go.

Shouts of "He's mine!" and "I saw him first!" filled my ears.

Clint rolled his eyes and gave me a look that said, "Help me."

I stepped in. "Ladies, please don't bruise my friend. I'm sure he'll be happy to dance with each of you." I leaned in and whispered to Mimsy, "Be a dear and let Marjorie have him first. She's older and won't last long." I winked.

Mimsy grinned. "Better dance with her first, darling. She's usually in bed by ten." She glided away before Marjorie had a chance for a retort.

Sean strode in, took Mimsy's hand, and guided her around the polished floor. That put a smile on her face.

Gwen's boyfriend, Clint, danced with the Banyan Isle dowager, while Gwen danced with an elderly tycoon from Jupiter Island. I turned and almost bumped into Greyson.

"Jett, may I have this dance?" He offered his hand.

As we glided around the room, he said, "Thanks for breaking up that dispute between Mimsy and Marjorie. I've never seen them so angry."

I laughed. "Poor guy was just trying to do a good deed."

He shook his head. "The things we do for charity."

"That reminds me, do you know a young woman named Muffy Murdoch?"

"Muffy? Oh sure, she's a socialite from Palm Beach, blonde, early twenties. We haven't dated, but I've danced with her at some of the clubs we frequent. Is she a friend?"

I nodded. "She went missing from Club Bacchus Monday night, and I've been hired to find her. I'm asking everyone who might know her if they saw her that night and maybe know something that will help. Did you see here there?"

"She was with the usual crowd. We danced a few times, and she danced with my buddies too. Talk to Matt Hanson, Nate Briscoe, and Blake Collins."

"I did. They said you were all there that night."

"Yeah, we like that new club. They have a superb wine list, and the place is always filled with fun people. You should go."

Oh boy! Every suspect gave me warning vibes, including Blake. They couldn't all be killers, could they? Maybe my trusted intuition had gone haywire.

A young blonde cut in to dance with Greyson, and Sean snagged me. He whispered in my ear, "The older women don't like Greyson. They think he's hiding something because he's so secretive and has all the windows barred."

"I agree with them, but we'll have to do something drastic to prove it." I spotted him snuggling close to his blond dance partner. "He admitted he has a basement but said it's just a wine cellar."

"A wine cellar with a hidden dungeon for blond prisoners, I bet." He unconsciously tightened his hold on me. "We'll nail the bastard and save Alannah."

"If he has Alannah, he might have Kerri too."

The dance ended, and Blake walked up holding a glass of red wine in one hand and a whisky in the other. He was about to hand me the wine when Bitsy Belvedere, a wealthy middle-aged lush, grabbed it out of his hand and downed it.

"Thanks, I needed that," she said and handed him the empty glass. Seconds later, she gasped and collapsed on the floor. Foam bubbled out of her mouth and nose as she twitched and jerked. Then she froze, and her wide-open eyes stared at nothing.

Bitsy was dead.

Sean grabbed my arm. "Don't drink or eat anything." He glanced around, searching the crowd for potential threats.

It had all happened so fast. Blake handed both glasses to me and said, "Hold these. I'm calling for backup, a county M.E., and a CSU."

Greyson pushed through the crowd, and his eyes widened when he saw me. "What happened here?"

"Bitsy grabbed a drink meant for me and dropped dead soon after drinking it," I said, watching his eyes for any sign of guilt.

He managed anger and outrage. "That's terrible! Who brought it to you?"

Blake answered, "I did. I got it from a bartender over there." He pointed across the room at a bar along an inside wall where all the bartenders were blond women.

Greyson glanced at the bar. "Which woman handed you the wine?"

"It was a man with really strong cologne." Blake scanned the crowd. "I don't see him now. He was late twenties and muscular with brown hair and eyes."

Greyson frowned. "All my bartenders are women. What was he wearing?"

"A standard black tuxedo. Are you saying he doesn't work for you?" Blake asked.

"I made a special request that all the catering and serving staff be blond women." He shrugged. "I like blondes. No men were hired for this."

Several Banyan Isle police officers arrived, and Blake waved them over to us.

"Keep people away from the body, and don't let anyone leave." He instructed them to look for the guy in his late twenties who served him the wine. Then he turned back to me. "Sorry. That was a close call. Are you okay?"

"No. I feel terrible about Bitsy, especially if the poison was meant for me. You'd better check if your whisky was poisoned too." I handed him both glasses.

Blake frowned. "Wait at your table with your friends. You might've been the target, but we can't be sure of anything yet. Everyone might be at risk." He used the band's microphone to warn guests to remain in the ballroom and not drink or eat anything.

Sean led me back to our table where we joined Gwen and Clint.

Gwen asked, "What happened? Did an old geezer have a heart attack?"

"That would've been bad, but preferable." My stomach churned as I explained.

"OMG! You think Blake tried to poison you?" Gwen asked.

"It's possible, but he seemed as surprised as I was when Bitsy died."

Sean jumped in. "If Blake was telling the truth, an imposter posing as a bartender handed him the wine intended for Jett."

Clint shook his head. "Sounds like your enemies switched gears when the snipers failed and sent in an assassin with poison."

I bit my lip. "Geez, I hope not, but it does seem like that's what happened."

"But how did the assassin know the wine was for you, unless Blake told him?" Sean asked.

"Or there was no assassin, and Blake poisoned the wine," Gwen said.

"But what's his motive?" Sean asked.

"He doesn't seem to have one, unless he's doing it for someone else," I said. "No, that can't be right because he protected me when a sniper shot at me during dinner at the Seafood Bar."

"You told me he used the table as a shield after the first shot missed," Clint said. "He might've been covering for himself once you knew there was a threat."

"Maybe, but I doubt it. He never did anything suspicious like Carl did with me."

"Then how did the assassin know the wine was for you?" Gwen asked.

I shrugged. "I'll ask Blake about it when he's not so busy. Maybe another guest heard him order the wine and asked him who it was for, and the imposter bartender overheard it."

Sean suggested, "Maybe Blake was the target, and the M.E. will discover that both drinks were poisoned."

I glanced across the room at Blake. "I bet he never thought of that possibility because he'd naturally assume the poison was meant for me."

Clint nudged me. "Does Blake have any enemies?"

"I have no idea." I realized how little I knew about him personally.

TWENTY-SEVEN

My tablemates and I speculated endlessly, gave statements to the police, and were home by midnight. Tim parked the Hummer in front and walked in with Sean and me.

"Saw all the cops. What happened at the ball?" Tim asked.

I hung my head. "You should probably lock me in a panic room with plenty of armed guards outside."

He sucked in a breath. "Tell me."

We sat on a sofa in the great hall. "Bitsy Belvedere drank a glass of wine meant for me and died within seconds. And that's not all. I don't have any proof, but I think Kerri and Alannah are Greyson Prescott's prisoners."

That got his attention. "Two questions: Who tried to poison you, and do you want me to rescue the women?"

I gave him a brief rundown of what happened at the ball. "Rescuing the girls is complicated. We have no hard evidence they're there." I explained our options.

"Are you suggesting we wait until he's out of town, then disarm his security system and search his home?"

"Unless you have a better idea," Sean said. "We're worried my daughter and Kerri might not be kept alive much longer."

He hesitated a moment, then said, "Try the dog charity ploy first. At the very least, Darcy's dogs will let you know if the women are or have been there."

"Okay, but can you verify what sort of security system he has while we organize the dog mission?"

"I'll get right on it." He paused. "Be careful, Jett. If you're right about him, he's a ruthless serial killer with lots of resources at his disposal. There's a reason he's never been caught." He paused. "And please, stay inside your house for now. Good night."

I slid into bed wondering if Greyson was a kidnapper and killer. Matt was also a definite possibility. But so was Nate, and maybe Blake. Maybe they all helped each other, or maybe they were innocent and just gave off bad vibes. I felt certain they were guilty of something. But did one of them take Kerri and Alannah? I hoped it wasn't the same guy who took Muffy and possibly buried her under a septic tank. I'd know that answer tomorrow when Darcy had the suspicious tank dug up.

Sleep eluded me for a few hours as I tossed and turned, worried I wouldn't find the women in time.

I woke to doggie kisses from Pratt and Whitney. They were such a comfort to me, especially since my longtime love, Mike, left me to join the FBI and then ghosted me.

Seemed like male friendships weren't a problem, but my romantic relationships always ended in disaster. Time to end my early-morning pity party. Better to focus on my P.I. apprenticeship with Darcy and forget about romance for a while, especially since Carl helped my kidnappers, and Blake may have tried to poison me. I sure was bad at choosing men.

My security guards assured me my land and the nearby area was sniper free. After taking the dogs for a run, showering, and dressing, I joined Sean and Karin on the back terrace for breakfast. It was good to be out in the fresh air, and Karin made delicious ham and cheese omelets.

"Is today when Darcy has that septic tank dug up?" Karin asked.

"Yep, I'm meeting Gwen and her there later this morning, if I can convince Tim I'll be safe." I grabbed a mini muffin.

"Are you expecting to find the missing girl from Palm Beach?" Sean asked.

"Darcy's dogs indicated Muffy is there, and my gut told me the same thing. I hope we're wrong, but I doubt it." I bit my lip and stared at the ocean.

Sean gently placed his hand over mine. "Wear a Kevlar vest, and I'll protect you."

"I'd appreciate you coming. We can benefit from your years of experience with homicides." I glanced at my watch. "We'll leave here in an hour."

Tim joined us at the table. "I have that info you wanted about Prescott's security system."

"That was fast. Would you like some breakfast?" I asked.

"Just coffee. I ate earlier." Tim accepted a cup from Karin.

"Can you hack into Prescott's security or circumvent it?" Sean asked.

"Doubtful. It has several layers of firewalls and three backup power sources." He took a sip of black coffee. "It's wired to prevent physical tampering as well as hacking. The Pentagon would do well to have a system like that."

"That means we'll need Darcy's dogs to find probable cause to justify a search warrant." Sean looked at me. "Think they can do that?" He sounded desperate.

"Yes, but it'll be tricky. We'll need to get the dogs inside his mansion and then *accidentally* lose control while they run through the place and find the women's scents. We'll prime them with their clothes before we knock on the door. Kerri's mother dropped off her underwear from her clothes hamper, and Sean brought Alannah's with him."

"The sooner the better." Sean looked at Tim. "Thanks for the security system intel."

I touched Tim's arm. "Can you do a deep background check on Matt Hanson and Nate Briscoe while we investigate that septic tank?"

"Consider it done, but you aren't going anywhere unless you wear a vest and take extra security with you."

"Don't worry. All the bad guys from the Everglades operation are either dead or in jail, so they won't have an opportunity to hire more assassins, and Sean is armed and will accompany me." I showed him the vest under my shirt.

"Okay. Take my car." He handed me the keys to his bulletproof Humvee and pushed back his chair. "Stay vigilant out there." He excused himself and left.

Sean and I helped Karin clear the table and carry everything into the kitchen.

"Thanks. Now you two head out to Equestrian Estates. I'll clean up here." She shooed us out of her kitchen.

———

We met Darcy and Gwen at the property with the suspect septic tank. She had Laddie, Dobie, Max, and Tiny with her. Tiny was a huge Great Dane.

My hair swirled in the light breeze as I scanned the area with high-powered military binoculars. "No snipers in sight."

Darcy looked at me with moist eyes. "It doesn't look good for Muffy. The odds of all four dogs being wrong …" Her voice trailed off, and she bit her lip.

Just then a truck arrived towing a trailer carrying heavy equipment. Five minutes later, an excavator lumbered off the trailer and across the yard to the dig site.

We stepped back with the dogs while the operator dug out the septic tank and set it beside the hole. Scents of dank earth and decay wafted through the air. The dogs showed no interest in the tank, but once again, a snake camera was fed into the neck to verify no one was inside. As before, it was empty.

Darcy's dogs leaned over the hole, sniffed, sat, and barked once, indicating Muffy was indeed buried under where the septic tank had been installed.

The assassin stood beside his black SUV and checked the area. No one in sight.

He opened the hatchback and pulled out a new Barrett 50-caliber sniper rifle. His navy jumpsuit had a Palm Beach County Water Management patch on it, and he wore sunglasses and a ballcap. After one more look, he slung the heavy rifle over his shoulder.

Didn't succeed at the Breakers, but I'll nail her this time. She'll never spot me from this far away. He grinned. *I'll earn that fifty grand today.*

He slowly climbed to the top of the water tower with a thirty-seven-pound rifle on his back and settled on a spot with a clear view of the property where an excavator was digging. Instead of attaching the tripod, he rested the barrel on the railing.

A relatively calm wind of 6-8 mph made his job easier. He snugged the butt against his shoulder and adjusted the high-powered scope. After scanning the site, he found his target, the woman with the long black hair.

He took careful aim.

TWENTY-EIGHT

"Something's wrong." I glanced around the dig site. "I'm sensing strong danger vibes."

Sean scanned high places in the distance. "Did you check that water tower?"

"It's so far away." I focused my binoculars on it. "Everyone, down behind the excavator!" A bullet whistled past my head as I dived behind a huge wheel.

Shots pinged off the heavy machinery as we hid behind it with the dogs crouching beside us.

Gwen called the Palm Beach County Sheriff's Office. She identified herself and said, "A sniper on a water tower has us pinned down in the backyard of 787 Eventer Lane in Equestrian Estates. We need someone to take him out, and we also need an M.E. and a CSU to remove a body we found under a septic tank."

"I'm so sorry about this," I said when the shots ceased. "The Feds said everyone was locked up."

"Nobody move," Sean said. "The shooter is waiting for us to come out in the open."

"Nah, he bolted. We're safe now." The truck driver, who had thick black hair, stood, and a 50-caliber bullet destroyed his head, splattering the ground with blood and brain matter.

Darcy gasped and pulled her dogs against her.

Nausea gripped me as I looked away from the bloody corpse, doubting my vest could save me from a large, high-velocity bullet like the one that destroyed his head.

Gwen called PBSO. "The sniper on the water tower just killed a man with us. How long until SWAT takes him out?" She listened and said, "Understood. We'll stay down."

Sean asked, "What did the Sheriff's Office say?"

"The shooter is trapped on the tower, but officers in squad cars are pinned down. SWAT has a long-range sniper setting up five hundred yards away. They'll call me when it's safe."

Ten minutes crept by like a lame tortoise.

I tried not to look at the truck driver's bloody corpse lying a few feet away. "Sorry I've been such a fool and endangered your lives," I said to my friends. "After the poisoning attempt, I thought the snipers were done trying, and so did the FBI. This is terrible."

Darcy reached out and patted my arm. "No need to apologize."

Gwen's cell phone trilled. She answered, listened, then said, "Good. Thank you." She stood. "All clear. The shooter is dead."

I stood gingerly, peeked at the water tower with my binoculars, and blew out a sigh.

Everyone brushed off their clothes and glanced at the water tower.

I eased around the excavator and peeked into the hole left by the septic tank. The process of digging it up had disturbed the earth beneath it. Something tiny glinted in the sun, so I peered around for something to reach down there. A long pool pole lay inside the screened-in porch.

I grabbed the pole and jogged back to the hole. The tool easily reached six feet down to the bottom. Using the netted end, I scraped away some dirt and uncovered a hand sticking out of plastic wrap. It had pink fingernails and a diamond tennis bracelet on its wrist. The diamonds sparkled in the sunlight.

We waited another fifteen minutes for the forensic team to arrive and retrieve the body. When they uncovered the woman's face, we identified her as Muffy Murdoch, and explained she was the missing Palm Beach socialite we'd been hired to find.

Darcy frowned. "Judging by her rosy cheeks and cherry lips, it looks like cyanide poisoning. At least her family will have closure and a proper funeral for her."

"I hope they find evidence linking one of our suspects to her body. I'd like to nail her killer." I stared at Muffy's corpse. She had been such a lovely, vibrant young woman. Her family and friends would be devastated.

Sean studied the scene. "This looks like the work of an experienced serial killer."

"What makes you say that?" Gwen asked.

"The attention to detail—wrapping the body in plastic and burying it where it was unlikely to be found. Very clever." He nodded at Darcy's dogs. "If you women hadn't traced her movements so quickly and brought the dogs to sniff her out, she would've been down there forever." He petted the dogs. "Darcy's dogs have given me hope Alannah will be found, hopefully alive."

I sighed. "First, we have the unhappy task of informing Muffy's family." I dreaded the drive to Palm Beach. There was no easy way to deliver bad news.

Sean took us aside. "Ladies, if you want to catch this killer, you'll need to work backwards. Look for new homes with recently installed septic tanks and local unsolved missing-women cases during those times."

"You're saying we need to establish a pattern with connections to missing women," Gwen said. "That's a great idea."

"Yeah, especially since we can't prove Blake, Matt, Nate, or Greyson killed Muffy unless his DNA is found on her body." I frowned.

"Even then, the killer could say his DNA was present because he danced with her," Gwen said.

"Darcy, do your dogs only find the scents you give them?" Sean asked.

"No, they're also trained cadaver dogs." She smiled proudly.

"Good. If you find matching cases, you can have the dogs check nearby septic tanks and maybe locate more bodies." He paused. "Can they locate a cadaver under a septic tank containing human waste?"

She nodded. "Bodies have a different scent than excrement, and the tanks don't use chemicals, just bacteria that feeds on the waste."

"Maybe a mountain of circumstantial evidence will be enough to convict the killer," Gwen said.

"I'll start searching the Internet as soon as I get home." I looked at Gwen. "Do you want to be there when Darcy and I deliver the bad news to the Murdoch family?"

"I guess I'd better, especially since they live in my jurisdiction." Gwen sighed. "I hate this part of the job."

Tim and several of his retired SEALs arrived in Humvees. He strode over to me.

"Jett, I heard about what happened on our police scanner. I insist you come home with us now and let your friends finish up here." He took my arm. "I'll drive you in my Hummer, and my men will drive in front and behind us. No more messing around until the threat is neutralized."

"You're right, and I'm sorry. I should've listened to you, and maybe that truck driver would still be alive." I bit my lip and turned to Sean. "We're riding with Tim."

TWENTY-NINE

Gwen called the next morning and told me the scene with Muffy's family had been heartbreaking and emotionally draining. I wished we could've found her alive. As it was, I felt like I'd failed Muffy's parents, Bitsy at the ball, and the truck driver who died. Those drug smugglers and their quest for revenge had to be stopped. And even though I wasn't able to save Muffy, maybe I could catch her killer and save other women from meeting the same fate.

Karin read my face when I pocketed my phone. "Sorry, Jett. I know you were expecting to find her body, but that doesn't make it hurt any less. Is there anything I can do to help you catch the scum who killed her?"

"Here's the thing: I'd hate for him to kill another woman because I took too long to catch him, but at the same time I think maybe a different person, possibly Greyson Prescott, took Kerri, and her time might be running out. And if I don't find a way to stop those smugglers from sending assassins, more innocent lives could be lost, which would kinda be my fault." I sighed. "Which case do I focus on first?"

Sean broke in, "If there's any chance you can find Kerri alive, you should pursue that lead first, and I'm not saying that because I want to find my daughter." He paused. "Gwen assured us she'd encourage the

PBSO to lean hard on the suspects. If nothing else, it might make the murderer stop killing while the heat is on."

"Then I'll ask Darcy to meet us here with her dogs, and we'll go door-to-door collecting for animal shelters. I'll wear the long blond wig." I pulled out my cell phone and made the call.

"Stop at every house along the way so Prescott won't be suspicious. You wouldn't want to trigger him killing the girls to hide his crimes," Sean said.

"Right and we'd better be well armed." I trotted upstairs to retrieve a weapon.

When I returned, Sean was decked out in tourist attire with binoculars hanging from his neck. He said, "I'll wander around, taking photos from the sidewalk, and scanning for shooters." He nodded at me and strode out the door.

Darcy arrived with Max and Laddie wearing their work bandannas. She said, "I brought one fierce-looking dog and one friendly-looking one to balance things out."

"Good thinking. I've got change in case someone pays cash."

"I'll hide Kerri's and Alannah's underwear inside my shoulder bag," she said. "The dogs will get the scents right before we approach the Prescott home."

"Yeah, but first, we'll knock on doors between my house and our target. That means seeing my ex-boyfriend's parents, who live three doors down from me." I sighed. "Oh, well."

I dreaded going to Mike's parents' house because I assumed it would lead to awkward questions. When we reached their door, it was opened by Mike's younger sister, Priscilla.

Prissy said, "Jett? Is that you? When did you go blond?"

"It's just a wig for a different look." I thumbed at my mentor. "I'm sure you remember Darcy. You met her at my charity ball a few months ago, and Max and Laddie are her trained work dogs."

Prissy petted the dogs. "They're magnificent. What can I do for you?"

"We're collecting donations for local animal shelters," Darcy said.

"Of course," Prissy said. "Come in and I'll grab my purse."

We stepped inside and waited a few moments for her to return. I whispered, "Let's hope Greyson invites us in like this."

Priscilla returned with a large check. She looked at me. "Sorry things didn't work out with you and Mike, Jett. He's loving the FBI training at Quantico, but we have no idea where he'll be sent after he graduates."

"Yeah, I'm sorry too, but I'm glad he's happy. He'll have a great future with the FBI." I turned toward the door. "Thanks for the donation. Give my best to your parents."

We tried the next home and then my lawyer's house, but no one was home, so we went to the Prescott mansion. I spotted Sean farther down the sidewalk. He was pointing his cell-phone camera at various homes, like a tourist taking photos.

Darcy held the open plastic bag under her dogs' noses. "Take scent and find." She pointed at our target home.

We buzzed for the gate. When it opened, we strolled up the hill to the front door and knocked. A muscular man answered the door. He looked to be in his late twenties with brown hair.

"Hello, I'm Greyson's neighbor, Jett Jorgensen, and this is my friend, Darcy. Is he home?" A cloud of cheap cologne wafted over me.

He stared at me. "Miss Jorgensen has black hair."

"This is a wig. I like variety. Now, will you please let Greyson know we're here?"

He looked at the dogs with suspicion. "Wait here." He closed the door, and the lock clicked.

The door opened a few minutes later, and Greyson said, "Jett? You look stunning as a blonde." He grinned. "A pleasure to see you again, and my apologies for the tragic accident at the ball."

"No need to apologize. It wasn't your fault." *Or was it?*

He glanced at Darcy. "Who is this lovely redhead with the dogs?"

I introduced them and explained, "We're here to collect donations for local animal shelters. May we come in?"

He hesitated and gave the dogs a nervous look as they strained on their leashes like they were eager to come in. "Please forgive me. I'd love to let you inside, but I'm allergic to pet dander. Let me make up for it with a generous donation." He pulled out his wallet and handed me five one-hundred-dollar bills.

"Thank you, Greyson. Sorry about the dogs. We didn't know you were allergic." I smiled at him and pretended I believed his lie. "We'd better keep going. Have a nice day."

We backed away as he closed the door, and then we strolled down the driveway beside his lush lawn. The dogs stopped and sniffed the grass. A gentle breeze from the southeast blew across the manmade hill.

Laddie and Max strained at their leashes, pulling us toward the lawn.

Darcy glanced at me. "They relieved themselves an hour ago. Should be good till we get home." She yanked them back to the driveway.

THIRTY

Blake pulled up in his unmarked police car and got out. He strode over to us. "Hi, ladies, what's going on?"

"We're collecting for animal shelters. Care to donate?" I asked with a smile.

"Jett? I didn't recognize you at first. You look good as a blonde." He glanced at Darcy and the dogs and pulled out his wallet. "I don't have a lot of cash on me, but here's a hundred."

"Thank you, Blake. Every dollar helps." Darcy stuck out her hand. "I'm Jett's P.I. mentor, Darcy McKay, and these are my trained K-9s, Max and Laddie."

Blake shook her hand. "Beautiful dogs."

"Thank you. We assist police departments all over the county, and my dogs help solve cases." She patted their heads, proud of her fur buddies.

Blake grinned. "I can see how your dogs help garner donations too." He turned to me. "Jett, any chance you'd have time to ride with me today after five?"

"I'd love to, if you don't mind going with a blond, potential target." I waved as he strode to his car.

He turned back. "No worries, Jett. The Feds checked and said the sniper on the water tower was hired before his employer was arrested. You should be good now."

"Thanks for telling me." I waved.

"Let's go two houses farther and then head back to your place." Darcy led the dogs south on the sidewalk.

Sean met us when he crossed the street. "Did you get inside?"

"No, he claimed he's allergic to pet dander." I glanced back at Greyson's mansion. "Then Blake stopped by and asked me to go riding with him this evening."

"Good. You might find out more about his buddies," Sean said.

Blake picked me up at quarter after five, and we headed west to Wellington where his polo ponies were stabled. I wore my long, blond wig in case more assassins lurked nearby.

"Have you encountered any shooters since the guy yesterday?" he asked.

"No. I can't be certain yet, but like you said, the Feds think he was a holdover from before the drug smugglers were arrested, trying to finish the job."

"Maybe he was the same guy who fired from a boat outside the Breakers. Makes sense he'd try to complete the contract. Good thing he's dead now."

Blake parked and led me to the stables as the scent of hay and horses filled the air. His steeds whinnied as we approached their stalls. I helped him saddle and bridle them.

"I'll show you the bridle path. It's wide, flat, shady, and circles the polo fields along the fence line." He mounted a polo pony named Tracker.

I climbed aboard Dash and followed Blake to a sandy trail, which muted the hoof beats as our horses ambled along it.

"The broad trees on either side make a thick green tunnel, and it's so peaceful." I rode beside Blake and enjoyed the steady breeze.

"Yeah, it's nothing like a pounding game of polo, but my horses love this." Blake stroked Tracker's neck.

"I'm hoping you can help me with my case." I gazed at him. "You said you were at Club Bacchus the night Muffy Murdoch went missing. Do you recall anything else since the last time we discussed it?"

Blake's posture stiffened and Tracker's ears perked. "You still haven't found her?"

"We recovered her body under a septic tank. This is a murder case now." I studied his face.

He frowned. "She seemed fine when I danced with her, but I didn't notice what she did after that. Sorry."

"Did you drive there in your BMW or ride with Greyson in his new Bentley?"

"I told you, I have my own Bentley. In fact, Greyson, Matt, Nate, and I all have identical ones. We got a fleet rate." He sounded defensive about the car, but was that because he was guilty of something or because he didn't want to appear inferior to Greyson?

I wanted to deflect possible suspicion about my car question, so I said, "I prefer your Bimmer—I'm more of a sportscar person."

"The BMW is fun to drive, but the Bentley is a better family car. The nanny drives a minivan, and my housekeeper has a Chevy Volt." He chuckled. "Good thing I have a four-car garage."

"I have plenty of room in my garage because a hundred years ago it used to be a stable for ten horses." I gazed down the long, shady trail. No one in sight. "I'm thinking of building an enclosed walkway to the house for use during inclement weather and adding a porte cochere in front of the main entry door."

"Good idea. You should call Nate for an estimate. He'll give you a good deal."

"There's another contractor I've used in the past, Caldarelli and Sons. I'll compare Nate's bid to theirs. I need someone who can match Valhalla's Nordic architecture."

He grinned. "I love that it looks like a Viking castle. My family heritage is mostly Norse with a little English and Irish sprinkled in." He turned to me. "My son, Ryan, is fascinated with castles."

"I'd be happy to give him a tour. Why don't you bring him over sometime?"

"Thanks. I'll check his schedule and give you a call."

"You could bring your puppy too. He'd enjoy playing with my dogs."

"Sounds perfect. Hans is housetrained now—well, most of the time."

"My dogs haven't met any children yet, but I'm sure they'll be fine with Ryan."

"Let's aim for next weekend."

A loud bang made me duck onto the horse's neck while my heart rate skyrocketed.

"Relax, Jett." He pointed at a dirt road. "That old pickup truck just backfired."

"Oh, I see it. Looks like it's trailing smoke from its tailpipe." I stroked my horse and sighed. "Whew, that got my heart going. Think it counts as aerobic exercise?"

"Let's put the horses in a brief canter—good for everyone's hearts." He nudged Tracker forward.

As we cantered along the shady trail, a steady breeze washed over us. I tried to think of another question that wouldn't sound too overt. I waited until we slowed to a walk and said, "Do you find it difficult dating while dealing with the demands of fatherhood and your new job?"

"It helps having a full-time nanny and a housekeeper. Both women are wonderful with Ryan, and he's making friends at school. I have dinner with him five nights a week and attend his school's sporting events. So far, everything is working out well. The key is balancing time with him and adult time with my friends."

"Sounds like you have it figured out. And getting him that puppy was a good idea."

"Ryan and Hans are best buddies—my son needs that." He hesitated. "It was tough losing his mom, but it's been over two years, and he seems to be adjusting. Moving here helped get us away from all the memories our old home held."

"What about you, Blake? How are you doing since her loss?"

"It helps to keep busy. The move to Florida was good for me too, and I love the easygoing lifestyle here." He turned to me. "And I enjoy spending time with you."

We picked up a trot until the final leg, walking back to the barn. All in all, a pleasant ride on superb horses.

I enjoyed brushing Dash and giving him carrots and an apple before we left the stable. Blake did the same with Tracker.

Later, as we pulled up in front of my home, he said, "Thanks for riding with me. We should do this again."

"Thanks for taking me, Blake. I'd love to ride with you again."

He walked me to my door and gave me a light kiss. "It almost seems like I'm kissing someone else with you in that blonde wig." He chuckled.

I waved as he drove away.

Why do my alarm bells ring around him? He seems so nice.

THIRTY-ONE

Darcy rang my doorbell the next afternoon. She had Max and Laddie with her. My dogs did a happy dance. They loved having her big guys around.

"Come in. Do we have something scheduled?" I asked as my dogs fussed over hers.

"We need to talk. Back terrace?" she asked.

"Yeah, the sniper threat's over." I led her through, and Sean joined us. Karin brought out coffee and fresh-baked chocolate-chip cookies.

Darcy sighed. "I messed up yesterday. My dogs were trying to tell me something, and I didn't listen."

"What are you talking about?" I asked.

"Greyson Prescott. First, they tried to pull me into his house, which we expected, but then they tried to go onto his lawn. I think the dogs picked up the scent of a buried cadaver. I should've let them investigate."

Karin, Sean, and I shared a collective jaw drop.

"I need to go back, get inside his gate somehow, and turn the dogs loose on his lawn." Darcy bit her lip.

"Would it be easier to sneak in from the beach side?" Karin asked.

"The fence is just as high in the back," Sean said.

My three friends looked at me. "What about Blake? Will he ask Greyson to let us in?"

"Doubt it. He's known him since they were buddies back in Boston."

Darcy held up stiff wires with little red flags. "I grabbed these cadaver stakes in case we get in."

"You're really sure about this, aren't you?" Sean asked.

Darcy nodded. "Laddie and Max were emotionally distressed ever since we left the Prescott property. They didn't understand why I wouldn't let them do their jobs. I feel awful."

"Call FedEx or UPS, say you need a package pickup, and give them Prescott's address," Sean suggested.

"Brilliant," I said. "We'll wait nearby and rush inside with the dogs when the gate opens."

Karin pulled out her cell phone. "I'll make the call." She stood and stepped away.

"Better call Blake as soon as the dogs find a body," Sean said. "He isn't going to like us sneaking in without his blessing."

"He'd never give his blessing." I shrugged. "We might be arrested for trespassing."

Karin returned. "A driver will be there in an hour."

"Sean, since we're skirting the law, would it be best to go there unarmed?" I asked.

"If the dogs find bodies, that means Prescott is a killer. We might need to defend ourselves." He checked his Glock 40.

"Okay, I'll get my pistol." I stood and headed inside.

FedEx arrived at 4:00 p.m. Darcy, Sean, and I rushed in behind the van and entered the lawn at the bottom of the hill. It wasn't long before FedEx drove away, and the gate closed, trapping us inside.

Darcy removed the dogs' leashes and instructed, "Search and find bodies."

The dogs sniffed the ground and moved upward. Max ran to a spot partway up the manmade hill, barked once, and sat. Laddie did the same in another spot nearby.

Darcy stuck a marker into the ground at each location.

I grabbed her arm. "Please tell me the dogs didn't just find Kerri's and Alannah's bodies."

She bit her lip and pulled out her cell. "They found two bodies. It might not be them, even though I primed them with their scents yesterday. They're trained to alert me any time they find a buried body." She dialed 9-1-1. "I'm calling this in."

We waited for an officer from the Banyan Isle Police to arrive, which took all of two minutes. Only it wasn't a patrol officer. It was Detective Blake Collins.

He pulled into the driveway, buzzed the gate open, parked, and leaped from the car. "What's this about two bodies? Where are they?"

Darcy pointed. "My dogs are trained cadaver dogs, and each one is sitting where a body is buried."

The sea breeze carried the sound of a jet ski zooming away from the ocean side of the house.

"He's getting away!" I poked Blake. "Do something."

"Who's getting away?" Blake asked.

"Greyson Prescott," I said. "He must've seen the dogs and realized they found the bodies. Now he's running away before you can arrest him for murder."

Blake crossed his arms. "I don't arrest people on your say so, Jett. First, I must see the bodies, and before I can do that, I'll need a search warrant to dig up his lawn. I don't know if a judge will sign off based on two dogs owned by a private investigator. I'll need real police dogs to confirm it."

"My dogs have assisted several police departments and located many buried cadavers. In fact, they recently located one in Equestrian Estates for the PBSO. You can call them and check," Darcy said.

Blake pulled out his phone and made the call. After a brief conversation, he said, "The sheriff confirmed your story. I'll contact the county D.A. to have a judge sign off on a search warrant. In the meantime, remain here with the dogs."

"But Prescott is getting away! You have to stop him," I shrieked.

Blake glared at me. "Not until I have probable cause."

Sean looked like he was about to vomit.

I squeezed his hand. "It might not be Alannah."

Blake tapped my shoulder. "Who are you talking about?"

Sean flashed his NYPD credentials. "I'm searching for my missing daughter, Jett is looking for a kidnapped girl, and we have reason to believe Prescott took them."

Blake barked at us, "You'd better be right. He's a powerful man with strong political connections."

A K-9 deputy from the Palm Beach County Sheriff's Office pulled up. He let his dog out, held his leash, and commanded him to search for a body. The dog pulled him halfway up the hill, barked once, and sat at a different place than Darcy's dogs. After marking the spot with a tiny red flag, the deputy commanded the dog to search again. He alerted to another body fifteen feet south and slightly downhill from where Laddie sat.

Blake jogged up to him and pointed at Darcy's dogs. The deputy's dog sniffed beside them and alerted to bodies where her dogs sat. Each place was marked with a red PBSO flag.

Darcy, Sean, and I joined them.

Darcy asked, "Would you like my cadaver dogs to help continue the search?"

The deputy nodded. "Use these to flag the graves." He handed us several markers and then called for a county forensics team.

I checked the time and turned to Blake. "Now will you send someone to look for the jet ski and arrest Prescott before he gets away?"

Another glare. "Don't tell me how to do my job." He stormed away.

Sean squeezed my arm. "I can't stand not knowing—feel like I'm going to puke."

I nudged the PBSO deputy. "We're looking for two women who might still be alive. Any chance we can use our dogs to search inside the house?"

He glanced around at all the red flags. "Have you got a search warrant?"

"One for the grounds to dig up bodies is in the works," I explained. "All these graves should provide exigent circumstances for a search inside, don't you agree?"

He frowned. "That's not my call. Detective Collins is the ranking officer, and this is his crime scene. You'll have to check with him." He turned his attention back to the search dog.

Sean heard what the deputy said and strode over to Blake. I rushed after him.

"We need to search the house now, before they kill any women held inside." Sean stood toe to toe with Blake. "I'm asking you as one detective to another. Please. My daughter might still be alive."

"Sorry, I don't have a search warrant for inside the house, and we haven't actually dug up any bodies yet."

Sean stood his ground. "Exigent circumstances. Lives are at stake."

Just then, a PBSO officer arrived with the search warrant for the grounds, and a county CSU pulled up.

Blake strode over to the county van, pointed at the nearest red flag, and said, "Dig there first."

The Crime Scene Unit went to work with shovels, digging in the area marked. The ground was soft, and they made rapid progress. Soon the hole was six feet deep, and they stopped digging.

Blake looked down and pulled out his cell phone. After making a call, he waved us over. We rushed to the site, hoping neither Kerri nor Alannah were inside.

A corpse wearing a wedding gown lay partially exposed in the dirt. The body was decomposed beyond recognition with mostly bare bones remaining under the dress and long blond hair on the skull.

Sean blew out a burst of air, like he'd been holding his breath. "Not Alannah or Kerri. Corpse has been buried too long." He glanced up at the mansion and said in a loud voice, "We need to get into that house."

Blake heard him and walked up to the entrance door. He knocked loudly, but there was no response.

I looked at the windows facing us and noticed how dark they

looked. Sunlight glinted off steel barriers that had dropped down behind the glass, sealing off windows that were already barred on the outside. Talk about overkill. Prescott didn't want anyone coming inside his home. What or who was he hiding?

I yelled, "The house has been sealed with steel barriers. We might not be able to gain entry without explosives."

Blake said, "I'll call SWAT. They'll get us inside."

A SWAT team arrived at 6:15 p.m. They used a battering ram on the door. That broke off a portion of thick oak, exposing solid steel behind it. Next, they tried door explosives, which didn't even dent the steel.

The SWAT commander said, "Search for other entries."

Meanwhile, Darcy's dogs found several more burial sites. So did the deputy's dog.

I called Tim and explained the situation. "Any ideas how we get inside?"

"Have they checked the roof? There might be a way in from above. If not, they'll need stronger explosives so they can blow a hole in the house."

"I don't think SWAT will be receptive to my suggestions. I'll keep you posted, but just in case, can you blow it open?"

"Jett, I want to help you, but I don't want to spend the next twenty years in prison. I can get the necessary explosives, but I'll need to work with the police."

"I understand, and I would never want to cause you legal troubles. I'm just trying to find a way to save Kerri before it's too late. Thanks, Tim."

I spent the next two hours watching SWAT try everything short of blowing up a section of the outer wall. They even tried getting in through the roof. Turned out it was reinforced with steel, and then they ran out of explosives.

During that time, more men with shovels were brought in to facilitate the digging. They couldn't risk using machinery that might damage the bodies or destroy evidence. At last count, fourteen bodies had been found. All were young blond women wearing wedding gowns. None were Kerri or Alannah.

Darcy and the deputy took the dogs to the other side of the hill, and they found more burial sites. Every time a marker was set, the dogs found more graves.

It was getting dark when I tapped Blake's shoulder. "Has anyone found Greyson Prescott or his jet ski?"

He hesitated. "I'm sorry. By the time my men located his jet ski, he was long gone. They checked with the airport. His private jet took off almost two hours ago and left the country. If he lands somewhere with no extradition—"

I interrupted, "He'll get away with mass murder, and he's probably already taken steps to hide large amounts of money in case the authorities freeze his bank accounts." I shook my head and walked away before I was tempted to say something I'd regret.

What if he left Kerri and Alannah trapped inside the house? Did he kill them before he left? Was there time? Maybe he poisoned them. My stomach churned just thinking about the possibilities.

THIRTY-TWO

Earlier

Kerri rolled over on the steel-framed bed, moaned, and pushed herself upright against the metal headboard. She knuckled her bloodshot eyes, crusted from dried tears, and glanced around. *Still in this scary room, and I thought the Everglades were hell on earth.*

Someone had snatched and imprisoned her. Were they from the smuggling base in the Everglades? *Why am I here? The guys from the swamp said they'd sell me, but the guy here just plays board games with me. No one would pay for that.*

She surveyed her ten-foot-square, concrete-floored prison with masonry walls and ceiling, no windows, an adjoining bathroom, and a steel door with one lock. Her ankle ached from a heavy metal anklet connected to a long chain anchored to the steel bed. She wiped away new tears. *What would Jett do? Not sit around.*

Her clothes and shoes were gone. She'd been given a long, cotton dress and soft slippers but no underwear. Her captor hadn't raped or harmed her. Instead, they played board games in the morning and chess in the late afternoon. She guessed the time because it was before the meager dinner they fed her. Worried she'd anger him, she hadn't tried to win, and his creepy skeleton mask made it difficult to concentrate anyway.

Never saw his face, so would he keep his promise to let me go if I won? Doubt it. Better plan an escape.

During their previous chess match, her captor mentioned she was a much better player than other guests. *Are there more prisoners? If I could meet one, maybe ...*

After searching the bathroom, she focused on a small table with two chairs in the bedroom. She looked under the furniture, searching for something to pick locks. Nothing. Then she checked for a box spring under her mattress but found wood slats.

Kerri stared at the disturbing picture hanging on the wall beside the table—a Salvador Dali painting titled *The Face of War*. She gently lifted the frame and peeked behind it. A stout mounting wire stretched across the back. Just what she needed, but she dared not take it now. *Better wait until late at night.*

A loud click sent her jumping onto her bed moments before her captor entered. His skeleton mask seemed out of place with his navy Armani suit and ruby cuff links.

"Ready for another game? You can go first." He placed a chess set on the table.

Kerri sat across from him and asked, "Am I the only girl you play with?"

He seemed surprised by her question. "Why? Are you jealous?"

"No, but if I practice with someone, it might increase my odds of winning and going home." She gave him a hopeful smile. "Would that be possible?"

His cold blue eyes pierced her. "No one ever suggested that. I'll think about it."

"Can I ask one more question?"

He sat back. "Go ahead."

She hesitated. "Do you get angry if your opponent wins?"

"Of course not. Take your best shot."

Kerri inherited a high IQ from her parents, and was president of the chess club at her prep school where she was undefeated.

They were only five minutes into the match when she made the decisive move. "Checkmate."

The masked man balled his fists and clenched his jaw. A loud knock on the door interrupted the tense moment.

"Excuse me." He stood, slipped into the hallway, and closed the door.

Loud words were muffled, but it sounded like a heated exchange. Then the door lock clicked, and the voices faded away. She waited what seemed like an hour, but the masked man never returned. *What happened? Should I risk picking the lock?*

The lock clicked open again, and a young, muscular, dark-haired man she didn't recognize entered, trailing an overpowering cloud of cheap cologne. His dark eyes radiated evil.

"Hello, I'm Ron." He grinned. "My boss, the masked guy, told me before he left that I can do whatever I want with you, so you'd better be real nice to me." He leaned close and licked her face. "Yum. Teenagers taste good. I'll be back with some duct tape, and we'll have lots of fun on the bed." He cackled gleefully, left, and locked the door behind him.

Kerri cringed, wiped her face, and listened at the door. *This might be my only chance.* She lifted the painting off the wall and laid it upside down on the bed. The mounting wire was wrapped around itself at either end. She went to work unwinding it. A sharp end punctured her finger, and blood dripped onto the valuable canvas.

She wiped her hand on her dress and hurried to remove the wire. Once she had it off the eye bolts, she bent it together at both ends to create two lock picks. Her hands trembled as she worked at unlocking her ankle chain. *He might return any second.*

It took many tries before the lock disengaged, and the anklet fell away. *Never dreamed the mystery novels I read would help me someday.* She ran to the door and worked the wires again. *Must hurry!* The door lock was easier to pick than the anklet. In moments, she heard the familiar click and opened the door a crack. Holding her breath, she paused and listened.

Silence.

Kerri slipped out and turned the thumbscrew, locking the deadbolt. Two doors with locks like hers were on the same side of the hall. She gingerly rotated the thumbscrew on the nearest one and eased the door open. *Hope Ron isn't in there.*

A blond girl lay on the bed in the fetal position, softly mewling. Wide-eyed, she gasped when she spotted Kerri, who held a finger over her lips as she closed the door.

"Hi, I'm Kerri." She smiled. "We've gotta leave before Ron comes back. The guy with the skeleton mask is gone."

The young blonde sat up and wiped her moist eyes with her hands. She backed against the headboard when she noticed blood on Kerri's dress.

"It's nothing. I accidentally punctured my finger." She held it up. "What's your name?"

"I - I'm Alannah Sullivan. Been here maybe a few weeks. How did you get in?"

"I'm a prisoner too. I used a mounting wire from a painting to pick the locks." Kerri lifted Alannah's ankle. "Let me get this off you." Now that she had some experience, she picked the lock faster. Soon the ankle chain fell away. "Let's go. We might have one more person to rescue." Kerri took her hand and pulled the frightened girl from the bed, peeked out the door before entering the hall, and said, "Follow me."

They stopped at the third door, and Kerri turned the handle. She peeked inside. A blond girl in a wedding dress lay motionless on the bed.

"Quick, let's free her." She hurried inside.

When she grabbed the girl's arm, it was cold. Her eyes stared straight ahead, and except for rosy cheeks and cherry lips, her skin had a grey pallor. No pulse.

"Oh, God." Kerri wiped her hands on her dress, sucked in a breath, and turned to Alannah. "She's dead. Time to go. Be very quiet."

Alannah's jaw dropped, and she stared at the corpse. After two weeks of emotional trauma, she couldn't think clearly. The dead girl only made it worse.

"Come on!" Kerri pulled her away and down to an office at the end of the hall. It was empty. "Quick, search for a phone and keys."

They rummaged around but didn't find anything useful.

"The exit must be at the other end of the hall." Kerri hurried back the way they'd come, and Alannah followed. The hall door was locked.

She picked the lock and carefully opened the door. A dark stairway led upward.

"Follow me, Alannah. We're getting out of here." Kerri climbed the stairs.

Another door at the top was also locked. "At least all the locks are the same." She picked that one and then slipped quietly through the door with Alannah close behind. They found themselves inside a tiny, pitch-black room.

"Feel around for a doorknob." Kerri ran her hands over the walls until she found a lever. She pulled it, and a bookcase swung open into a library. There was a closed door on the opposite side of the dark room, dim recessed lights in the ceiling, and tall windows covered with heavy drapes. She closed the bookcase, ran, and opened the draperies.

Instead of seeing outside, she found a steel barrier covering the windows. "Oh, no. The house is sealed."

"How will we get out?" Alannah asked.

"I'm not sure, but we'd better hide from Ron while we figure this out."

THIRTY-THREE

Two county medical examiners attempted to ascertain a preliminary cause of death for all the victims. They said most of the corpses had been buried too long for an obvious C.O.D., but some had died within the past few months. They suspected the women had been poisoned, since all the bodies lacked any signs of trauma. Tests would be performed later to confirm their suspicions.

Odors of fresh dirt and rotting flesh wafted past me as I stared at the open graves and wondered if Kerri and Alannah were trapped inside the mansion. Did Prescott have time to poison them before he fled? Did he leave an accomplice behind to do his dirty work? We'd never know unless we found a way inside. I called Tim again.

"Hey, I'm still at the Prescott property. SWAT is unable to breach the sealed house. Earlier, we heard someone escape on a jet ski, and an hour later, Prescott's private jet left the country." I paused. "I think I'm missing something. Any thoughts?"

"Did anyone see him exit the house and ride the jet ski?" Tim asked.

"No, we didn't even know he had one." I gazed down the hill covered with deep holes and scanned the waterfront.

"Is there a structure on or close to the beach?"

"Yeah, he has a small building facing the ocean. The cops found an ATV hooked to a sled at the water's edge. They assumed he used it to tow out the jet ski."

"Did they search that building for a tunnel entrance to the mansion?"

"I don't think so. Let me check and I'll get back to you." I strode over to where the SWAT commander was conferring with PBSO deputies and the lead detective I dated.

Blake blocked me. "Sorry, Jett. Police business only. Move back."

"We don't have time for this." I sidestepped around him to the SWAT commander. "There might be a secret tunnel to the house."

"I warned you." Blake grabbed me from behind while the other law enforcement officers formed a semi-circle in front.

The SWAT leader said, "Tell us what you know."

"I'm a private investigator hired to find and rescue Kerri Lyons. I believe she's locked inside that house with Alannah Sullivan, the daughter of an NYPD detective. The structure on the beach might have a hidden escape tunnel connected to the house, and every second counts if you want to save those young women."

Sean stepped forward and showed them his NYPD badge. "She's telling the truth. Please, let her go and save my daughter."

The SWAT commander glared at Blake, and he released me.

"Okay, you've said your piece, Jett," Blake said. "Now stay out of the way."

I backed away with Sean and watched the SWAT team zigzag around the graves on their way down to the beach with Blake and his officers close behind. "Fingers crossed they find a tunnel."

A few minutes after the cops reached the beach shed, a loud explosion shook the ground, and smoke rose from the area.

"That was way too big for blowing open a door," Sean said. "The tunnel must've been boobytrapped."

The brave officers were not seriously injured, but one man suffered a broken arm, another had deep lacerations, and many had cuts and bruises from flying debris.

The SWAT commander briefed Sean and me. After explaining what happened to his men, he said, "That entrance is now completely blocked by the collapsed tunnel. No way into the house. Sorry."

"What's next?" I asked. "Will you blow open an outer wall?"

"Without proof someone inside is in imminent danger, we have no legal authority, and there's no indication anyone is still there. The homeowner fled the country, and my men need medical treatment." He brushed blood off his arm and strode away.

I buried my face in Sean's shoulder and bit my lip, frustrated. Then I sucked in my breath. "I'm not giving up. There must be a way inside."

He hugged me. "Earlier, you said a guy answered the door and then went to get Prescott while you and Darcy waited outside with the dogs, right?"

I replayed that moment in my mind. "Yes, but both men could've left on the jet ski, or the other guy might be in the house." I paused. "Unless he died in the tunnel explosion."

Sean looked into my eyes. "Let's assume he's still in the house. He'll want to escape arrest. If I were him, I'd wait until late tonight and sneak out past the police guards. When he does, you and I will be waiting with Darcy and her dogs."

"And we'll have two retired Navy SEALs with us. Nobody gets past them." I pulled out my phone and called Tim.

After I relayed all the events so far, he asked, "How many bodies did they dig up?"

"Twenty-one. The grounds are a mess. One of the M.E.s told me they'll have to store most of the bodies in hospital morgues until they can do all the autopsies."

"And none of the victims were Kerri or Alannah, right?" Tim asked.

"Right."

"Then they're probably trapped in the house, possibly with the guy who answered the door. I'm assuming he's Prescott's accomplice. Otherwise, he would've let the cops in."

"Think he'll try to escape late tonight?"

"With such a high body count, the D.A. might get a court order, and SWAT will blow their way in tomorrow morning. If he doesn't bolt tonight, he'll be caught and charged with multiple murders."

"That's a strong incentive. Can we count on you and Kelly to assist us?"

"Have you cleared your plan with the cops in charge?"

"Um, no." I gazed over at Blake, pacing in front of the house. "Banyan Isle's lead detective is close friends with Prescott, and he's being a condescending jerk to me, letting his ego get in the way of good police work."

Tim gave me a one-word reply filled with exasperation, "*Jett.*"

"Hey, the SWAT commander liked me, and the Sheriff's deputies liked working with Darcy and her dogs, but they're not in charge. Blake is the problem, but he won't keep watch all night. He'll post no more than one or two Banyan Isle patrol officers as guards, because the island's police force is so small."

"What are you hoping to accomplish tonight?" Tim asked.

"Catch the guy when he sneaks out and make him tell us where Kerri and Alannah are. No explosives. Just a recon and recover mission."

"We'll meet at your house at 2100." He hung up before I could say anything else.

Holding hands, Kerri and Alannah hurried into a long, dark hallway dimly illuminated by a few tiny, recessed emergency lights in the ceiling. They rushed along, frantically listening for Ron. Just as they were even with a door on the right, footsteps clacked on the hardwood floor, and they ducked inside.

Kerri gently closed and locked the door. The dark room had dim lights in the ceiling. She froze. "Ron's been here recently. I smell his disgusting cologne."

"Yeah." Alannah sniffled. "My nose is clogged from crying, but even I can smell it." She reached over and tried a wall switch. Nothing.

"Looks like a fancy office. Maybe we can find a phone." She strode to a large antique mahogany desk.

After a careful search, the women couldn't find one, so they tried the desktop computer. It wouldn't function.

Alannah used a letter opener and removed the back. "It's missing the hard drive. I'll keep this blade in case we need a weapon."

"Keep looking and hurry. He might come back any second." Kerri opened a cabinet and found a fax machine. She pushed the power button. "It works!"

"Know the fax number for someone who can help us?" Alannah asked.

Kerri thought a moment and smiled. "Yeah, my hunky flight instructor. He rescued me from a scary situation in the Everglades."

"Tell him my dad is NYPD Detective Sean Sullivan."

She sat at the desk, pulled out a pen and paper, and wrote: EMERGENCY!!!!! I'm Kerri Lyons, and I'm trapped in a huge mansion sealed with steel barriers. I freed NYPD Det. Sean Sullivan's daughter, Alannah, from a locked room, but a guy named Ron intends to rape and murder us. Please save us! I'll try to unseal the house, but don't count on that. Godspeed.

Kerri dialed Hunter's fax number, fed the note into the machine, and hit SEND. She knew the number from when she faxed him a document for her flight training. It was only one digit different from his cell phone, which she'd called many times to book flights.

THIRTY-FOUR

We were all decked out in black when Darcy arrived at 9 p.m. with her four big dogs. She too was in black attire, and the dogs wore their work bandannas with GPS locators. My nine-month-old pups were thrilled to see the big boys. Soon they would be trained like her dogs.

"Recheck your weapons before the SEALs arrive." I racked the slide on my Glock 26, concealed in a lower-back holster, and checked the SIG Sauer P365 in my ankle holster. Remembering how Sophia always carried extra ammo, I smiled and slipped a loaded magazine into my pants pocket. *I missed her.*

Sean watched us and said, "Remember, we need him alive so we can find the girls."

Karin petted the dogs. "What's the plan for your boys, Darcy?"

"Find and protect the girls. They'll have their scents. When they hear a door or window open, they'll charge into the house."

"And we'll grab the bad guy," I said.

"Sounds good." Gwen turned when the doorbell boomed "Ride of the Valkyries."

"Tim and Kelly must be here." I opened the door.

They were dressed in black combat gear with night-vision helmets.

Rifles with night scopes were slung across their backs, and their thigh holsters held pistols. They looked at us and smiled. I guess that meant they approved. Or they found us comical. I was never sure what they were thinking because they weren't big talkers.

"We did a recon on the way here," Tim said. "There's only one Banyan Isle cop guarding the Prescott mansion because SWAT thinks it's empty."

"Yeah," Kelly agreed. "The cop circles the building once every thirty minutes, then sits in a chair out front and stares at his phone."

"No moon tonight, and it's cloudy. Should be easy to sneak past him on the ocean side." I glanced from Kelly to Tim. "How do you guys want to handle this?"

"Our target will probably exit onto the back terrace, run to the beach, head south to the hotel, and steal a car," Tim said. "We'll intercept him."

"I'll hide with my dogs close to the terrace so they can rush in if a door opens," Darcy said.

"Should we go now?" I asked.

Tim glanced at his watch. "He could bolt any minute, but chances are he'll leave after midnight." He exchanged a look with Kelly. "Blake doesn't trust Jett and her crew to stay out of this. He might swing by. It'll look suspicious if everyone's gone, but their cars are here. And Karin should be home to tell him Jett went to bed early. He's sure to check your whereabouts too, Gwen."

Sean added, "He's right. Five people are enough, and if Blake gets suspicious, he could ruin our chances of saving the girls."

"That makes sense. I'll go home and change. Karin should do the same here. Call as soon as you know anything, no matter what time it is." Gwen hugged us and left.

"Sean's rental car is in my garage." I grabbed the remote-control door opener. "Darcy and Tim can hide their cars there too."

"Just Darcy. We left the Hummer on a side street near the Prescott mansion," Tim said.

We waited with the dogs in the great hall while Darcy parked in my garage. When she returned, Karin joined us wearing shorts and a T-shirt.

"Don't worry. If Blake stops by and gets too nosy, I'll text you." Karin hugged me. "Happy hunting." She grabbed my dogs' collars so they wouldn't follow me outside.

Except for a gentle breeze, a few crickets, and the soft lapping of waves on the shore, it was silent when we gathered on my back terrace.

Darcy instructed her dogs, "Quiet. Stay close."

The German shepherd and Doberman blended into the darkness with the Labrador and Great Dane close behind as we headed across my backyard to the beach.

"Stay vigilant," Tim warned. "Our target might already be out here, and he's probably armed."

"If he's near, the dogs will alert us." Darcy gathered her furry friends when we reached the beach, and Kelly assumed the lead.

Tim brought up the rear as we walked single-file close to the fence and bushes on the oceanside of my property, heading south. A mild sea breeze washed over us under a dark, cloudy sky, and the fence hedges of neighboring homes shielded us along the way.

The tunnel explosion left a big hole in the perimeter fence enclosing Prescott's backyard. We halted near the debris field to regroup and receive assignments from Tim. He and Kelly studied the grounds and the mansion on the hill with their night-vision binoculars.

Tim glanced at his watch. "The cop just made his rounds. That gives us thirty minutes to settle into our hiding spots." He turned to Darcy. "See the bushes along the back terrace? Can you and your dogs hide there?" He passed her his binoculars.

She took a quick look. "Yeah, we'll hunker down, and I'll keep an eye on the terrace door." After returning the binoculars, she said, "Watch out for the open graves."

Before anyone moved, my phone vibrated. "Wait, it's Hunter." I answered, and his tense voice worried me.

"Jett, I got a fax from Kerri. I'll read it and then text it to you."

I put my phone on SPEAKER so everyone could hear him.

When Hunter finished, I said, "I'm outside the Prescott mansion with four friends and Darcy's dogs. It's sealed with steel barriers. This must be where Kerri and Alannah are imprisoned."

"What can I do?" Hunter asked.

"Call Gwen and have her get the address associated with Kerri's fax and text me. Then bring the fax to my house and wait with Karin. I'll call if we need you."

"Okay. Keep an eye on the doors and windows. Maybe Kerri will find the control box and disengage the steel barriers."

"Talk soon." I pocketed my phone and saw hope in Sean's eyes. I squeezed his shoulder. "Alannah is alive. Gwen will verify if she's in this house."

Tim looked at Sean. "She's your daughter. You want us to call in SWAT or handle this on our own?"

"The perp has security cameras that show only one guard on duty. He'll wait until the guard's out front and sneak out the back. But if he sees a SWAT team surrounding the house, he'll use the girls as shields or maybe kill them and himself."

"Agreed. Want to wait for confirmation she's in there?"

"Yeah, unless he comes out now."

"We'll hold here and watch the house while we wait for Gwen's call."

Tim and Kelly kept their NV binoculars trained on the Prescott mansion. No one said anything while we waited, and my heart pounded. Ten minutes passed like a snail on tranquilizers.

Gwen called me, and I put it on SPEAKER. "Kerri's fax came from Prescott's house."

"Good. We're in the right place. I'll call when we know something." I pocketed my phone.

Tim aimed a sniper rifle with a sound suppressor and shot out a camera mounted high on the mansion's oceanside.

Kelly did the same until all the cameras on the east side were silently destroyed, preventing the perp from spotting us climbing the hill.

"Ten minutes before the guard does his rounds," Tim said. "Darcy, you and your dogs go now. We'll cover you and wait until he finishes his circuit."

She ran through the opening, sprinted up the hill, dodging graves, and ducked behind the bushes beside the terrace's three-foot-high base, the dogs settling beside her.

Kelly kept watch with his night-vision binoculars. "Those dogs are amazing. They do exactly what she says. She's giving them the girls' scents now."

Sean frowned. "I hope the girls find the control panel before that guy finds them."

Tim nudged him. "We brought grenades. One way or another, we'll get inside."

Once the guard was out-of-view, we stood, ready to deploy.

"Sean, I want you in that gazebo close to the terrace," Tim said. "Jett, wait behind that banyan tree by the fountain. Kelly will cover the backyard, and I'll cover everyone. Don't forget to watch out for open graves. Go!"

We ran uphill into Prescott's backyard and took our positions. As I waited, I wondered what was going on inside. Did Prescott's henchman find the girls?

THIRTY-FIVE

Kerri closed the cabinet holding the fax machine and prayed that Hunter had received her message. "Where would they put a security control panel?"

Alannah glanced around. "Maybe in this office, hidden like a wall safe."

They peeked under the paintings, and Kerri found a safe behind a reproduction of the *Mona Lisa*. No security panel. "Maybe it's in a room farther down the hall. Let's go look."

Alannah gripped her arm. "What about the scary guy? Does he still think we're locked in the basement?"

"Don't know, but he doesn't seem to be looking for us. Better hurry before he discovers we escaped." Kerri inched open the office door and listened.

No footsteps outside.

They slipped into the dark hallway and eased the door shut. The next room held velvet sofas and a black lacquered grand piano on a Persian carpet. Red velvet draped the windows. No hidden electronics panel. Nearby, a door clunked closed, and they froze.

"Quick, in here." Kerri darted into a storage closet. Large books of sheet music stored on shelves were set back just far enough from the door to allow the girls to stand in front. She closed the door and sealed them in complete darkness.

Someone entered the room. Heavy footsteps strode across the oak floor to the central Persian carpet, then over to the velvet curtains, and back again. The entrance door closed with a soft thud.

They remained hidden, barely breathing. Two minutes later, the door opened and closed again, as though someone had closed it the first time without leaving.

The girls trembled and held hands for fifteen minutes in the dark closet, then they slipped out. The music room was empty, but a faint scent of Ron's cheap cologne lingered.

"Sounded like he's looking for us." Kerri cracked open the door and listened for footsteps before they ventured back into the hallway.

Silence.

They hurried through every room on both sides of the hall. No security panel.

"Hope it isn't upstairs," Alannah whispered. "Ron could trap us up there."

"We should find the kitchen and arm ourselves with knives. Maybe it's at the end of this hallway."

They edged around a corner and found a door leading into a huge ballroom with round tables and matching chairs bordering a central dance floor. Inside, faint security lights recessed into the ceiling provided minimal light with dark shadows everywhere. They paused and listened.

Silence.

Steel barriers blocked the tall windows. Sheer red curtains cascaded over the dark steel, and life-sized statues of Greek gods and goddesses bordered the windows and French doors.

"The double doors probably lead outside," Alannah said, "but those darn metal barriers are blocking them."

"No place to hide a control panel on this side, unless it's in a statue. Check them while I search that back wall." Kerri headed there while Alannah scanned the statues.

Good thing I took that course in Greek mythology for extra credit.

Kerri found a painting of Apate, the Goddess of Deceit, mounted on the wall with tiny hinges on one side of its frame. She swung the painting open and spied the elusive control panel. "Eureka!"

Alannah hurried over to her.

Kerri said, "There's a lot of switches here. Not sure which ones control this room. If I select the wrong one, I might set off an alarm."

"Flip all of them and run for it."

"Okay, stand over by the French doors before I do this. If it works, don't wait for me. The barriers might be on a brief timer. Run outside and get help in case they close before I get there."

"Okay, but I'll shove a statue in the doorway first. Maybe it'll hold the steel up if it drops down again." Alannah ran to the doors and pushed hard at the base of a heavy marble statue of Hera, slowly edging it in front of the door. Finally in place, she waved.

Kerri flipped several switches, and the steel barriers slowly retreated into the walls above the doors and windows. Alannah opened a French door, kneeled, and shoved hard, moving the statue into the doorway.

A strong scent of cheap cologne drifted past Kerri. *Oh my god, he's here!*

She sprinted for the open door, but someone hit the engage and lock switches.

A bullet pinged off the marble statue beside her, and Alannah sidestepped through the door an instant before the steel barrier slammed down onto the life-sized goddess. The frightened young woman froze as four big dogs charged her. They slid to a stop when the sculpture split and crumbled under the weight of the steel barrier. Hera's severed head rolled up against Alannah's left foot.

She glanced down at it as the dogs surrounded her protectively, wagging their tails and licking her hands. Relieved they weren't attack dogs, she petted them.

Everyone ran forward as Darcy said, "Good dogs! Heel."

The dogs sat beside their boss, and Sean hugged his daughter.

"Alannah, are you hurt, baby?" Her worried father checked her over.

Tears streamed down her face as she caught her breath. "I'm okay, Dad, but the bad guy is shooting at Kerri. Please, save her!"

Halfway across the ballroom, Kerri pivoted when a bullet pinged off the polished oak floor beside her. She ran to one side, dodging tables, and jumped behind a big statue of Zeus. Her heart raced as she peeked at the open door—close but not close enough. The steel barrier groaned, and the goddess statue holding it up split, piercing the silence like a thunderbolt. Pieces of marble broke off and shattered onto the floor. Her only escape route would be blocked any second.

She balled up the wire she'd used as a lock pick and tossed it at a statue twenty feet back. The clattering drew his attention, and he fired at the marble goddess. Just as Kerri spun around to run, the barrier crashed down, chopping off Hera's head. The heavy steel decimated the statue and slammed onto the floor, cloaking the huge room in darkness.

Trapped!

Pin-point lights in the high ceiling did little to penetrate the Stygian gloom in the vast ballroom. Kerri crouched behind Zeus's muscular legs and tried to spot her stalker, but it was too dark.

A beam from a mini flashlight swept the room. It barely penetrated ten feet ahead of her adversary.

"Come out, come out, wherever you are." He cackled. "You can't get away from me." He crept forward, stopping every few feet and listening.

She waited, helpless, as the light swept closer. Would the statue hide her? She held her breath when he aimed the flashlight at Zeus. The beam reflected off the steel behind her, revealing her hiding spot.

"I see you. Come out now, and I won't shoot."

She darted into the darkness and dived under a table. Then she scrambled on her hands and knees from one table to the next, breathing hard.

The flashlight beam missed her as she worked her way around to the back.

She paused, listening.

Silence.

Trembling, she slowly stood and crept toward the hallway door.

A beam of light from behind illuminated her.

"It's an easy shot from ten feet. Turn around and hold out your hands."

She turned and froze. "I-If you give up before anything bad happens, you'll get off easy. The guy in the skeleton mask was the killer, right?"

"Yeah, but I'll be charged with all the murders anyway." He waved the gun and handed her a long zip tie. "Put this around your wrists."

Her hands shook, and she dropped it. "S-Sorry." She fought back tears.

He snatched it up, slipped it over her hands, and tugged it tight. At least her hands were in front of her.

He shoved her. "Hurry—down that hall to the library."

When they entered the familiar room, he pushed her toward the bookcase with the hidden door, then pulled on a narrow book. A portion of the bookcase swung open.

He pushed her through the small room beyond and through an open door on the other side. They descended the stairs to the basement, but instead of entering the hall with the prison rooms and office, he shoved her behind the stairwell.

A thirty-six-inch-square wood panel opened when he tapped the adjacent panel.

"Down on your hands and knees. Crawl in there." He jammed the gun barrel into her back.

Kerri crawled into the pitch-black tunnel. The flashlight's beam only reached a few feet beyond them as the hidden door closed with a soft whoosh.

The dark passage stretched ahead of them, dank, musty, and silent.

THIRTY-SIX

I toed Hera's severed head. "That was close, Alannah. Who was shooting at you?"

"A guy named Ron, and he's after Kerri! Hurry and save her!"

I turned to Tim. "Can you guys blow open the door?"

"We'll try. Everyone get down against the terrace border and hold your ears." He waited while we took cover.

Darcy and I inserted ear plugs and handed extras to Sean and Alannah. Then the four of us covered the dogs' ears with our hands.

The SEALs placed grenades against the lower corners of the door with the smashed statue, pulled the pins, sprinted toward the yard, and dived off the terrace.

Both grenades blew at once, and we waited for the smoke to clear. The steel was bowed at one end, leaving a small opening in a bottom corner that looked big enough for the dogs to crawl through and maybe Darcy or me. Our muscular, broad-shouldered, male companions would never fit.

I removed my ear plugs and nudged Tim. "Got any more grenades?"

"In my Hummer, but I'm sure the cop out front called in that blast." He frowned. "We'll be arrested before I can get them."

"No!" Alannah screamed. "Dad, I can fit. *Please*, let me save Kerri." She reached for his weapon.

"No way, sweetheart. I'm keeping you safe." Sean hugged her close.

I turned to Darcy. "Quick, send in the dogs." While she gave them Kerri's scent again, I pulled out my cell and called my lawyer, who lived next door.

He answered, "Hello, Jett, did you hear that explosion?"

"Yeah, that was us. We're trying to rescue a kidnapped girl from the back side of the Prescott mansion. We're about to be arrested, so please come and help us."

"Be right there." He hung up.

I pocketed my phone and climbed onto the terrace as Darcy wriggled through the small opening after her dogs. Although I was taller, I was narrower and slipped through the opening before the cops charging around the corner could stop me. I slid through sideways and pulled my feet clear a second before hands grabbed for me and missed.

Blake shouted, "Dammit, Jett, get back out here right now!"

I ignored him and sprinted after Darcy. Her dogs disappeared into a hallway.

She pulled out her cell which had a tracking feature that displayed the dogs' GPS signals. Four red dots moved on the screen, and we ran after them.

Hands on hips, Blake glared at Tim. "What's going on? Did you set off the explosives?"

Tim pointed at Sean's daughter. "Meet kidnap victim Alannah Sullivan who just escaped. She has a lot to tell you."

Alannah sobbed and wiped away tears as she explained how Prescott drugged and kidnapped her in New York over two weeks ago. "Kerri helped me escape right before the barrier slammed shut again, and Ron might shoot her." She clutched his arm. "Save her!"

"I'm calling in SWAT." Blake pulled out his phone and made the call.

When Blake pocketed his phone, Tim tapped his arm. "Darcy and Jett are in there with an armed suspect who knows every inch of that house. Let my team help them."

He frowned. "I have a job to do, and I warned you people to stay out of this. You're all under arrest for interfering with a police operation. Wait over there." Blake nodded at a spot on the terrace, but he didn't handcuff them.

A tall, distinguished-looking gentleman with silver hair, wearing an expensive suit and silk tie, rounded the corner and spotted the civilians. He strode over and said to Tim,

"I'm Niles Lockwood, Jett's lawyer, and yours too, I presume. Where is she?"

"We're helping Jett and Darcy rescue two girls. This one's safe now with her father." Tim made the introductions, then pointed at the blast hole. "The women crawled inside, and there's no telling what might happen in there with an armed assailant. If we wait for SWAT, it might be too late. Think you can convince the cops to let us continue the rescue op?"

We found the dogs in the library pawing at a bookcase. Max nudged a book with his nose.

"Obviously, there's a hidden door." Darcy petted the dogs as I pushed and pulled on various books without success.

"Max, where's his scent?" Darcy asked.

The German shepherd nudged the same book again with his nose. It was a rare first edition of *The Theory and Practice of Gamesmanship* by Stephen Potter.

I grabbed the narrow spine and pulled straight out, releasing a spring-loaded latch. The bookcase door swung open, and the book slid back in place. "Better put a big book against the door, or it might close and lock after we go in." I grabbed a thick volume and shoved it into the opening after we slipped inside.

The dogs rushed through a tiny room and down a staircase. Their feet pattered on the wood as we crept behind them. They ignored a door at the base of the stairs and ran to a wall behind the steps.

Four noses sniffed a thirty-six-inch-square wood panel on the wall.

"Oh, geez," I whispered. "I hope that isn't a tiny escape tunnel." The bottom of the panel was level with the floor, and the idea of crawling through there gave me the creeps.

Darcy whispered, "Max, where's his scent?"

The big, honey-colored dog sniffed beside the area the dogs were interested in and pushed his paw against it. The tunnel door swung open.

Darcy whispered, "Good boy," as she blocked her dogs from entering. "If he hears us coming, he might kill Kerri. Max and Dobie will sneak up silently and neutralize him."

I nodded, and she directed the two dogs into the tunnel and kept the Great Dane and Labrador behind to help find the tunnel exit. She carefully closed the door so it wouldn't make a noise and then checked her phone screen.

Two red dots moved south about fifty feet and then made a right-angle turn east. She sent a text to Tim: *Perp and Kerri are in a second tunnel heading toward the beach with Max and Dobie in pursuit. I'm bringing Tiny and Laddie to locate the tunnel exit. Jett's guarding the entrance.*

Tense, she showed me the text.

I nodded and whispered, "Hurry!"

She rushed away with her dogs.

Kerri crawled slowly, her head and back occasionally bumping against the tunnel roof. "Are you sure there's an exit?" Her voice was a high-pitched squeak.

"Claustrophobic, are ya?" He chuckled.

Her hand landed on something long and slimy. She froze and screamed.

"What?" He poked her with his handgun.

"S-snake!!!!"

He shined the light on it. "Relax. It's dead. Keep moving."

She remained motionless. Loud, rapid breathing signaled her panicked state. He reached forward and pushed her buttocks. Her stiffened body kept shaking.

"You're my shield. No time for panic attacks. Keep moving." He gave her butt another shove.

She remained glued to the floor. "Y-you can't shoot me—you need me, and y-you might not fit past me."

"Whadaya want?"

"I'm s-scared. Gimme the flashlight so I can see what's in front of me."

He rolled it between her hands and knees, and she grabbed it. The light illuminated a short section of tunnel, but the blackness seemed to stretch into infinity.

She took a deep, calming breath and steeled herself.

Now or never.

She mule-kicked him in the face hard enough to break his nose and kept kicking, hoping to knock him out so he wouldn't shoot her.

Fierce growls reverberated behind her amidst blood-curdling screams.

Kerri froze, fearing a wild animal was about to attack her.

The overpowering scent of Ron's cologne now mixed with the acrid odors of blood and urine.

She flinched and gasped when something warm and wet splattered onto her right hand and arm. Her heart racing, she shined the light on herself. Blood covered her right side.

Not her blood.

She twisted around and fearfully looked back with the light. Ron lay flat with a German shepherd on his back and the dog's jaws clamped around his right wrist, which bled profusely. The vicious bite had made him drop the weapon. Farther back, a Doberman sank his teeth into Ron's right ankle, and tugged him backward, away from her.

She blew out a sigh and slowed her breathing.

Must be Darcy's dogs. Bless her.

Kerri reached back between her legs and grabbed the handgun.

Better escape while the dogs have him pinned down.

She crawled forward like she was in a race for her life.

The screaming and growling faded into the distance, and she never looked back.

THIRTY-SEVEN

Alannah yelled, "This is taking too long. *Do* something before he kills them!"

Blake pulled out his phone and hit speed-dial. "SWAT, what's your ETA?" He listened. "Fifteen minutes? Drive faster."

"*Drive faster?*" she wailed. "*That's* his solution? Dad, help her! You heard the gunshots when I escaped."

Sean looked at Tim and Kelly.

Tim shrugged. "If our lawyer can get Blake to agree, I can grab a few more grenades from my Hummer. Should be enough to get through that damaged barrier."

"Well, Niles? Any ideas?" Kelly asked.

He nodded and strode over to Blake. "Detective Collins, I'd hate for you to be held responsible for innocent deaths because you're impeding a rescue operation. The SEALs assured me they have what's necessary to breach that barrier before it's too late." He paused. "Lots of witnesses if the women die because of your actions." Niles arched his brow and stared him down. It had the desired effect.

Blake barked orders. "Render whatever assistance these people require."

Tim said, "I need a ride to my Hummer where I have additional explosives."

Blake looked at a patrol officer. "Take him there now."

While they were gone, the others paced back and forth, eyeing the hole.

Five minutes later, Tim and the officer returned.

Tim waved Kelly over. "We'll tape four around that hole." He yelled, "Anyone inside, get away from this door, and everyone out here, down behind the terrace."

Tim and Kelly waited until the cops and civilians were clear. Then they set the grenades, pulled the pins, and dived for cover. The ear-splitting blast shook the ground, and gunpowder smoke permeated the air. When the smoke cleared, there was a much larger hole in the barrier.

The men ran toward the opening just as Darcy stepped through it with two of her dogs. She looked at Tim. "Didn't you get my text?"

"No. Where's Jett?"

"Yeah, where's Jett?" Blake asked.

"She's in the basement guarding the entrance to a second tunnel." She glanced down at her phone. "We gotta find the exit before the gunman gets there with Kerri. Tiny and Laddie will help. The other dogs are in the tunnel." Darcy swallowed hard when she noticed the red dots on her screen weren't moving anymore. She prayed her furry partners hadn't been shot as she ran downhill toward the beach.

Tim glanced from the house to the beach. "Kelly, help Darcy. Sean, hold my rifle and stay with Alannah and Niles. I'll find Jett." He ignored the cops and rushed into the mansion.

"I'm coming with you." Blake ordered his men to search the house as he rushed in after Tim.

———

Kerri reached the end of the tunnel where a black leather duffel bag lay beneath a metal hatch that locked from the inside with a simple slide bolt. She took a moment and unzipped the bag. Inside, her light revealed clothing, lots of cash, a handgun with several extra magazines loaded with ammo, and three passports from different countries, all with Ron's photo. After zipping the bag shut, she hesitated and listened.

Nothing but distant screams and growls.

She unbolted the lock, and the hatch sprang open outward. Her light illuminated the faces of two big dogs. She recognized one.

"Laddie, good boy, remember me?" She offered him her hand.

He wagged his tail and kissed her fingers.

"Thank God!" Tears flooded her face.

"Good dogs." Darcy pulled them aside.

"Kerri, where's the gunman?" Kelly asked, his sidearm ready to fire.

"I have his gun." She handed it to him. "And here's his escape bag. His name's Ron, and he's about halfway back in the tunnel."

He holstered his weapon, shoved the other gun into his waistband, set aside the bag, lifted her out of the open hatchway, and cut her zip tie. That's when he spotted the blood. "How bad are you hurt?"

"It's not my blood." She sniffled, wiped her face, and turned to Darcy. "Do you have a German shepherd and a Doberman?"

Her mouth went dry. "Yes, have you seen them?"

"Yeah, they saved me. Bit the crap out of the bad guy and made him drop his gun. Had him by the wrist and ankle when I crawled away." She hugged Darcy. "Thank you!"

I opened the tunnel door and listened. Loud screams and growls filtered through from a distance.

Crap! I need to crawl in there and find out if Kerri's okay.

The time for stealth was over. I kicked the door panel until it broke off the hinges. At least I'd be able to get back out, and if anyone came looking for me, they'd find the open tunnel door.

A long, dark passage only big enough to crawl through stretched ahead of me. *Wish Tim were here. Nothing scares him.*

I couldn't see anything, so I activated my cell phone's flashlight, which illuminated ten feet of tunnel. I steeled myself and crawled inside. My heart rate skyrocketed as I moved forward as fast as possible in the tight space.

The dank, musty air carried a faint scent of cheap men's cologne.

About fifty feet in, the tunnel made a sharp turn toward the beach. When I crawled around the turn, the cologne grew stronger, and the screams and growls grew louder. *The dogs must've found Prescott's henchman.*

I crawled even faster as the odor of blood and urine washed over me. It wasn't long before my light displayed Dobie's rear end as he tugged on someone's ankle.

Darcy's dogs knew me well. We'd been on many missions together. I yelled, "Max, Dobie, hold."

The dogs remained still but kept their grips on the perp as I eased closer. My light revealed a muscular man face-down with Max on his back, the dog's jaws around his right wrist, and Dobie's jaws around his right ankle. I shined my light ahead of the man.

No Kerri.

"Please, help me. That teenage bitch broke my nose and left me with the hounds from Hell." The man whined, "They're killin' me. I'm gonna bleed ta death!"

He sounded nasal, like his nose was indeed broken. Score one for Kerri.

"Max, release and guard." The nimble German shepherd let go of the guy's wrist, moved in front, turned around, and faced him.

"I can't reach you, but your hands are free now. Tear off part of your shirt and bandage your wrist. And don't make any threatening moves or he'll rip your throat open."

I shined my light over the perp. The guy wiped his face, blew his nose, and started ripping his shirt.

His jeans were soaked in the crotch area, and his body trembled like he was on a vibrator bed. While he tore his shirt into strips, I checked his ankle. Blood oozed between Dobie's jaws, still clamped around him.

"Dobie, release and guard." I waited as the dog let go and backed away a foot.

"Reach back and hand me a strip so I can bandage your ankle."

He handed me a length of cloth, and I asked, "Where's the girl?"

"She crawled to the beach exit—probably long gone." He sniffled and coughed.

Once his wounds were wrapped, I asked, "Which is closer from here, the house or the beach?"

"House."

"Can you crawl backwards, or should I have the dogs drag you?"

"No dogs!"

"Start back slowly. If you try anything, I'll shoot you, and they'll bite you."

"Who the hell are ya?"

"Your worst nightmare. Now, back up." I crawled backward, and the dogs kept pace with the perp, watching his every move.

Such good dogs. Darcy trained them well.

THIRTY-EIGHT

Tim raced through the huge home with Blake on his heels. He assumed the entrance to the basement would be well hidden. Based on his experiences at Jett's castle, he decided the library might be a good place to start. When he found the room, he spotted a thick book on the floor on the far side, propping open a bookcase door. He crossed the room and glanced down at the title: *The Encyclopedia of Serial Killers*.

Blake picked it up. "Can't believe Prescott kept this in his library."

Tim ignored him and continued through a small room and down a staircase. A door at the bottom led into a hallway with three doors on one side and one at the end. The first two doors opened to empty bedrooms that had obviously been used as prison cells. The third room had an occupant on the bed.

"Blake, over here." Tim hurried to the young blonde. Her eyes were open, and her cheeks and lips were cherry red.

"Classic signs of cyanide poisoning." Blake touched her. Her body had long since lost its rigor. "Probably dead a few days."

"Yeah, but where's Jett?" Tim strode to the door at the end of the hall and opened it. "Nothing but an empty office." *What am I missing? She must've left that book so we'd look in the basement.*

Blake pulled out his phone and called for a medical examiner and a crime scene unit.

Meanwhile, Tim hurried back to the stairs and paused. *Was that a growl?* He eased around the staircase and found an open entrance to the second tunnel.

No Jett.

He drew his weapon and crawled inside the dark passage. After flipping down his night-vision goggles, he continued forward. Forty feet ahead, relief flooded him when he spotted Jett crawling backwards toward him.

"Jett, you okay?"

"Yeah. The dogs nailed the perp, and he'll probably need stitches."

"*Probably*? I'm frickin' dyin' here!" Ron yelled.

"Shut up or they'll bite you again." She glanced back at Tim who had crawled nearer. "I can't get out of here fast enough."

He tapped her foot. "Flatten onto your back, slide under and past me, and I'll bring him in."

"Hold up a minute," she said to Ron. She stopped and rolled onto her back. Tim grabbed her feet and pulled her partway under him. Then he grasped her hips and slid her farther back.

When she was directly under him, she looked up and smiled. "It's awfully nice of you to let me out of this hell hole. Thanks."

"Don't be too quick to thank me. Blake's in the basement."

"That's okay." Her face was inches from his, and she gave him a quick kiss before sliding past him.

She missed seeing the big smile on his face afterward.

———

Blake was waiting for me when I backed out of the tunnel.

"Jett, what the hell?" He offered me his hand.

"Couldn't wait—had to save the girls." I brushed dirt off my clothes.

"Where's the second girl—the one named Kerri?"

"She saved herself and crawled out to the beach exit. Probably waiting for us outside." I glanced down at the tunnel.

"Where's the gunman?"

"Crawling back here with Darcy's dogs and Tim—should be coming out soon."

Blake hesitated. "Do I need to get Darcy down here to control her dogs?"

"Not necessary—they obey me." I crouched down and peeked into the tunnel. "Here they come now."

Tim backed out first, followed by Dobie, Ron, and Max. I offered Tim my hand and a big smile.

"Thanks for letting me out first." I gave him a hug, and he hugged back.

Kerri's abductor was shaking and bleeding, and his face was swollen and bloody. His broken nose was smashed, and he wobbled when Tim pulled him to his feet.

"I-I need a hospital." He took a step toward me, and the dogs snapped and snarled at him. He screamed and peed himself again.

Tim ignored him and the dogs and turned to Blake. "Would you like to take charge of the prisoner?"

"With pleasure." He pulled out handcuffs and cuffed the perp over his bandaged and bloody wrist.

"Max and Dobie, stand down and heel." The big dogs stopped guarding Ron and sat beside me. "Good, boys." I petted them and asked Blake, "Okay if we go outside now? I'd like to check on Kerri, and Darcy will want her boys back."

"You and Tim go ahead with the K-9s, and I'll follow behind with the perp."

We made our way upstairs and out to the terrace. Kerri was there with Darcy, her other dogs, and everyone else.

Kerri ran up and hugged me so hard it almost squeezed the air out of my lungs.

I pulled out my phone and called her parents. Her mother answered in an anxious tone. I said, "Kat, it's Jett. I have Kerri. She's safe. Here she is." I handed Kerri the phone, and she sobbed while rattling off everything that happened so fast her mother probably didn't understand half of it.

After she paused to catch her breath, she said, "Mom, the cops want me to go to the Banyan Isle ER to get checked out. Will you and Dad come and get me?"

She smiled at her mother's answer, said goodbye, and handed me the phone.

Blake and another cop dragged Ron from the house. His right wrist and ankle were bleeding as he limped between them.

Kerri glared at Ron and said to Blake, "If you'd like easier access to the house, the security control panel's hidden behind a goddess painting on the ballroom's back wall."

Blake said, "Thank you." He jerked Ron. "We'll take you to the hospital before we lock you up." He recited his Miranda rights as he dragged him to a police car.

I hugged Darcy and told her dogs how wonderful they were. Then I accompanied Kerri in an ambulance, while Sean and Alannah went to the ER in another ambulance. Tim and Kelly waited with Niles and a Banyan Isle Police officer to brief the SWAT commander, who arrived as we left.

―――――

Alannah and Kerri were examined by ER doctors who assured us they were unharmed and in good condition, except for the psychological trauma, which might require a long recovery.

Doctors Kat and Riley Lyons rushed into the room where I waited with Kerri. After lots of hugs and a few tears, everyone calmed down.

Riley looked at me. "Did they catch the scum who took Kerri?"

I filled him in on all the players. "The Feds nailed the drug smugglers who were responsible for your daughter's kidnapping. We caught the man who helped her captor, but Prescott, the serial killer, is very wealthy and escaped to a non-extradition country."

Kat broke in, "So he'll get away with all the murders and terrorizing our daughter?"

"Not if I can help it." I gave them a reassuring smile. "We'll nail the bastard. That's a promise."

Sean and Alannah walked in. She hugged Kerri, and she and her dad met Kerri's parents.

Sean said, "Expect the FBI, probably tomorrow morning. They'll want to gather as much evidence as possible against Ron and his boss, Prescott."

Kat put her arm around Kerri. "Whatever we can do to help put away those horrible men."

"Your brave daughter is quite the heroine," Sean said. "She escaped her cell and rescued Alannah. They might not have survived if it hadn't been for Kerri."

Riley smiled. "We're very proud of her."

"Thanks, Dad. Please take me home now, but first, stop and get me a cheeseburger. I'm starving."

Kat smiled lovingly and caressed her daughter's cheek. "You may have whatever you want, my darling daughter."

THIRTY-NINE

Sean and Alannah spent the night at my house, and we met with Niles, Tim, and Darcy the following morning for breakfast. Hunter was there too, having spent the night with Karin. She made us a delicious breakfast of fresh fruit, western omelets, whole-wheat toast, and lots of strong coffee to jolt us awake after the late night.

My loud doorbell rang as we lingered over our meals.

Hunter jumped up and returned with two Feds. He introduced us and said, "These ladies replaced Agents Taylor and Barnes in the Miami Field Office. Meet Special Agents Ruth Jacobs and Jody Smith." He was smiling, and so were they. Not surprising since women were always charmed by him.

Both agents were super-fit, attractive blondes who looked like they could wipe the floor with us. They exuded confidence, and their eyes held a friendly but fierce intensity.

"Thank you for coming." I invited them to join us for breakfast.

"Just coffee, please," Agent Smith said.

"Same for me," said Agent Jacobs.

Alannah asked, "Have you caught Greyson Prescott?"

"Ron Burns ratted him out, but Prescott fled to his estate in the Maldives—no extradition," Smith explained. "According to Burns,

Prescott always wore a skeleton mask when he was with his captives. Think you could pick him out of a lineup if we catch him, Alannah?"

"I'll never forget the ice-blue eyes behind the mask—so scary, and his deep voice."

"Good. We're hoping the other survivor, Kerri Lyons, will also spot him in a lineup," Jacobs said. "Otherwise, we only have Burn's word for twenty-two murders."

"What about the skeleton mask?" I asked. "Maybe it has Prescott's DNA."

"We couldn't find it. Must've taken it with him when he fled," Smith said.

"He probably plans to use it on new victims in the Maldives," Darcy said.

"Dad, we can't allow that monster to get off," Alannah said.

"Sweetheart, there's not much the FBI can do if Prescott is hiding somewhere with no extradition."

Hunter smiled at the FBI agents. "I think I speak for everyone here when I say that we already have far more confidence in you two than we ever had in your predecessors. Is there any chance you could lure him to a place where you can arrest him?"

"He's an intelligent adversary," Jacobs said. "Luring him out, if ever, would probably be a few years down the road."

"Agents, I understand you're limited by international law, but there might be another way." I glanced at my lawyer. "Niles, would it be legal for me to offer a million-dollar bounty?"

He gave the Feds a nervous glance. "Depends on what the bounty is for. If you're asking that Prescott be caught and turned over to the FBI, no problem."

Tim put down his coffee. "Hold off posting a bounty, Jett. You don't want to alert him and end up dealing with a bunch of cowboys. I know some retired SEALs who are international bounty hunters. They always get their man."

"I like that idea," Hunter said. "Let pros handle it."

"I'll put up half the bounty and pay all their expenses," Darcy said.

"And a company jet will be available for their use," I said. "Call them."

"Your P.I. firm has jets?" Sean asked.

"My late parents' company, Jorgensen Industries, has a small corporate fleet." I drained my coffee.

Tim made the call then told us, "The team leader just delivered a felon to the FBI in D.C. He can be here by five this evening for a meeting."

"Should I send a jet for him?" I asked.

"No, he's flying commercial into PBI," Tim said. "I'll pick him up and bring him here."

"Plan to stay for dinner," Karin said. "I'll make steak Diane with red potatoes and asparagus."

"Sounds good," Hunter said. "I need to take care of some things, but I'll be back in time to meet the bounty hunter and dine with everyone."

"Wait a minute," Agent Smith said. "If this isn't handled right, you could be charged with kidnapping."

"Not if they have a contract with a licensed bounty hunter, and Prescott is delivered unharmed to the FBI," Niles said.

"Okay, but keep us in the loop," Agent Jacobs said.

"We still have several questions about last night and everything that came before," Smith said.

She and her partner questioned us for two hours. Afterward, Jacobs said, "That was one of the most remarkable accounts I've ever heard."

"Yeah," Smith agreed. "You're our kind of women. Well done!"

I walked them to the door and promised to keep them informed.

Tim and his friend drove up right on time and rang my Viking doorbell. I opened the door, wondering what the bounty hunter would be like.

An attractive, fit-looking, fortyish man wearing a tailored suit stood beside Tim. He smiled at me with his perfect white teeth. I guess I was expecting someone harder looking, maybe with a few scars and a short buzz cut, but this guy sported a full head of light brown hair parted to the side and looked like he just stepped off the cover of GQ.

"Welcome to my home. I'm Jett Jorgensen." I held out my hand, and he kissed it.

"Bob Metz—honored to meet you."

My dogs sniffed him and wagged their tails—good sign.

"These are my Timber-shepherd pups, Pratt and Whitney. I'm training them to assist me in private investigations."

Bob ruffled their fur. "Beautiful dogs. I can see the wolf in them. Must be super smart."

"And easy to train. My uncle gave them to me. He's waiting for us in the great hall with everyone else." I led them into a room with a cathedral ceiling, ancient wall-mounted weapons, and Viking battle paintings. Tall windows showcased the sea.

Sean and Hunter stood when we walked in. I introduced the men after Bob met Darcy, Gwen, and Alannah.

Bob and Tim took leather seats opposite Hunter and I with the others flanking us on both end sides of the rectangular seating arrangement.

Karin strolled in and introduced herself before serving single malt Scotch to the men and wine to the ladies. She smiled and retreated to prepare dinner.

Sean helped us fill Bob in on Greyson Prescott's extensive criminal history, and Alannah added what he put her through.

I ended with, "So you can understand why it's so important for us to bring that monster to justice. Can you help us?"

"Definitely." Bob savored his Scotch. "When would you like us to grab him?"

"What sort of timeline would you recommend?" Gwen asked.

"Ideally, we'd wait a month and let him settle in while we research his home in the Maldives. That way he'll think no one's coming after him."

"What about after you snatch him?" Hunter asked. "I imagine it'll be tricky getting him past authorities in the Maldives. He probably paid them to protect him."

Bob smiled. "We have our ways. We'll hand him over at the FBI headquarters in D.C. or to the agents in the Miami Field Office, your choice."

Hunter grinned. "You'll want to hand him over to Agents Ruth Jacobs and Jody Smith in Miami."

Tim nodded. "He's right. I met them, and they'd be the perfect ones to bring him in, especially since they're both blondes, and Prescott hates blondes."

"He'll probably have security guards," Darcy said. "Will you be able to take him without killing anyone?"

"We use special tranquilizer darts. No one gets hurt. When they wake up, we're long gone, and the drugs insure they remember nothing—easy peasy." He glanced at me. "Should I coordinate with you for use of your corporate jet?"

"Yes." I handed him my card.

Darcy gave him a check for fifty thousand. "This will cover your initial expenses. After you hand Prescott over to the FBI, submit a bill to us if you have additional expenses, and we'll add that amount to your million-dollar bounty check."

"Thank you," Bob said. "This should cover expenses."

"How many men are on your team?" Sean asked.

"We operate with four men, but we have access to more if the op calls for it."

"How many do you think you'll need to nab Prescott?" Alannah asked.

"Four will be plenty—your guy's a lightweight compared to the drug lords and illegal arms dealers we've taken."

Karin strolled in and announced, "Dinner is served in the dining room—looks like rain outside."

Everyone followed her into the formal dining room, which held a long, wide mahogany table that seated forty-four. The walls were covered in teal silk matching the upholstered chairs. Portraits of Viking ancestors lined the walls with paintings of my Cherokee relatives added to the gallery. We gathered around one end of the massive table.

Bob and Tim sat on either side of me with Hunter on the end and everyone else scattered around us. Karin served the meal and then sat beside Hunter.

After we'd settled into our meal, Tim said, "I hate to bring this up, Jett, but I think your new Banyan Isle detective might be involved in something illegal with Prescott."

"Blake was obviously protecting him, but I assumed that was because they'd been friends since back when they both lived in Boston."

"Hard to believe he knew him that long without suspecting his buddy was a killer," Sean said.

"And what about Nate Briscoe and Matt Hanson?" Gwen asked. "Maybe they were all in this together."

Bob took a sip of red wine. "Did the other men bolt too?"

"Nope, I checked," Gwen said.

"Once the Feds have Prescott in custody, they might offer to eliminate the death penalty if he rats out his friends," Tim said. "Then you'll know if any of them were in on it." He nudged me. "In the meantime, better not chance dating Blake."

"I'll keep my guard up, but I might go out with him again just to see what I can dig up."

Tim shook his head. "Be careful, Jett."

"We still have to find out who killed Muffy Murdoch," Darcy said. "Hiding bodies under septic tanks doesn't fit Prescott's MO."

"Yeah, nailing him for both crimes would be too easy," I said. "It was probably Matt or Nate."

"If you ladies find out who did it, and you're certain but can't prove it, call me. My team can help you."

I smiled at him. "Good to know. We'll keep you in mind."

When the evening drew to a close, Bob said, "I'll text you with updates."

"Need a place to stay tonight?" I asked.

Tim answered, "He's staying with me so we can catch up."

Bob took my hand. "Thanks for the offer, Jett. I'll be in touch."

After they left, I huddled with my friends and Hunter. "I have a good feeling about the bounty hunter. His team will nail Prescott."

"I agree," Hunter said.

Everyone nodded.

Sean looked at us. "If you want to nab Muffy's killer, backtrack on missing girls in the vicinity of new septic tanks connected to Briscoe or Hanson. Build a case."

"Right," Darcy said. "Maybe we can nail her killer before he flees the country too."

"Yeah, they're rich enough to do what Prescott did if they know we're onto them," Gwen agreed.

"Make them think you blame Prescott for Muffy's death," Sean suggested.

I nodded. "We can act like no one suspects them for anything now that Prescott has fled to the Maldives."

"Jett, I can't thank you and Karin enough for your hospitality. I'm taking Alannah home tomorrow as soon as I can book a flight, but I'm just a phone call away if you need my help with anything."

"Forget the airlines. You're going home on a company jet. They fly to New York on business a lot. I'll call the flight department." I pulled out my cell.

"Sean, we might run a few things by you on the phone if you don't mind," Gwen said.

"Call any time, ladies. I'd love to help you catch the killer or killers."

After a brief chat with Jorgensen Industries' flight dispatcher, all was arranged. "We have a Gulfstream jet flying to La Guardia tomorrow morning at eight, and you two are on it."

"Thank you, Jett, for everything." Sean hugged me.

Then Alannah hugged me. "I'll always be grateful to all of you for saving me." She went around the table, hugging people.

Everyone said their good-nights and good-byes, and I headed off to bed.

FORTY

I had just returned from a morning run with the dogs when my doorbell boomed Wagner. I opened the door, and Blake greeted me with a smile.

"Good morning, Jett. Got time for a chat?"

"Of course. Want to join me for breakfast on the terrace?"

"Just coffee, thanks. Can we speak in private?"

I nodded and led him out through the terrace French doors. "We'll sit at this table for two. Karin will understand."

"Are the Sullivans still here?" he asked, taking a seat.

"They flew back to New York early this morning. Sean wanted to get Alannah home and away from her nightmare."

"That's understandable." He hesitated. "I want to apologize for my behavior the other day and night. I've been friends with Greyson for years, and I never imagined he was a serial killer. I should've believed you and not protected him."

I looked into his sincere eyes. Either he was an expert liar, or I'd misjudged him. "It's just that you're a police detective, and it's hard to understand how you could know him for so long and not notice anything strange going on."

His face flushed. "The thing is I rarely spent time at his place. We went boating a few times when my wife was alive, and I often played chess with him. He never gave any indication he was leading a secret life."

"Ron Burns ratted him out. Too bad the Feds won't be able to arrest him." I sipped my coffee.

"Yeah, no extradition from the Maldives. He'll be stuck there the rest of his life."

"Looks like he'll get away with twenty-two murders." I frowned. "FBI agents told me they'll keep tabs on his activities, but they doubt he'll ever leave his island refuge and risk arrest."

"Twenty-three murders if we count Bitsy Belvedere, probably poisoned by Burns under orders from Prescott to kill you." He stirred his coffee. "What about Muffy Murdoch? Think he killed her too?"

I lied, "We think he ran out of burial space at his home on the hill and started hiding bodies under septic tanks. There might be more victims besides Muffy."

"At least her parents were able to have a funeral, thanks to you and your team."

I sighed. "I hate cases that involve people I know. It's heart wrenching."

"You knew her from a ball you held at your home a few months ago, right?"

I nodded. "Now that you know the truth about Prescott, can you look back and recall a few things that were suspicious, like maybe the deaths of his mother and sister that made him super rich?"

He shook his head. "That was an accident. Their yacht exploded while they were sleeping aboard."

"How do you know he didn't cause the explosion?"

"He was sleeping on board too. It was a fluke he didn't get killed."

"What happened?"

"It was a warm, starry night, and he decided to sleep on an air mattress on the bow and enjoy the fresh sea air."

"Let me guess—their staterooms were in the stern, and the explosion was in the vicinity of the engine room?"

Blake nodded. "Prescott dived off the bow before the yacht was engulfed in flames, and he swam to shore, which was about a hundred yards away."

"He could've orchestrated the explosion and slept on the bow for an alibi."

"That would've been risky. He could've been killed."

"Not if it was a big yacht. How long was it?"

"A hundred and fifty feet."

"There you go."

"No, because he was in Boston until right before the boat left the harbor," Blake said. "He never entered the engine room during the voyage or after they dropped anchor off Martha's Vineyard. And he didn't swim around the boat."

"How do you know that?"

"The crew survived because their bunks were in the bow section. They testified at the inquiry that Prescott couldn't have done it."

"Maybe Burns used scuba gear and rigged it under cover of darkness, or your friend hired someone else." I shrugged. "He could afford it, and we know he's a killer."

He hesitated. "Yeah, I guess maybe Burns could've placed timed explosives under the engine room for him."

"I'll call our new FBI agents and tell them to ask him about it."

"Why bother? They already have him for all those other murders."

"You're a detective. Don't you want to know the truth?"

He frowned. "The more I learn about Prescott, the more embarrassed I am that I didn't realize he was a sick criminal." He sighed. "I feel like each new revelation is more proof of my incompetence as a detective."

I patted his hand. "Don't be so hard on yourself. He fooled lots of people for years."

"Thank you for being so understanding, Jett. I really like you, and I'd hate it if my former friendship with him ruined my chances with you."

"Don't worry. I'm not going anywhere. We should go riding again soon."

"How about this evening? I'll pick you up at 5:15."

"Sounds good. I love exercising your horses."

He stood. "See you later today."

After he left, Karin sat across from me. "How'd that go?"

"He's hiding something, and I'll find out what it is this evening. He's taking me riding."

"Anything new about our serial killer neighbor?"

"Yeah, I think he arranged for someone to rig his mother's yacht to explode and kill her and his sister so he could inherit billions."

"What did Blake say about that?"

"He was way too quick to deny it. Makes me wonder if he had something to do with it."

Karin stared out at the sea. "Maybe you should take a hard look at how Blake's wife died. Didn't you tell me his son inherited a huge trust fund that Blake controls?"

"That's right. I'll research her death and ask him some questions tonight."

I strode into my study and fired up the computer. It was easy to find articles about Blake's wife's fatal accident. It got a lot of coverage because she was a famous author and prominent socialite in Boston.

The accident report stated she'd spent a week alone at their mountain cabin in New Hampshire, finishing a new novel. She left at dawn to drive home in her Range Rover. The gravel road to her cabin was steep and winding. As she headed down the mountain, she hit a pothole, and her right front wheel fell off just as the road curved sharply to the left. Her car missed the turn, went over a cliff, and smashed into a giant boulder, killing her instantly.

I stared at the report. Nobody checks their lug nuts before they drive. Someone could've loosened the right front wheel's lug nuts so they'd pop off after hitting that pothole. And Blake probably made sure he had an alibi for the time it happened. Someone else did it for him. A trusted friend? Prescott?

I researched property owners within twenty miles of Kim and Blake's cabin and discovered that Prescott owned a cabin five miles from theirs. Where was he that morning or the night before? Did he rig Kim's wheel in exchange for Blake rigging his mother's yacht? If so,

Blake would want to make sure Greyson was never brought back to the US to stand trial and rat him out.

Although this was all mere speculation on my part, it wasn't that farfetched. Proving it would be difficult, but Blake's reaction to some careful questions would help me decide if my intuition about him was right. How could I trick him?

I had several hours to formulate a plan while I researched missing women in the vicinity of new septic tanks. I found six in the past year. Each young blond woman vanished without a trace. Lots of new septic tanks had been installed within a twenty-mile radius. I emailed the info to Darcy. She'd go and check each site with her cadaver dogs. If we found any victims, we'd have to determine whether Nate or Matt had a connection to the property or the victim.

Lots to do.

FORTY-ONE

Blake picked me up in his BMW, and we headed west over the Banyan Isle Bridge to Wellington.

On the way, Blake said, "Ryan's doing well. He's making new friends and loves being on the soccer team at Banyan Isle Prep Middle School."

I gazed at the heavy traffic. "How are things going with your German shepherd puppy? I hope Ryan plays with him often."

"Oh, yes. Ryan and Hans are best buddies. Frisbee is their favorite game."

After a forty-five-minute drive, we pulled into the parking area for the stables. The familiar scent of hay and horses wafted over me. Tracker and Dash seemed happy to see us. They were cooperative as we put on their saddles and bridles. Soon we were riding side by side.

I said, "I love this trail. It's so peaceful and shady."

A gentle breeze ruffled his blond hair. "Yeah, I find it relaxing, and the horses like walking on the smooth trail."

The sandy path muted their hoof beats.

"Blake, are the Feds hassling you about the Prescott case?"

"Those female agents came down hard on me—made me feel like a fool. Now they won't tell me anything about the case. Know if they made any progress?"

"They're looking into anything connected to him, including the explosion of his mother's yacht." I glanced at Blake and noticed he tensed up at my comment. I continued watching him. "They're also looking into a mountain cabin he owned in New Hampshire. They think he might have more bodies buried up there." *Now for the biggie.* "Did you know his cabin is only five miles from yours?"

His body stiffened and his voice quavered. "No, he never mentioned it."

"Oh, geez, I'm sorry. Wasn't that near where your wife had a fatal auto accident? I didn't mean to stir up bad memories."

He coughed. "Let's talk about something else. Have you closed the Muffy Murdoch case?"

"Not yet. We want to see if Prescott buried more bodies under septic tanks. There are several missing women we're looking into. It could take a while. The Feds want us to keep them apprised."

He frowned. "Yeah, so they can take credit if you find anything."

"I'm used to that. My ex did the same thing."

"You two had a long history. Are you over him?"

"We haven't had any communication since he left to train for the FBI." I sighed. "He left a hole in my heart that'll take time to heal—makes it hard to trust again."

He ran his hand through his hair. "I understand. It was two years after Kim's death before I felt comfortable dating."

Did he really grieve her death, or was he faking it to avoid suspicion? I wondered. Some men were expert liars, especially sociopaths. Was Blake one? My inherited intuition warned me not to trust him.

We finished our ride an hour after we started, and I helped him water and brush the horses. Caring for animals always had a calming effect on me. Blake seemed to enjoy it too.

On the drive home, we made small talk. Then I asked, "Besides the murders at Prescott's, have there been any crimes on Banyan Isle since you started?"

"Nothing major. Mimsy Farnsworth thought someone stole her fat poodle, but I found Muffin waddling down the street, begging for food from tourists." He laughed. "Mimsy keeps putting the dog on a diet. Every time she does, he escapes."

"That's it? No other crimes to solve?"

"Petty stuff—a stolen bicycle, a domestic dispute that got a bit heated, and trespassing on the Lockwood estate." He shrugged. "Except for the murders you mentioned, this job has been low stress."

He parked in front of my home and walked me to the door.

"I hope Banyan Isle stays laid back now." I kissed his cheek. "Thanks for a lovely ride."

When I stepped inside, I found Tim waiting for me in the foyer. He seemed worried.

"Hey, Jett, how was your date?"

"I probably smell like a horse, so let's chat outside on the terrace." I led him to a table where a steady ocean breeze washed over us.

Karen brought iced tea and joined us. "What happened with Blake."

"I have a theory, and based on his physical reactions to my comments, I might be right." I took a sip and continued. "I think Prescott murdered Blake's wife in exchange for Blake killing his mother and sister."

Tim leaned forward. "I thought both incidents were ruled accidents."

I explained what I suspected and why. "The deaths in Prescott's family resulted in him inheriting billions, and Blake's wife's death gave him control over a huge trust fund inherited by his young son."

Karin nodded. "It would be easy to plant a timed explosive under the yacht's stern, and if it was set for when the tide was going out, the current would carry away the evidence. Didn't you say they were anchored a hundred yards offshore in deep water?"

"Yes, and Blake is a certified scuba diver." I took another sip.

"Blake's wife died after her right front wheel came off on a steep road, right?" Tim asked.

"Yep, easy peasy, if the lug nuts had been loosened almost all the way off," I said.

Tim frowned. "Impossible to prove unless Prescott rats out Blake to avoid the death penalty."

"And a sharp lawyer could claim he's lying to save himself," Karin said.

"That's a possibility, especially since I don't think Blake killed anyone else. His wife's murder was motivated by greed, unlike Prescott, who enjoyed killing lots of women." I petted my doggies.

Tim reached out and put his hand on mine. "Don't underestimate him, Jett. If Blake had his wife killed, and murdered Prescott's mother and sister, he's responsible for three murders. That proves he'll kill again if it benefits him."

"Tim's right," Karin agreed. "Every minute you spend with Blake is risky. You might be his next target."

"Why would I be a target?"

"Blake plays the long game," Tim explained. "He probably plans to win you, marry you, get you to change your will in his favor, and then arrange a fatal accident."

"Well, there's no chance of that happening. I could never fall for someone I don't trust, and I definitely don't trust Blake."

Karin nudged me. "Then it's time to stop dating him. You've probably learned all you're going to from him."

"She's right, and I'd sleep better if you stopped seeing him," Tim said. "Protecting you is challenging enough without you dating a suspected killer."

I rolled my eyes. "Okay, you two convinced me. No more outings with Blake, not even to ride horses."

My cell rang. I answered and heard Darcy's excited voice.

"Jett, my dogs found two bodies so far—one under a septic tank at a home built by Nate, and another under a septic tank at a home bought and sold by Matt."

"Holy cow! Think they're in it together?" I asked.

"Looks that way, but we have to prove it. I'll continue checking properties with my dogs. Do another deep dive into their backgrounds. Maybe we missed something."

"Okay. Call if you find more bodies, and I'll keep you in the loop on what I find."

When I pocketed my phone, Tim and Karin looked at me expectantly. I filled them in.

"While you research them, I'll use my sources and see what I can find," Tim said.

"Good idea," Karin said. "And Jett should call Sophia's mobster sons and ask if they know anything."

"Alrighty, let's get cracking." I stood. "Thanks for offering to help, Tim. Call me if you dig up any dirt on Matt or Nate."

We parted ways, and I headed upstairs for a shower. After I dressed in shorts and a T-shirt, I called Sophia's older son, Dominic.

"Hey, Jett, did ya find that girl?" he asked.

"Thanks to you, we followed her killer's trail from Club Bacchus to where she was buried under a new septic tank."

"Did ya catch the killer?"

"Still working on it. Any chance you have dirt on local property developer Nate Briscoe or real estate investor Matt Hanson?"

He hesitated. "Was Briscoe at the club when the girl went missing?"

"Yeah, and so was Hanson."

"You didn't hear this from me—we think Briscoe killed his pregnant girlfriend, Crissy Sanders. There's a strong possibility he buried her in or under a new septic tank that replaced the old one in his backyard."

"Did someone dig her up?" I asked, shocked.

"No one looked there. Sounds like he did the same thing to your missing girl. Did ya find her on a property he owns?"

"Yeah, we found her in Equestrian Estates, a new development his company built."

"Do me a favor, Jett. Hold off on checking Briscoe's septic tank until I get back to ya. Make him think ya suspect someone else."

"Okay, I'll wait. Thanks for your help, Dom."

"My pleasure." He hung up and left me wondering what he had in mind.

FORTY-TWO

As soon as my call with Dominic ended, I checked my list of missing blondes. One of them was Crissy Sanders. I called Darcy. "You aren't going to believe what Sophia's oldest son told me about Nate, but we have to keep this on the QT until Dom gets back to me." I told her everything.

"Wow, it's looking like Nate and Matt are in this together," Darcy said.

"Or Nate is trying to make it look like Matt is the killer. I doubt Matt knows about Nate's dead girlfriend. That's not something you tell people. I'm surprised Nate didn't bury her on one of Matt's properties."

"Maybe he didn't get the chance because he had to hide her body fast."

"We need to figure out if they're both killers, or if Nate's the only one."

"Jett, is there any chance Prescott did it all? I mean just because the M.O. with the bodies is a little different doesn't mean he didn't do it."

"True, and the timeline fits, but what about Blake? Any chance he's involved?"

"Hard to know," Darcy said.

"Seems like he's only motivated by financial gains." I told her my theory about the pact between them.

"Sounds plausible, but we can't prove it." She switched topics. "So far, I've told the police we suspect the bodies under the septic tanks were put there by Prescott, like we agreed."

"Good. Assuming Nate's dead girlfriend is where Dom thinks she might be, let's look for the other three women on the list. We'll gather as much evidence as possible while I wait to hear back from Dom."

"My dogs are eager to keep up the search. They love working." She paused a beat. "Maybe you should stop seeing Blake now that you suspect he's a killer."

"No worries. Tim and Karin already convinced me to steer clear of him."

"That's a relief. See if you can find anything else on Nate or Matt, and first thing tomorrow morning, I'll continue the search for more bodies. Good night."

After breakfast, I looked up Crissy Sanders and found the news reports about her disappearance. None of the reporters or her family knew she was pregnant. How did Dom know? Nate had been questioned by police but downplayed his relationship with Crissy. He tried to make it look like they'd only gone out a few times. She'd been missing two months, and no trace of her had been found. Did Prescott kill her? She was a blonde, and he could've met her through Nate.

I thought about Sophia's eldest son, Dominic DeLuca, *don* of the most powerful New York Mafia family. I guessed he might use the info about bodies buried under septic tanks as leverage to obtain something his people wanted before burning that bridge with Briscoe, owner of a huge construction company. I hoped he didn't want Nate to bury a body in concrete in exchange for Dom not telling anyone about Crissy. I had to tread lightly. After all, Dom was doing me a favor, and I didn't want to become entangled in his scary business affairs.

Back to Nate. He built two huge housing developments west of

Royal Palm Beach. We found Muffy buried in Equestrian Estates, but the new home was owned by Matt as an investment property. Prescott could've known about the locations. The two bodies Darcy found yesterday were in Nate's other new community, Country Estates, a few miles from his previous project, and Matt had bought one of the homes there too. Again, Prescott could've chosen those sites to frame Matt or Nate if the bodies were found.

I decided to interview Matt again and hopped on my Harley. I took a chance he'd be at his office on Flagler Drive. When I gave my name to his receptionist, he came out wearing a big smile.

"Jett, good to see you." He took my arm and led me into his office. "Take a seat." He held the chair for me.

"Thanks for seeing me, Matt. I was in the area and hoped you'd be here."

He ran his eyes over me. "What can I do for you?"

"This is a bit awkward because you and Prescott are friends, but I'm hoping you'll help me."

"We *were* friends—not anymore."

"Good. I'm helping the Feds build a case against him for Muffy Murdoch's murder and the murders of several other women buried under septic tanks."

"What makes you think he's responsible?" Matt seemed very interested.

"We're working on the theory that he ran out of burial space on his Banyan Isle estate and took advantage of his friendship with you and Nate to find out about new homes scheduled to receive septic tanks." I paused. "He would've asked in an innocent way not to arouse suspicion. Can you recall any conversations like that with him?"

He seemed pleased with my question. His eyes lit up, and he glanced up like he was trying to recall. He gave me the impression he intended to capitalize on the opportunity to throw suspicion away from himself. Or maybe he was just a fair-weather friend who enjoyed throwing Prescott under the bus.

"Now that you mention it, I recall several times that he asked about new housing projects Nate was building and whether I'd bought any spec houses there. If I said yes, he'd ask if anything needed to be done before the house was ready to sell."

"And that's when you told him about a septic tank scheduled to be installed?"

"Yeah. I assumed he was interested in real estate investments." He rolled his eyes. "Never guessed he was scouting burial sites."

"Prescott is very clever. That's why he's never been caught." I leaned forward. "The Feds suspect he arranged for his mother's yacht to explode so he could inherit the family's billions."

"Sounds plausible, but it's probably too late to prove it. Aren't twenty-two murders enough for the Feds?"

"The problem is the evidence for those crimes is circumstantial. The killer wore a skeleton mask when his victims saw him, and the Feds can't find the mask."

He sat back. "What about Ron Burn's testimony?"

"A sharp lawyer will say Burns killed the women and ratted out Prescott to save himself. Prosecutors need more."

"What about the two survivors? Don't they know which one did it?"

"That's not a sure thing. They'd have to remember his eyes and voice and pick him out of a lineup of similar masked men." I frowned. "That's why anything you or Nate can tell us might make a difference."

He grinned. "I'm happy to help. Wouldn't want my good reputation tarnished."

I tried to look sorry when I said, "I hate to tell you this, but bodies have been found under septic tanks on properties you own. That's why I was hoping you'd remember something that would help us nail Prescott."

A flicker of panic crossed his eyes. Then he feigned anger. "That bastard! He's trying to frame me for his crimes."

"You and Nate. Bodies were found under tanks on his properties too."

"Have you told him?"

"Not yet." A quick smile. "I came to you first."

"Thanks. I think he's in his office this morning. Want me to take you there?" He buzzed his receptionist. "Check if Nate is in."

His office was on a lower floor in the same building. Matt escorted me there, and his friend ushered us inside.

"Jett has news that'll have a negative impact on us." He nodded at me.

I told Nate about the bodies. "Can you recall if Prescott ever asked about when a septic tank would be installed on one of your properties? We think he was scouting burial sites for his victims."

He stiffened and glanced at Matt, who gave an almost imperceptible nod. "Yeah, now that you mention it. I assumed he was looking to invest. Never knew about the women he killed."

"If he manages to weasel out of the charges related to the bodies on his Banyan Isle estate, your testimony could help the Feds nail him for these other murders."

"Good, but is there any way we can avoid the bad publicity this will generate?" He waved his hand. "A home's value drops if buyers know it was the site of a murder."

"Oh, nobody thinks anyone was murdered there. The Feds are confident all the women were killed in Prescott's basement and moved elsewhere for burial." I glanced at them. "I could be wrong, but I don't think a body buried in the ground and then removed has the same impact as a murder inside a home. The publicity might actually help sales."

Matt raised his eyebrows. "She could be right."

"When will this hit the news?" Nate asked.

"Soon. PBSO dug up the first body earlier today." I glanced at Matt. "Sorry. I think that one is behind a house you own."

"That's okay, Jett. Thanks to you, I'll have time to spin it in my favor when reporters call me."

"Expect someone from Law Enforcement to ask you guys the same questions I did."

Nate glanced at his watch. "We'd better call our lawyers and circle the wagons. Thanks for the heads up, Jett."

"Call me if you think of any other properties Prescott asked about." I smiled and waved as I headed out the door.

It was obvious both men were hiding something. I already knew one thing Nate was hiding. Dom was never wrong about stuff like this. Was Matt a killer too? Seemed like Hunter, Tim, and Tim's men were the only good guys I knew. How could there be so many killers in my sphere of acquaintances? Maybe I was wrong about Matt. Either Greyson, Nate, or Matt was the septic tank serial killer. Blake hadn't been here long enough for that.

I was about to put on my motorcycle helmet when my cell rang. Dom was calling.

"Hey, Jett, go ahead with whatever ya need to do about Nate Briscoe. I suggest ya get cadaver dogs out to his home today before he has a chance to move the body."

"Thanks, Dom. Give my best to Marco."

"I will, and Ma says hello. She's havin' the time of her life in Italy with Count Medici."

"I'm glad she's having fun, but I sure do miss her."

"She'll kill me if she finds out I told ya first, so act surprised when she calls." He chuckled. "Aldo asked her to marry him. The wedding is in Italy, and you're invited."

"OMG! I thought he might ask her. This is exciting news. I can't wait to hear about her dress and all the wedding stuff."

He laughed. "She'll want ya to stand up with her. I'll walk her down the aisle, and Marco will be one of the groomsmen. Beyond that, I don't know what she has planned."

"Think she'll call me today?"

"Count on it. Take care, Jett."

I pocketed my phone and grinned. Sophia and Aldo getting married—it was good to have something happy to look forward to.

I made one more call before donning my helmet. "Darcy, I just received a green light from Dom, and time is critical. See if your PBSO contacts can get a judge to grant a search warrant for Nate's backyard. We must find Crissy's body before he has a chance to move it."

"I'll get right on it."

I fired up my Harley.

FORTY-THREE

Now that Darcy's dogs had found over thirty buried bodies, counting the ones on Prescott's estate, she had a reputation for never being wrong about suspected sites. The same judge who'd granted the other search warrants gave her permission to check Nate's backyard. I met her there. So did a deputy from the Palm Beach County Sheriff's Office.

Darcy brought all four cadaver dogs, and we walked around the house and screened pool to where a septic tank was buried. The dogs eagerly sniffed the ground and converged on the same spot near the back fence. Each dog barked once and sat.

The deputy radioed for a Crime Scene Unit and a backhoe. It took about an hour for the heavy equipment to arrive and dig up the septic tank. Once it was set aside, the dogs ignored the hole and circled the tank. With the help of the heavy equipment operator, CSU techs pried open the tank and discovered a decomposed body inside. This one wasn't wrapped in plastic like the ones buried under septic tanks.

All the noise and commotion alerted the neighbors, and one of them called Nate.

He rushed into the backyard. "What's going on?"

I ran to him. "Sorry, Nate. Because they found bodies on your other properties, they got a warrant to dig here too."

His eyes were wild with panic when he spotted the septic tank and the CSU techs. He spun around and face planted into the broad chest of a six-eight PBSO deputy.

"You're not going anywhere, Mr. Briscoe." The deputy handcuffed him.

Darcy nudged a tech. "We think her teeth will match the dental records for Crissy Sanders, who went missing two months ago, and her unborn baby's DNA will match Nate Briscoe."

He nodded. "Thanks. Could save a lot of time identifying her and nailing her killer."

I texted Dom: *Found it.* I wasn't expecting an answer.

Darcy and the dogs joined me. She said, "We're done here. I'm taking them home. If this one is Crissy, all the missing blondes have been found."

"Who owned the burial properties?" I asked.

"Matt owned three, and Nate owned two, plus this one."

"Were all the women you found, except this one, wrapped in plastic?"

"Yeah." She glanced back at Nate. "You think Crissy is the only one Nate killed?"

"Maybe." I shrugged. "The body here doesn't match the others. Serial killers usually stick to a pattern."

"The D.A. will want a quick result. He'll pin all the septic-tank bodies on Nate. The guy has a connection to every site, and he owns a company that builds and installs septic tanks. Makes him look guilty for all the murders."

"The prosecutor will argue the body here wasn't wrapped because Nate didn't have time to prepare it like the others." I shook my head. "If somebody else killed all those women, he'll get away with it."

"How will we prove who did it?" she asked.

"Maybe a blonde will go missing while Nate is locked up and Prescott is in the Maldives. Guess we'll have to wait and see."

I arrived home just in time to receive a call from Sophia in Italy. "Hey, Jett, how the heck are ya?"

"Better now that I hear your voice. I miss you. How's it going with Aldo?"

"Couldn't be better. We're getting married soon, and I want ya to be my maiden of honor."

"Congratulations! Are you excited about becoming Contessa Sophia?"

She laughed. "Hard to imagine myself as royalty, but Aldo makes everything easy."

"When is the wedding?"

"Two weeks from tomorrow in Sicily. You'll stay with us at his villa and so will the rest of our gal pals and their men. The ceremony will be held in an ancient church up the hill from the villa." She paused to catch her breath. "I need you, Karin, Mona, Gwen, and Darcy to come ASAP so we can pick out our dresses in Milan. Aldo has a designer waiting with an army of seamstresses poised to make whatever we order in one week."

"Why the rush?"

"I'm a senior citizen, and Aldo is in his early seventies. We can't afford to waste time. Can you and the girls fly to Milan tomorrow? I'll meet ya there."

"Mona is vacationing with Snake at his ranch in Texas. I'll call her and see what I can arrange."

"I want Snake, Hunter, and Clint in the wedding as groomsmen. They'll room with Mona, Karin, and Gwen who will be my bridesmaids along with Darcy, but the men don't have to come until two days before the nuptials so they can participate in the rehearsal and pre-wedding festivities. Marco will escort ya down the aisle, and a relative ya haven't met will escort Darcy, but if you girls want to bring dates, we have plenty of room." She hesitated. "I realize this is short notice, but it will mean the world to me, and I promise everyone will have a fun time."

"This is exciting. Let me make a bunch of phone calls, and I'll get back to you ASAP." I found Karin in the kitchen and gave her the happy news. "Call Hunter and tell him to dust off his tux."

Karin grabbed her cell phone and made the call while I called Gwen. She was thrilled for Sophia and agreed to come. I hung up so she could call Clint while I called Mona in Texas.

"Hey, Jett, we saw on TV how busy you've been with that serial killer on Banyan Isle. Nice going." Mona Wang, a Korean-Irish American in her mid-twenties, had spiked black hair and brilliant green eyes that enhanced her Goth/steampunk style. She was my resident hacker and computer expert.

"I have big news." I filled her in on Sophia's plans. "I'll send a jet tonight for our brief dress-shopping trip, and later for you and Snake if you two will agree to come."

After a few moments of explanation from Mona to Snake, he grabbed the phone and said, "Hell yes, we'll come. Ya'll come and get Mona while I get my tux cleaned. I'll be ready to roll when the jet returns for us. Here's Mona."

"Mona, my jet will pick you up at the Signature Aviation terminal at DFW tonight at seven. You'll land here before we depart for Milan. This'll be fun. See you soon."

Darcy was next on my list. After I gave her the good news, I asked, "Any ideas who can take care of my fur babies while I'm gone both times?"

"Pratt and Whitney can stay with my dogs. Dad and his new wife, Sally, will take good care of them."

"Thank you," I said. "That's a big worry off my mind."

She sighed. "This will be loads of fun, except—"

"Except what?"

"You and I will be the only ones going solo. Do we want to take our chances with young, testosterone-filled Mafiosos, or should we hire escorts?"

"I've been through enough lately," I said. "I'm not keen on fending off randy mobsters, but I don't want to hire strangers either."

"Tim and Kelly are single, aren't they?" she asked.

"Think so." I thought about them. "They're comfortable in any environment, look hot in tuxedoes, and are totally badass, which will discourage the Italians."

"You know them better than I do, so ask them, okay?"

"Alrighty, I'll call Tim now." I hung up and waited for him to answer.

"Hello, Jett. Everything okay?"

"Good news for a change—Sophia and Aldo are getting married in Italy in two weeks."

"That's great and I assume you're attending?"

"That's why I'm calling." I sucked in a breath. "I realize this is a big ask, but I need you to be my escort for all the pre-wedding and wedding festivities, and Darcy needs Kelly to do the same for her. She and I are the only women without boyfriends, and we don't want mobsters putting the moves on us. We need two badass guys nobody will mess with."

"Where will all this take place?"

"Aldo's palatial villa in Sicily and a nearby church. I'll provide a private jet and anything else you guys need. You'll both be staying at Aldo's." I held my breath, hoping he'd agree.

He hesitated, probably taken aback by my request. "Let me check my schedule and make some calls. I imagine we'd wear tuxedoes for the formal affairs and linen suits for the other events. Ask Sophia if we need tails for the wedding and if Aldo can provide firearms for us."

"I'll call her right away. I really hope you guys can come." I hung up and called Sophia.

"No tails because the ceremony is at two p.m., and Aldo will provide weapons for Tim and Kelly. I'll put your escorts in rooms next to yours. Can't wait to see ya."

Ten minutes later, Tim called back. "Jett, we'll go. When is our flight?"

"I'm flying to Sicily eleven days from now, and my jet will take you and Kelly there the next night. Aldo's driver will pick you up. Plan to depart PBI from Signature Aviation at ten p.m. You'll arrive the next afternoon local time, well before the rehearsal dinner. And

Tim, thanks a million. I really appreciate this. You just saved us from a big worry."

"No problem. Want us to be bodyguards or play boyfriends?"

"Um, let me get back to you on that." I hung up thinking boyfriends could be fun. Tim and Kelly were both handsome, manly men.

I'd have to ask Darcy.

FORTY-FOUR

After flying all night, my friends and I met Sophia in Milan, where she hugged us and said, "Hey, girlfriends, thanks for coming. I really missed ya. We're gonna have fun today." Her auburn hair was perfectly coiffed, and her hourglass figure was showcased in a silk blouse and designer jeans.

"Let's get this party started." I towered over her slender, four-foot-ten frame. All thoughts of catching murderers were replaced by choosing pretty dresses.

We rode in a stretch limo to the bridal shop and settled on a long, comfortable sofa where we sipped Prosecco while models wearing the latest wedding fashions paraded past us. Sophia decided on a fitted cream duchesse silk wedding gown, and we chose fitted, formal-length, silk bride's-maid dresses with halter tops and open backs. We would each wear a different pastel color of our choice, making for a lovely, late-summer tableau.

"Thank you, ladies," the shop owner said. "We'll bring the dresses to Sicily three days before the wedding to ensure they fit properly." He bid us farewell. "Have a lovely afternoon."

Sophia linked arms with Gwen and me. "Next, I'm taking everyone shopping for pretty outfits to wear on pre-wedding days, at the rehearsal dinner, and the morning of the wedding." She grinned. "Aldo said we can spend as much of his money as we want, so don't hold back."

We shopped for two hours, then stopped in a café for drinks and a nice meal.

I made a toast to Sophia, and then she said, "Now that the wedding stuff is done, tell me what's been happening back home."

We took turns filling her in on the missing persons, kidnapping, and murder cases.

"Whoa, you girls have been busy. Sorry I missed all the action."

After the meal, we piled into the stretch limo and headed for the airport.

On the way, I asked everyone, "What do you think of Darcy's idea to have Tim and Kelly escort us to the wedding festivities so we don't have to fend off unwanted suitors?"

"That depends—will they be acting as your bodyguards?" Sophia asked.

"They're willing to pose as boyfriends or bodyguards. Which do you think would work best?" Darcy asked.

Gwen, Karin, and Mona exchanged glances and giggled.

Then Gwen said, "Tim and Kelly are boyfriend material. You should go for that, and maybe they'll become real boyfriends by the end of this."

Everyone nodded, grinning.

I looked at Darcy and shrugged. "Alrighty, boyfriends it is."

Sophia elbowed me. "Which one's yours?"

"Tim's mine, and Darcy will be with Kelly."

"I've always liked Tim," Sophia said. "And I've lost count of how many times he's saved you."

"Yeah, he's always been there for me," I said. "They're both awesome guys and easy on the eyes."

The limo pulled up to where our jets were parked, and Sophia said, "I'll take all your new stuff back to Sicily for ya, and I'll see ya there three days before my wedding."

We took turns hugging her before she boarded Aldo's jet, and then we cleared Customs, hopped aboard the Jorgensen Industries jet, and headed home.

After takeoff, I asked my friends, "What are the chances we catch the killer or killers before we return to Italy for the wedding?"

"I thought you already wrapped it up," Mona said. "First, you caught the wedding-dress killer's accomplice, Ron Burns, and then that property developer, Nate Briscoe, who they're calling the septic-tank killer."

"Nate probably killed his pregnant girlfriend and dumped her in his home's septic tank, but he may not have killed the girls who were found wrapped in plastic underneath other septic tanks," I explained. "That was a different M.O."

Mona's jaw dropped. "Who do you think did it?"

Darcy answered, "Greyson Prescott or Matt Hanson."

"But I read that Prescott buried his victims on his Banyan Isle estate, and they were all dressed in wedding gowns." Mona glanced from Darcy to me. "The women under the septic tanks weren't wearing wedding gowns, were they?"

"Well, no, but he might've changed his burial ritual when he ran out of space for graves on his estate," I said.

"You don't really believe that, do you?" Gwen asked.

"No, I think Matt did it." I explained, "He was too eager to throw Prescott under the bus when I gave him the chance."

Mona sat up straighter. "We should check properties Matt owns in other Florida counties and cross-reference missing blondes."

"Yeah, see if one went missing after Nate was jailed," Darcy said.

"What's the name of Matt's company?" Mona opened her laptop.

"MHRI, which stands for Matt Hanson Real Estate Investments, based in West Palm Beach," I answered.

She tapped the keys. "Bingo! Three new houses in Weston." She showed us the screen.

"Check if they have septic tanks," Gwen said.

Mona's fingers danced across the keys. "Yep, two homes were recently completed with the tanks installed, and the third home will have its tank installed day after tomorrow." She pointed at a map on the screen. "The houses are on adjacent lots in the new Willow Lake Estates in Weston."

"Does Matt have them on the market yet?" I asked.

Mona checked. "The two completed ones are available for purchase now."

"Any missing blondes within ten miles?" Gwen asked.

"Ooh, here's one who went missing the day after Nate was arrested, so he couldn't have taken her." She showed us the news story. "Looks like they aren't making a big thing out of it yet because they aren't sure if she ran off with a guy she met at Weston's trendy new nightclub, Hashtag."

"Matt could be our guy," Darcy said. "I'll make an appointment for us to view those houses and bring my dogs."

Mona chuckled. "Right, Darcy. Isn't your business motto, *The Nose Knows*?"

"Yep, nobody fools my fur buddies." Darcy gave Mona a high five.

The women settled in for several hours of sleep during the night flight home.

Later, an announcement came over the airplane's speaker system, "Good morning, Ladies. It's six-forty, and we're on final approach for Palm Beach International Airport. The weather is sunny and seventy-five degrees. We'll be on the ground in fifteen minutes."

Jon, one of the company's handsome young flight attendants, checked that our seats were upright and out belts were fastened. He told Mona, "Miss Wang, this airplane will depart for Texas as soon as the tanks are refueled and the new crew takes over. Should be about forty minutes. It's been a pleasure serving you. Have a good flight."

FORTY-FIVE

Six Hours Earlier

Valhalla Castle, Jett's ancestral home, stood dark and silent on Banyan Isle under a moonless sky. The pups were staying at Darcy's father's ranch outside Garnet while Jett and her friends were visiting Sophia in Italy.

One guard manned the gatehouse in between rounds checking the frontside of the six-acre estate. The other guard maintained a steady circuit around the oceanside backyard and boat docks along the northern inlet between the Intracoastal Waterway and the Atlantic Ocean.

A man wearing a backpack and dressed in black from head to toe crouched behind bushes bordering Jett's fence along the beachfront. He held a rifle loaded with tranquilizer darts and scanned the backyard through a night-vision scope. When the guard passed his position, he shot him in the upper arm, avoiding his bulletproof vest. The stricken sentry took a faltering step and crumpled to the ground, unconscious.

The man in black sneaked over to his fallen prey, pulled out the dart, and put it inside his backpack. He took the guard's radio and ran across the backyard and around the castle. Pausing at the structure's front corner, he checked the gatehouse with his scope. The second guard sat inside, checking his cell phone. Seizing the moment, the intruder sprinted to a banyan tree in the front yard, climbed to a lower branch, and waited with his rifle pointed toward the gatehouse.

Ten minutes later, the front guard began his rounds. When he passed near the tree, the masked assailant shot him. He stumbled, clutched his arm, and fell unconscious.

The intruder pulled out the dart, secreted it inside his pack, and took the guard's keys and code card. He sprinted to the front door, unlocked it, and entered. After finding the security panel in the study, he punched in the code and shut off the outside cameras. There weren't any cameras inside the house. He erased the past thirty minutes of security video, and then he planted high-tech bugs and tiny remote video cameras in numerous locations on the main floor and in Jett's bedroom suite on the fourth floor.

Two hours later, the intruder locked the entry door and returned the keys and code card to the unconscious front guard and the radio to the one in the backyard. He left through the beach gate and vanished into the night.

Tim woke to a trilling cell phone at 3:30 a.m. and rubbed his eyes. He grabbed the phone. "Tim Goldy. What's up?"

"It's Kelly. I'm at Jett's castle. Craig and Bill are unconscious. When they missed their check-ins with headquarters, the night shift called me. I drove over here and found them. They're at the hospital now."

"We're they shot?" Tim pulled on his pants.

"No bullet wounds, bleeding, or bumps on the head, but it was hard to check them in the dark. The doctors will figure it out."

"Has the home been burglarized?" He grabbed a polo shirt with his company logo.

"No signs of forced entry. All the outer doors and windows were locked, and it looks like nothing inside was disturbed. We'll know better when Jett gets home later this morning. I think her plane lands at seven."

"Anything on the security videos?" He had the phone on SPEAKER while he donned his shoes.

"I checked before I drove over here. The videos from one to one-thirty in the morning were erased, and nothing after that was recorded. Cameras must've failed."

"Check the control panel in Jett's study. I bet someone turned off the video feed."

"How could they get in? Everything was locked."

Tim locked his front door and headed for his Humvee. "Did the gate guard have his keys?"

"Yep, hooked on his belt loop like always."

Tim started the engine on his bulletproof behemoth. "I'll be there in twenty minutes. Call me as soon as you know whether those cameras were turned off from Jett's study."

Five minutes later, Kelly called. "You were right, Boss. The cameras were switched off at the home's control panel."

"Go in the kitchen and make some coffee. I'll be there in fifteen minutes, and we'll figure this out."

Tim pulled up in front of Valhalla Castle, and Kelly met him at the front door with a steaming cup of black coffee.

"Thanks. Have you heard from the hospital?" Tim took a sip.

"Just got off the phone with the ER doc. He said both men were shot with powerful tranquilizer darts. He mentioned an unpronounceable drug and said our guys should regain consciousness in a few more hours and fully recover."

"Good." Tim called his headquarters. "I want new locks installed everywhere on the Jorgensen estate today and send over our bomb-sniffing dogs right away." He glanced at Kelly. "I want to verify this place is safe before Jett and Karin get home." He sipped the hot coffee. "Better wait for the dogs before we start poking around."

"Yeah, I'd hate to set off a boobytrap." Kelly opened the front door. "Let's wait on the outside steps."

The men sat on the stone steps and finished their coffee.

Tim expected fast response times from his employees, and he wasn't disappointed. It wasn't long before a black Chevy Suburban pulled up, and two men unloaded their bomb-sniffing dogs, both Belgian Malinois.

"Thanks for coming so fast. We'll start in the middle of the ground floor. I'll follow Pete and his dog through every room in the south wing, while Kelly goes with Steve in the north wing. When we reach the study, I'll take my team up the secret passage to Jett's bedroom where we'll check the turret rooms and the roof. Kelly will take the other team up the hidden passage from the ballroom into Jett's parents' suite and check the north turrets and roof. Then we'll work our way through the fourth floor to the central staircases and continue down, searching the third and second floors. Any questions?"

The men shook their heads, and the dogs seemed eager to get started. The dogs each checked half of the great hall and then turned south and north.

Pete's dog was fast, but efficient. He checked everything he could reach. Then Pete lifted the excited K-9 so he could sniff high up along the walls before they continued to the next room. Forty minutes later, they'd covered about ten-thousand square feet, including the study.

The door to the hidden passage was part of a floor-to-ceiling oak bookcase along the southern outer wall. Tim pulled out a black leather-bound book titled, *The Murders at the Rue Morgue and Other Short Stories* by Edgar Allan Poe. Behind it, he pushed a round wolf-head emblem embedded in the wood, and part of the bookcase swung open. A whiff of musty air greeted them from the dark, winding staircase.

"Send the dog ahead," Tim said, waving Pete forward.

The men followed the Malinois up four flights of stairs to the turret room in the southeast corner of the castle where he waited for further instructions.

Pete pointed up the turret stairs. "Want to check the roof first or the bedroom?"

"The roof." Tim waited while the dog climbed another flight of spiral stairs to the roof door. No explosives.

They entered the flat concrete roof area bordered by parapets and waited while the dog searched. They met the other team in the middle.

"Nothing in the north wing so far, but we haven't checked any rooms on the fourth floor or below," Kelly said.

"Same with us. Let's check the fourth floor and continue down," Tim said.

The dogs wagged their tails and galloped back to their respective turret doors in the opposite corners. Two hours later, they met in the foyer.

Steve asked, "What's next?"

"The garage, the front yard and gatehouse, and the backyard and boat docks." Tim opened the front door. "We'll start with the ten-car garage."

The men and dogs finished their searches just as Jett and Karin pulled up in Jett's SUV with Pratt and Whitney onboard.

Jett jumped out and froze when she spotted the guards with the K-9s. "What's up, guys? Can I let my dogs out?"

FORTY-SIX

Before Tim had a chance to answer, a man pulled up in one of Trident Security's trucks. He joined the group and set down a metal toolbox and a satchel filled with locks and keys.

"I'm ready to change the locks, Mr. Goldy."

"Good. Start with the front door." Tim strode over to Karin and me. "There's been an incident. Bring your dogs inside, and we'll tell you about it."

I snapped the leashes on Pratt and Whitney while the K-9s headed for their vehicle, and Tim opened my front door. My dogs greeted him and Kelly and followed me inside the house.

Everyone settled in the great hall, and I removed the dogs' leashes.

"Guys, the suspense is killing me." I glanced from one man to the other. "Did anyone get hurt?"

"Not exactly." Tim gave us a quick recap of everything that happened while we were gone. "We don't know why the intruder did what he did. Let us know if anything is missing. I held off searching for bugs until we finished checking for explosive devices. Our K-9s from the bomb unit just finished clearing your house and grounds."

My cell phone trilled. I answered, and Darcy said, "Jett, someone shot my guards with tranquilizer darts, then erased the security footage and turned off the cameras. Is everything okay at your place?"

"Nope. Same thing happened here. Is anything missing?"

"Don't know—haven't had time to check yet, but nothing seems out of place. What about Gwen's house?"

"It looked normal when we dropped her off. Her chef and house manager were both there while we were gone, and her security guard didn't say anything about an intruder."

"Right. Good. What are you doing about this?"

"Tim is having my locks changed. He checked everywhere for explosives and will search for bugs. You should probably do the same."

"Okay, my dogs can sniff for bombs. Let me know if your guys find anything. Do you still want me to make an appointment to see Matt's properties in Weston tomorrow?"

"Yeah, we need to know if he's guilty. I'll call those FBI agents in Miami and let them know what we're up to. They might have a theory about our intruders."

"I'll try for an appointment at eleven tomorrow morning."

"Eleven sounds good. I'd like to wrap this up as soon as possible."

"Me too. I'll let you know."

I pocketed my phone and told everyone what happened at Darcy's house while her pets were staying at her dad's place.

"Sounds like the intrusions might be related to a case you two are working on," Kelly said.

"Yeah, they're trying to nail Matt Hanson for the septic-tank murders," Karin said.

"Excuse me while I call the Feds in Miami." I walked away and called the number.

Special Agent Ruth Jacobs answered. "What can I do for you, Jett?"

I brought her up to speed on the break-ins and our plans for checking Hanson's properties in Weston tomorrow morning. "We suspect he might be responsible for all the septic-tank murders except Nate's girlfriend."

"Why?"

"Nate was in jail when the most recent woman went missing. If she's buried under Matt's septic tank, it has to be him, right?"

"Sounds plausible, but aren't you taking a big chance going there without a police escort?"

"Gwen is a detective with the Palm Beach Police, and Darcy and I will be armed and accompanied by her four big dogs. Hanson doesn't stand a chance against us."

"If he knows you're coming, he won't want the dogs to find that body." She paused. "Don't call today for tomorrow's appointment. That gives him time to move the body and set a trap."

"Good point. I'll call Darcy and tell her to call in the morning, so he won't have time to do anything."

"Ask her to set the appointment with one of his realtors. Maybe then Hanson won't know about it until after you find the corpse."

"Thanks for the good suggestions, Agent Jacobs. I'll keep you posted." I dialed Darcy. "Have you called Hanson?"

"No, I've been busy checking my house. What's up?"

I explained what the Fed suggested. "I'll be ready early tomorrow in case we have to accept an earlier appointment."

"Okay, I'll wait until first thing tomorrow and text you with the meet time."

"I wonder if Hanson broke into our homes to search for evidence we might have on him," I said. "What do you think?"

"It's possible, especially if he found out we were in Italy. Maybe Blake told him."

Kerri hugged her mother. "Love you. Sorry you have the early shift in the ER today. Hope it goes well."

Her mother squeezed back. "Be careful jogging." Kat glanced around. "Where's King?"

"Don't know." She peeked under the kitchen table. "He was here a minute ago."

"Find him, please. I can't handle another missing family member. I'll wait."

"Okay, Mom." Kerri hurried away and checked the bedrooms.

She found the tri-color Cavalier King Charles spaniel snuggled against her sleeping father, smiled at the cute scene, and trotted back to the kitchen. Chuckling, she said, "He climbed in bed with Dad."

"Your father's sleeping in a little. Don't forget to wake him before you leave for school." Kat grabbed her keys and said, "Love you," on her way out the door.

Kerri slipped her cell phone into an armband, adjusted her earbuds, and locked the door behind her. She jogged to a shaded trail near her family's house on Jupiter Island. *It's good to be home safe knowing all the bad guys are locked up or out of the country.*

The sun peeked above the horizon, and the grass glittered with early-morning dew as her ear buds filled her head with music from her favorite Taylor Swift album. Rounding a corner, she swerved right to avoid an oncoming runner on the narrow path.

The handsome man in his early thirties seemed vaguely familiar. *Do I know him?*

Primeval alarm bells drowned out Taylor's lyrics, and icy shivers tingled her spine as she slowed her pace for a quick glance behind. Before she turned, something sharp stung her back. She spun around and faced her attacker while she reached back and pulled out whatever was hurting her. Confused, she examined the tiny dart in her hand.

He grinned, and she froze, her wide eyes focusing on his menacing eyes.

When the man moved closer, his body blurred. She collapsed, and the maniacal grin on his distorted face disappeared into a black fog.

The runner slipped the tiny dart into his pocket and tossed Kerri's cell phone into a nearby pond. He zip-tied her wrists and ankles, gagged her, then carried her through the trees and deposited her in the cargo area of his SUV, concealing her with a blanket. He drove off Jupiter Island and headed south on US1 before cutting over to I-95 South.

Traffic was light at such an early hour. Forty-five minutes later, he turned onto I-595 West in Broward County and drove twenty miles to Weston. He parked in the empty garage, closed the electric door, and opened the rear hatch on his SUV. Kerri was still unconscious when he carried her inside the house.

My phone pinged with a text from Darcy as I finished breakfast with Karin on the back terrace. The text said our appointment in Weston was set for 10:00 a.m. With rush-hour traffic, it might take an hour and a half to drive there. I'd have to hurry. I called Gwen.

"Good morning, Jett. Are we on for Weston?"

"Yep, Darcy just made our appointment for ten, so I'll pick you up in five minutes." I pocketed my phone and dashed upstairs to grab my Glock.

Gwen was waiting outside when I arrived next door in my white SUV. She wore navy slacks with her police-issued Glock 40 holstered under a light-blue cotton blazer.

"Darcy will meet us there with her dogs." I drove over the bridge and headed for I-95 South. "I hope we nail Muffy's killer today."

Gwen nodded. "I don't think Nate killed her, even though he owns a septic tank company. Whoever buried the women under septic tanks used a different M.O. than he used with his pregnant girlfriend, who he put *inside* his septic tank."

My stomach churned. "I agree, but I keep getting this feeling that we're missing something important."

Doctor Riley Lyons awoke to wet doggie kisses. "Okay, King, I'm awake." He sat up and glanced at the digital clock on the nightstand.

Nine twenty! Kerri forgot to wake me at eight. She's usually dependable.

He dressed hurriedly, assuming his daughter had already left for school. King nudged him repeatedly and whined.

Riley looked down at him. "Sorry, boy, didn't Kerri let you out?" He strode into the kitchen, let King out, and spotted his daughter's school backpack on the counter. "Kerri?"

She wouldn't forget her backpack.

His mouth went dry, and his heart raced. He dashed to the garage. His daughter's car was still there. He ran back to the kitchen, snatched his phone off the charger, and called her.

No answer.

"Kerri!" he yelled as he ran through the house looking for her. No luck.

He activated the Find-My-Phone app on his cell phone to trace her location. The tracker indicated she was a quarter mile from the house on the shaded jogging trail.

Maybe she tripped and broke a bone. But why didn't she call?

He bolted out the door with King on his heels. When Riley reached her phone's location on the trail, he realized the tracker indicated it was thirty feet west of him.

He turned and swallowed hard. *Oh my God! It's in the pond!*

Don't panic. She'd never go in that mucky, snake-infested gator hole, especially after her Everglades nightmare. But why is her phone in there? Something bad must've happened. Fearing for his daughter, he waded in, following the locator beacon. *Good thing I bought her the waterproof model.*

The pond was shallow near shore, but the water soon was up to his chin as he slogged through it. His heart raced and his anxiety rose as he neared the location.

Ten more feet. Please, God, not Kerri.

When he reached the spot, he held his breath and ducked under, grasping around on the mucky bottom. His right hand landed on a thin, rectangular device. He grabbed it and anxiously thrust his hands out, searching for Kerri. His lungs ached for air when he burst through the surface.

Gasping, he stared at his right hand and noticed the sparkly pink cell-phone case with a big K on the back—Kerri's phone.

"No!" A hot knife twisted into his heart as he prayed his daughter had not drowned, mired in the muck. He shoved the phone into his back pocket and dived down, desperately searching for his only child.

FORTY-SEVEN

Darcy's big SUV was parked behind Matt's Bentley. She and her dogs waited inside the car with the engine and air-conditioning running until she spotted us pull in behind her. We exited and gathered with her team outside the house's front door.

"I thought we were meeting one of Matt's real estate agents." I rang the bell.

"She must've told him, and he took her place." Darcy peeked through the window.

No answer and no signs of movement inside.

"Let's check out back." Darcy and her dogs led us around to the backyard.

The dogs sprinted to an open hole bordered by a tall pile of dirt near the back fence. They sniffed around it and trotted back to Darcy.

Gwen walked over and looked down. "Seems a lot deeper than most holes for septic tanks."

"But the dogs didn't find any bodies." I petted them, and my phone rang. I pulled it out and answered.

"Jett, it's Riley Lyons." On the edge of panic, his voice cracked. "Kerri's missing. I found her phone in a pond beside a jogging trail. Police divers are coming to search."

"If she accidentally dropped her phone in the pond, she'd never go in there to get it." My gut twisted into a knot. "It's too soon to speculate, but if someone took her, it's possible he tossed the phone so he couldn't be tracked."

"I thought all the criminals who were after her are in jail or out of the country."

"Most of them are, but we're closing in on a guy right now who might know something. I'll call as soon as we have him."

"Please, find my daughter, Jett."

The anguish and tension in his voice made my heart ache. I pocketed my phone and told Gwen and Darcy what happened. "I can't believe she's missing again."

"Maybe Matt took her. Let's find him." Darcy headed for the French doors beyond the pool. They were unlocked. She turned to the dogs. "Stay."

We followed her inside, and I called, "Matt? Where are you?"

No answer.

"I'll check the front." Gwen strode through the long living room to the front door. "I don't see anyone outside the windows, and the door is locked electronically."

Seconds later, loud clicks came from the rest of the exit doors and windows.

I turned, and my mouth went dry. "The French doors are locked now." Goosebumps erupted on my arms as I checked the inner door to the garage near the front entry. "Also locked. Did he do this from somewhere in the house or lock us in remotely?"

Darcy said, "The windows are locked too. What if he plans to blow us up or gas us?"

Gwen pulled out her phone. "I'm calling 911." She checked the screen. "No signal. This house is obviously wired—might even have hidden cameras. If we break a window, it might trigger something lethal."

"Let's spread out and search for Matt and the control panel, starting with the ground floor. We'll meet back at the staircase." My heart hammered my chest as I headed for the kitchen. It was empty, and so was the pantry. No control panel hidden in a cabinet. A door revealed a rear staircase beside the pantry. I glanced up the dark, empty stairs and then met my friends back in the living room.

"Nobody down here," Darcy said. "We'd better check upstairs. The listing said this house has five bedrooms and six and a half baths, so he could be hiding anywhere, ready to pounce."

"I found another staircase by the pantry," I said. "I'll go up that way so he can't sneak past us."

"Be careful," Gwen warned. "He knows we're coming."

───

Upstairs, Darcy turned into the nearest poolside bedroom, while Gwen ducked into the opposite one. A slight breeze from a window alerted Darcy that it was not fully closed. She opened it wider, leaned out, and shouted, "Dogs! Rescue!"

After hearing Max bark an acknowledgment, she turned and crossed the empty room. A mirrored door opened to a large walk-in closet. She stepped inside. It was empty, except for a couple of tall cardboard boxes near the back. One box had small holes torn in it that could have been from shipping damage.

She stopped and listened.

Silence.

Wary, she drew her pistol and crept toward the boxes. When she was two feet away, something stung her in the neck. As she reached for her wound, the box with the holes sprang to life and slammed into her, knocking her to the floor. A heavy weight pinned her down, and the box was cast aside.

Feeling weak and woozy, Darcy gazed into the face of her attacker as he snatched the pistol from her limp hand.

He whispered, "The usual dosage doesn't take effect fast enough, so I took a chance on a stronger dose that might kill you." He shrugged. "I plan to bury you alive anyway." He grinned, and his features distorted as she sank into a bizarre black nothingness.

Carefully emerging from the closet, he stopped and listened, then sneaked across the hall. He didn't notice the open window, which had slid back down several inches.

He peeked into the opposite bedroom where Gwen searched a walk-in closet with four large boxes inside. When she bent over to check inside one, he crept behind her and shot a tranquilizer dart into her back. Then he sprang on top of her, pinning her to the floor, facedown.

Snatching the gun out of her hand, he whispered, "Your Glock won't help you now."

He waited until her eyes closed and her body went limp.

I crept up the back stairs into the main hallway, stopped, and listened for movement nearby. Nothing.

I slipped into the master bedroom that occupied that end of the house. Goosebumps erupted on my arms again, a chill ran down my spine, my heart raced, and an overwhelming sense of imminent danger enveloped me.

I paused and listened.

Silence.

Where is he?

I drew my Glock and glanced around.

Nothing.

The bedroom door was near a huge master bath and two walk-in closets. Tall, double windows dominated the other three walls, and a thick, cream-colored Berber carpet covered the floor.

There was no place to hide in the unfurnished bedroom, so I turned to the closet on the right side of the bathroom and looked inside.

I gasped and took a moment to get my heart rate under control.

The closet held a shocking surprise: a blonde in her early twenties, lying on the floor. Her skin had a gray pallor, except for her lips and cheeks, which were cherry red.

I checked her pulse. Dead, probably from cyanide poisoning.

No signs of a struggle.

Could be the missing girl from that club in Weston and probably killed elsewhere and dumped here. My stomach churned as I backed away from the corpse and listened for movement.

Matt must be the killer.

I sucked in a deep breath, stepped away, and eased open the bathroom door. An empty, glassed-in shower, toilet, and vanity sink on one side was separated by a half-wall from a Jacuzzi tub and a second toilet and sink on the other side.

Alarm bells clanged inside my head as chills tingled my spine. I spun around.

No one there, just eerie silence.

Steeling myself, I checked the other closet, my senses on high alert. When I looked inside, I froze.

Another surprise: Matt, sprawled on the floor, his eyes closed. My pistol at the ready, I checked his pulse. Still alive.

Who did this? Blake?

I pulled out my cell and hit 9-1-1. No signal up here either.

A device in this house is blocking all cell-phone signals. Someone planned this.

I must have stared at my phone a second too long. Something stung my back. I spun around, and someone dived into me and knocked me down. He pounced on me and pinned my weakened arms to the floor.

The room did a slow spin as a male voice said, "Hello, Jett."

I tried to recognize him, but his features were too blurry.

He grinned. "I'll bury you and your friends alive, then blame it on Matt."

I was fading fast. His face looked like a distorted reflection in a funhouse mirror as my world went black.

Darcy's super-smart dogs were eager to work. Earlier, Max, the big German shepherd, and his team spied their master yelling for rescue from a second-floor window. They raced around the house, searching for an open door or window, but found none.

Trained to use any means of entry, Max led his team to the back of the house. He leaped onto the rocky side of the pool's tall waterfall and scrambled up it. After climbing to the top, he jumped onto the slightly sloped roof overhanging the pool, and almost slid off the smooth tiles. He clawed his way up to the outer wall of the second story and watched his team struggle over the slippery roof tiles.

Max reached the barely open window, and his team joined him and went to work with their paws and noses, pushing and lifting. Soon it was open enough for Tiny's huge head to squeeze through.

The one-hundred-and-seventy-pound Great Dane pushed up the window with his strong neck and leaped inside. Nose to the floor, he found Darcy in the closet. Max, Dobie, and Laddie joined him, and they licked her face and arms, trying to wake her. When that failed, the Labrador stayed with her, and his three teammates spread out and searched for the other women and the man who had left his scent on Darcy.

Dobie found Gwen across the hall in another bedroom and stood guard over her while Max and Tiny followed the man's scent, searching for him and Jett in the silent house. A new scent detoured them to another bedroom.

Their noses led them to a closed closet door. The familiar scent of a girl they recently rescued was on the other side of that door. Max used his mouth as Darcy had taught him and turned the handle. He pulled the door open, and Tiny rushed in and licked Kerri's gagged face. Max joined him, both dogs wagging their tails and licking her.

The tranquilizer had worn off, and her eyes popped open. Once her vision cleared, she recognized Darcy's dogs. Knowing how smart they were, she rolled over and lifted her zip-tied hands away from her back.

Max carefully grabbed hold of the plastic tie and gnawed it until it broke. Her hands now free, Kerri pulled off the gag.

"Good dogs!" She held up her feet. "Max, chew this off."

The dogs knew from the scents they found there was still one girl to rescue and a bad guy to neutralize, so Max nudged Tiny to continue the search. As Tiny bounded away, Max chewed through the zip tie around Kerri's ankles.

She hugged him. "Thank you, Max. You're such a good dog. Where are Darcy and Jett?"

Darcy was just one bedroom away, and he led her there first. Kerri gasped when she spotted her motionless on the floor with Laddie on guard. She rushed over and found the dart in her neck, but her pulse was strong, so she hoped Darcy would wake eventually. Unlike Kerri, Darcy wasn't bound or gagged, which meant she wasn't expected to wake soon.

Kerri searched the unconscious woman and her shoulder bag, and found her cell phone and an empty holster. She tried calling 9-1-1, but she couldn't get a signal, then glanced at the time on the phone. "Oh, God, my parents must be worried sick."

Kerri petted the Labrador. "Good boy, Laddie. Stay and guard Darcy while Max and I find Jett."

Max nudged her, and she followed him across the hall into another bedroom, where she found Gwen in the same condition as Darcy and guarded by Dobie. Her weapon was missing too. She petted Dobie. "Stay with Gwen." Then she looked at Max and said, "Where is Jett?"

He sniffed the air and led her down the hall toward the master bedroom, ignoring the fourth bedroom, which was across from the one where he'd found her. He paused near the master bedroom's open door and raised his hackles. Then he bared his teeth and charged into the room.

FORTY-EIGHT

The previous day, Tim's team had successfully found and removed every bug and tiny video camera in Jett's castle, but he worried about what the intruder might have learned in the few hours before all the bugs were found.

He sat with Karin on the oceanfront terrace, while Pratt and Whitney napped at his feet. Glancing at his watch, he said, "I wonder if they found another body."

"I haven't heard anything," Karin said. "Jett promised she'd call as soon as they finished searching the property."

"Didn't you say the appointment was at ten?" He tapped his watch. "It's noon."

Before they could speculate further, Tim's phone rang. He answered, "Goldy here."

Tim's bounty-hunter friend, Bob Metz, said, "This might be an emergency. Prescott isn't in the Maldives. An actor lookalike was hired to impersonate him. We think Prescott returned to the States in disguise with a fake passport. Jett could be in danger, and we can't reach her, Gwen, or Darcy."

"I'll get right on it. Thanks, Bob." Tim ended the call and hit

Kelly's number on speed dial. "Kelly, bring the chopper and rifles and meet me at Jett's backyard, *now*."

"I'll be there in fifteen minutes."

Tim called Jett, Gwen, and Darcy, but the calls went straight to voicemail. He tried Matt's cellphone. No answer. He dialed 9-1-1, gave the address, asked for a wellness check, and explained what he suspected. Then he explained his concerns to Karin, checked his sidearm, and paced the deck waiting for Kelly.

Soon, thundering rotor blades replaced the gentle sounds of breaking waves on the shoreline. The helicopter had barely touched down when Tim jumped in. Seconds later, the bird rose into the sky and sped toward Weston.

Fifteen minutes later, Kelly landed on an empty lot across the street from the house. A lone cop stood outside the locked front door.

Tim and Kelly slung their rifles across their backs and held out their IDs as they approached the police officer.

Tim identified himself and explained, "I called 9-1-1. My security company is responsible for the safety of the women trapped inside this house."

"No one answered the door. How do you know they're trapped inside with a killer?"

"It's a long story, and there's no time. I'll take full responsibility for any property damage. We must save the women." Before the cop had time to object, Tim ran around to the back side of the house with Kelly and spotted the open window on the second floor.

"Better to sneak in up there than make noise breaking a window down here." He climbed up the side of the rock waterfall, and Kelly boosted him up to the overhanging roof. He reached down and pulled Kelly up. The two men ignored the deputy's protests and climbed through the window.

They found Darcy unconscious and guarded by Laddie, who recognized them from the night at the Prescott mansion. He wagged his tail.

"Good boy." Tim petted him. "Let me check her." He felt for a pulse. "She's alive. We'd better hold off calling an ambulance until we find everyone. Laddie, guard Darcy."

They found Gwen across the hall in another bedroom with Dobie guarding her. His wagging tail indicated he recognized them. They verified Gwen was alive, and Tim said, "I hope Jett's okay."

Kelly glanced around. "Yeah, I wonder where she and the other dogs are."

Somewhere in the distance, a woman screamed and yelled, "Dobie, help!"

The fierce Doberman rocketed down the hall like a fur missile and vanished into the farthest bedroom with the men racing after him.

Earlier, Kerri crept into the master bedroom and spotted Max leaping toward the man who'd shot her with the dart six hours ago. He was standing in a wide walk-in closet with Jett, a man, and Tiny lying unconscious behind him. Kerri's kidnapper raised his dart gun and shot Max in the chest seconds before the powerful dog slammed into him and knocked him to the closet floor. The dog's jaws were open and wedged under his chin, but the beast passed out before he could bite down.

Greyson Prescott shoved Max aside, sat up, and aimed his dart pistol at Kerri. She froze, but when he pulled the trigger, nothing happened.

"Dammit! Out of darts. Never dreamed I'd need this many. I have their Glocks, but guns are too loud." He shoved the dart gun into a back pocket, lunged to his feet, pulled out a switchblade, and flipped it open. "There's a grave prepared for you and your friends in the backyard with room for the dogs." He grinned. "I'll kill you now, but they'll be buried alive under a septic tank braced above them so they can suffer extreme terror before they suffocate." He thumbed at Matt. "He'll take the blame."

Seeing Jett and the dogs lying helpless filled Kerri with rage. "You bastard! I won't let you kill my friends." She tried a spinning heel kick she learned in taekwondo class, but the effects of the tranquilizer had not fully worn off, and she ended up falling into him.

He rolled her under him and raised the knife as she screamed for Dobie.

When Tim and Kelly reached the master bedroom, they spotted Max and Tiny sprawled in a large walk-in closet beside Jett and an unconscious man. Kerri was on her back, gasping for breath, fighting with a man on top of her. Dobie's jaws were clamped around his wrist on the hand that held a knife, and blood splattered Kerri's face.

She tried to pull the knife out of his hand, but Dobie jerked the man's wrist from side to side while snarling and biting deeper. The man struggled to fend off Kerri and push aside Dobie, but neither gave way.

Tim said, "Good boy, Dobie," and yanked the guy off Kerri. The bleeding man, no longer wearing a disguise, was easily recognizable. "You should've stayed in the Maldives, Prescott." Tim petted the big Doberman and said, "Release, Dobie." He grabbed the knife.

Dobie stepped back but never took his eyes off the perpetrator.

Kelly kept a weapon trained on Prescott while Tim cuffed him. "I'll guard him, Boss. Check Kerri and Jett."

Tim helped Kerri up to a sitting position and said, "You okay?"

She nodded. "Dobie saved me. The knife was an inch from my throat when the brave dog grabbed his wrist. Better check Jett."

He eased around to Jett and checked for a pulse. "She's alive."

"Good." Kerri wiped her face and cringed. "I'm covered with his blood." She bit her lip and fought back tears. "Please, call my parents. I wanna go home."

"We'll get you checked out at a hospital first." He turned. "Kelly, let the cop in and call for five ambulances and Kerri's parents. Then call those FBI agents in Miami and tell them we have their fugitive. Prescott can get medical treatment later."

"On it, and I'll warn the cops not to hurt the dogs." Kelly rushed from the room.

FORTY-NINE

Kelly and several Weston Police Officers waited with Prescott while Tim rode in an ambulance with Jett. Ambulances with the other women and Matt also headed for Weston Hospital.

"You call this first aid?" Prescott held out his bandaged, zip-tied wrists. "I should be in a hospital. I could bleed to death."

"We should be so lucky," a cop said.

"Relax, Prescott. Two blondes are coming for you." Kelly grinned. "That should make you happy."

"What blondes?"

"FBI agents I called especially for you." Kelly smirked. "This'll be a real treat. I know how much you like blondes, so, you're welcome."

"I demand to call my lawyer immediately!"

"Tell someone who cares." Kelly crossed his arms. "I'm private security."

Prescott turned to the cops. "Officers! Officers?"

The local police turned their backs on him.

A large black SUV skidded to a stop. The Feds must've driven full speed with their lights flashing because they arrived from Miami forty minutes after Kelly called. Agents Jacobs and Smith leaped out and hurried to the prisoner.

Kelly grinned. "Special Agents, it's my pleasure to hand over Greyson Prescott."

The FBI agents smiled at Kelly and then studied the killer with icy detachment.

Agent Jacobs turned. "Thank you, Mr. Mahone. We'll get back to you for a full report later. Are the women okay?"

"Everyone except a young, blond murder victim. Don't know her name. Jett and her team, along with Matt Hanson, were hit with powerful tranquilizer darts that rendered them unconscious. They were taken to a local hospital."

Agent Smith scrutinized Prescott. "This is all wrong. Your wrists should be cuffed behind you." She cut the zip-tie, yanked his arms behind him, and roughly clamped the handcuffs onto his wrists.

"Owww! You're killing me!" he squealed.

"Sorry. Did that hurt?" Smith grinned.

She unwittingly triggered memories of all the abuse meted out by his blond mother and sister.

Panicked, Prescott said to Kelly. "Don't let them take me. I'll pay you ten million."

Kelly chuckled. "Keep your money. Watching you squirm is worth a billion."

Agent Jacobs, unaware of Prescott's family history, said, "Huh, looks like your right wrist is bleeding." She glanced at Smith. "We'll have to get that looked at, eventually."

The women grinned at Kelly, then dragged their prisoner to their SUV.

Kelly smiled and waved as they drove away.

I woke with a splitting headache and blurred vision. Slowly, my eyes focused on a white ceiling. When the pounding in my head eased a little, I struggled to sit up, and Tim leaped from a chair at the foot of my bed and helped me.

"Where am I?" I reached for a glass of water, and Tim grabbed it and held it to my lips.

"You're at the Weston Hospital in a private room. How do you feel?"

"My muscles are rubbery, my brain's in a fog, and "The Anvil Chorus" is booming inside my head."

"Drink lots of water. It'll help flush out the drugs." He refilled my glass and held it to my lips.

I took a deep sip, and memories flooded my consciousness. "Gwen and Darcy! Kerri! The dogs! What happened to them?"

He gently squeezed my hand. "Relax." He explained all my friends were in similar condition in private rooms. "Kerri's unharmed, here with her parents. As for the dogs, Tiny and Max weigh the same or more than most women, so the tranquilizers weren't too much for their bodies. Darcy's father transported them to their veterinarian and looked after Laddie and Dobie. All the dogs are with him now and doing fine."

I rubbed my forehead. "There are things I need to tell the Feds—Matt and the dead blonde."

"No worries—Kerri filled us in on some of it. Prescott planned to blame all the murders on Matt."

"Now that he's in custody, did he rat out Blake?" I sipped more water.

"Yep." He glanced at his watch. "Right about now, those special agents from Miami are probably tricking Blake into confessing."

Doctors Riley and Kat Lyons tapped on the door and entered with their daughter.

Kerri rushed to my side. "You okay, Jett?"

"Yeah, thanks to you and Dobie." I grinned. "You're quite the heroine, young lady."

She blushed.

Riley asked, "Are you sure we're done with those monsters, Jett?"

I glanced at Tim, and he nodded. "We're sure."

Kerri grinned. "Good, because I have a date with a hot football player tomorrow night."

At the courthouse, FBI Special Agents Jacobs and Smith escorted Banyan Isle's Detective Blake Collins past his sister-in-law, who glared at him. Her lawyer had filed for emergency custody of Blake's son, and it was granted to her. The agents and Blake settled in an interview room with an expensive criminal attorney seated at Blake's side.

Jacobs began, "We have Greyson Prescott in custody, and he's throwing you under the bus to escape the death penalty for over thirty murders. What he doesn't know is that we're willing to offer you a deal that saves you from that fate if you give sworn testimony that Prescott asked you to kill his mother and sister in exchange for him killing your wife."

"Why does that help you if you already have him for multiple murders?" Blake asked.

"He gave you up for killing his mother and sister so he could avoid the death penalty for thirty murders," Smith explained. "But we want him to die for his crimes."

Jacobs continued, "Your wife's murder, along with his mother and sister, are separate crimes that could earn him the death penalty with your testimony." She paused. "I guess you got greedy—wanting control of your wife's trust fund—but you aren't a mass murderer like Prescott."

Smith nodded. "Yeah, you might do twenty years of a forty-year sentence with time off for good behavior and still have a life when you get out." She slid a document across the table. "This guarantees you avoid lethal punishment if you give a recorded statement under oath and sign a written statement afterward, detailing how the murders were committed and the exact agreement you had with Greyson Prescott."

Jacobs checked her watch. "We'll leave you to confer with your attorney, but we need an answer in forty-five minutes, or the Attorney General will demand you receive the maximum penalty."

Smith stood. "It would be a shame for Prescott to get off with life in prison while you get executed. Especially since he killed way more women than you did."

Blake leaned over and whispered something to his lawyer, who nodded.

"Stay," Blake said. "I'll do what you asked."

FIFTY

Gwen, Darcy, and I recovered from our final ordeal with Greyson Prescott in plenty of time to attend Aldo and Sophia's wedding festivities. Gwen's boyfriend Clint, Karin, and my Uncle Hunter joined us on the flight to Sicily.

Our Gulfstream jet landed at Palermo Falcone Borsellino Airport a few minutes after the one carrying Mona and Snake arrived from Texas, and we all rode together in a stretch limo to the Medici villa on Sicily's northern coast. On the way there in the bright sunlight, we told them how our cases turned out.

"So, that Prescott guy killed Muffy too?" Snake asked.

"Yeah," I said. "After twenty-two graves, he ran out of burial space on his Banyan Isle estate and started hiding bodies under septic tanks."

I slid against Snake and then against Hunter as the limo navigated the winding coastal highway under a bright blue sky.

"Prescott had a collection of hairs from Matt Hanson and Nate Briscoe that he planted on his victims," Gwen said.

Snake shook his head. "Nice friend."

"He framed them as insurance in case the bodies were found." Darcy rolled her eyes. "What a sick dude."

"How did you find out all this?" Mona asked.

"Ron Burns, his accomplice, had been holding back critical info. Once he was certain Prescott was in custody and couldn't hurt him, he made a deal to avoid the death penalty," I explained. "He told the Feds where to find Prescott's creepy skeleton mask and photos of the women in wedding gowns Prescott took before he killed them. Burns also admitted he buried the victims."

"I can't believe Prescott risked everything to come back and kill us," Darcy said.

Gwen shrugged. "He wanted revenge because we're the reason he had to leave the country."

"You're right," Darcy said. "He had a good thing going, and we ruined it."

"And he couldn't handle being bested by women," I interjected as we drove along the azure Tyrrhenian Sea. "Kerri told me he went ballistic when she beat him at chess."

Mona grinned. "Then it's a good thing Tim and Kelly rescued you girls, *again*."

Snake nudged me. "Where's Tim? Is he still up for playing your boyfriend this weekend?"

"He and Kelly will be here tomorrow before the rehearsal dinner, and yes, he'll play my boyfriend." My cheeks turned red.

"I bet he'd like to be the real deal," Mona said, grinning.

I rolled my eyes and blushed harder, if that was possible. "Probably not—I mean he's never asked me out or given any indication that he's interested." I glanced at my friends, and everyone was smirking. "Do you guys know something I don't?"

"Oh, please," Hunter said. "That man has rescued you more times than I can count."

"Yeah, but that's his job. It doesn't mean anything, right?" I nudged Snake.

He arched an eyebrow. "Remember when Mona's uncle sent that Korean gang to attack your castle? Bullets flying everywhere and dozens of retired SEALs defending, but who rushed directly to your room to save you?"

"Okay, it was Tim." I sighed and stared out at the sparkling sea. "Look, all my romantic relationships have had disastrous endings. Obviously, my dating judgment sucks, so if you're so sure about this, then ask Tim, guy to guy, and tell me his answer."

"First, we need to know what you want." Snake glanced around.

"Yeah," Hunter said. "How do you feel about him?"

Embarrassed, I wondered if my cheeks could get any redder. "He's the whole package—I mean, an awesome guy like that—he probably already has a girlfriend."

"How could he?" Gwen laughed. "He spends all his time protecting you."

Everyone snickered, fueling my embarrassment.

"Geez, I feel like I'm back in high school," I said, wishing I was on the huge yacht I spotted cruising offshore. "Give me a break, people."

Snake grinned. "All right, Jett, I'll ask him."

Hunter looked across at my mentor. "What about you, Darcy? Are you interested in Kelly?"

"Heck, yeah, he's a real hottie." She giggled. "Sign me up."

"So, you'd like me to make discreet inquiries?" Hunter asked, leaning forward.

She nodded. "God, yes. Get this ball rolling. I need a good boyfriend."

Everyone laughed, ready for a fun weekend.

Everyone except me. My gut roiled. *What if Tim's not interested in me?*

In my bedroom at the Medici villa, I turned from the wall mirror. "How do I look?" I smoothed the navy silk fabric of my low-cut cocktail dress. "He'll be here any minute."

My dear friend, Sophia DeLuca, mother of a powerful New York Mafia *don* and soon to be Contessa Medici, looked me over. "Jett, ya look beautiful, not that it matters. The guy's crazy about ya."

I bit my lower lip. "How do you know that?" Panic crept in as I looked at my feet and checked my matching navy-blue stiletto heels.

"This is me you're talking to." She raised her eyebrows. "Have ya ever known me to be wrong?"

I thought about that as I admired her four-foot-ten hourglass figure, decked out in a sensuous black cocktail dress and five-inch heels. I briefly reminisced about all our exciting adventures during the past eight months that I had known her. "Nope, never."

"Okay, then. Go out there and get your man." She strode to the ornate, hand-carved bedroom door and opened it.

I steeled myself and followed her down the curved marble staircase to a huge, tiled terrace overlooking the Tyrrhenian Sea. Her sons, Dominic and Marco, were standing near the cliff's edge, chatting with her fiancé Aldo, and Tim and Kelly.

Darcy tapped my shoulder, and I turned. "You look fabulous, Jett. Think Kelly will like my dress?"

Sophia turned and laughed. "Are ya kidding? With your figure, ya could stop traffic in that sexy red dress."

She glanced down. "I think it's more a burgundy."

"Close enough." Sophia laughed.

Someone tapped my shoulder. I spun around, and Tim was facing me. I threw my arms around his neck and hugged him. "Thanks for coming. I really need you."

He planted a gentle kiss on my neck. "Why?"

Flustered, I said, "Lots of reasons. You ... always make me feel safe, and I've needed that a lot lately." I didn't let go.

He squeezed me tighter. "Whatever you need, I'm here for you."

I spotted Snake and Mona twenty feet away, watching us. Snake smiled, pointed at Tim's back, and gave me a thumbs-up. He must have had a chat with Tim and confirmed that he was indeed interested in dating me.

Moments later, everyone was ushered into limos for the short trip up the hill to the church. We did an abbreviated run-through of the wedding ceremony so everyone would know their places and the order of events. Then we headed back to Aldo's villa for the rehearsal dinner.

When the group exited the limos, Tim took my hand and pulled me aside. "Before we go in, I'd like to ask you something." He stood close to me, and my heart raced.

"Sure. What is it?" I held my breath, not sure what he would say.

He gazed into my eyes. "Would you like to spend two days with me in Venice after the wedding? I've never been there, and we could enjoy the beautiful city together. What do you think?"

I exhaled and smiled. "I've always wanted to see Venice, and I'd especially love to be there with you."

"Good, then consider it our first date." He leaned in and gave me a kiss that left me breathless.

This boyfriend arrangement was turning out to be way better than I had hoped.

———

Sophia and Aldo's wedding drew royals and nobility from all over Europe—a gathering of the rich and famous, fashionistas, elites, and upper echelon Mafiosi. I didn't know most of the guests, but it didn't matter. Tim made me feel like I was the only person in the ballroom.

I was Sophia's maiden of honor, so Tim and I were seated near the happy couple at the reception table. In the short time I'd known her, Sophia had become a close friend and second mother to me. We lived together for eight months, and I would miss her more than she could imagine.

When the dancing started, Tim took my hand and guided me onto the dance floor. He gently drew me close and looked into my eyes. As we swayed to the slow music, our lips inches apart, I almost forgot to breathe, remembering that hot kiss he gave me outside.

One dance blended into another as our bodies remained glued together like magnets, and our lips brushed ever so lightly, sending jolts of electricity down my spine. I wasn't paying attention to where we were when Tim stopped dancing and encircled me in his arms. A quick peek revealed a shadowy area on the outside terrace.

He leaned in for a gentle kiss that slowly became more and more passionate. With my arms around his neck, I ran my fingers through his thick hair and lost myself in his embrace. My heart pounded so hard I could barely breathe. This man really knew how to kiss, and I looked forward to discovering what else he did well.

While Tim and I enjoyed a romantic and steamy stay in Venice, Darcy and Kelly did the same in Rome, and Sophia and Aldo honeymooned in the Maldives—yep, the same group of islands where Prescott had kept his hideaway, now tied up in numerous court actions.

I was home by mid-week, basking in the afterglow of much needed romance. The morning air was warm under a sunny sky as I gazed at the ocean from a lounge chair on my terrace. Tim was officially my boyfriend now, taking me on romantic dates twice weekly and making me feel special. I glanced down at Pratt and Whitney, who slept at my feet, happy to have me back. Life was good again.

As it turned out, Karin and Hunter had taken a side trip to England to visit her in-laws, and Gwen and Clint enjoyed a brief visit to Switzerland. Not to be outdone, Snake and Mona went on a hot-air balloon tour of several French châteaux in the wine country. Fun was had by all.

My dogs perked up when my cell phone rang. The call was from Sophia.

Her voice was filled with anguish. "Jett, I'm heartbroken and devastated. Aldo had a heart attack on our honeymoon, and I just brought his body home to Italy." Her voice cracked. "The funeral will be in Florence, and everyone can stay with me in the palace."

My heart sank. "Oh, Sophia, I'm so sorry. Would you like me to come right away?"

"Yes, please. I really need ya. My boys are helping with the arrangements and probate. Aldo had no children, and his close relatives have all passed on, so he left me his entire estate: the palace in Florence, his vineyards and wineries, his villa in Sicily, and all his financial holdings. It's a lot to process."

"Is there anything I can do to help?"

"Yeah, there is one thing."

"Anything, Sophia. Just name it."

"After everything's settled, I wanna come home to Valhalla Castle and live with you and the doggies again."

"We would love to have you back."

AFTERWORD

Banyan Isle is a fictitious residential barrier island on the east coast of South Florida in Palm Beach County, north of Singer Island and south of Juno Beach.

The exotic wildlife included in this book are abundant in Florida, and the Everglades covers a vast portion of South Florida.

The Piper Cub flown by Jett and Kerri is a real airplane, and the author owned and flew a Piper Cub Special.

Jett's Timber-shepherd dogs, Pratt and Whitney, are based on the author's dogs who enriched her life for fourteen wonderful years.

ACKNOWLEDGMENTS

First and foremost, I thank my Lord and Savior, Jesus Christ, for my many blessings.

I always appreciate the helpful comments from retired airline captain, aircraft mechanic, and vintage airplane restorer Jeff Rowland, who generously shares his expertise with me. Thank you, Jeff.

My sincere gratitude goes to my treasured critique buddies Fred Lichtenberg and George Bernstein.

Thank you to my beta readers whose observations are always helpful, with special thanks to Robert Metz and Linda Freeman.

Kudos to The Singer Oceanfront Resort and The Islander Grill on Singer Island, Florida. I spend many hours writing my books while enjoying fine cuisine and beverages in the fresh ocean air on The Singer's covered deck and delicious food and fun live music in The Islander Grill inside the Palm Beach Shores Resort.

Many thanks to my trusty editor, Suzanne Berglind, for lending her expertise.

ABOUT THE AUTHOR

S.L. Menear is a retired airline pilot. US Airways hired Sharon in 1980 as their first woman pilot, bypassing the flight engineer position. The men in her new-hire class gave her the nickname, Bombshell. She flew Boeing 727s and 737s, DC-9s, and BAC 1-11 airliners and was promoted to captain in her seventh year.

Before her pilot career, Sharon worked as a water-sports model and then traveled the world as a flight attendant with Pan American World Airways.

Sharon has enjoyed flying vintage airplanes, experimental aircraft, and Third-World fighters. She has flown many of the airplanes in her Samantha Starr Thrillers featuring a woman airline pilot and in her Jettine Jorgensen Mysteries.

Sharon's leisure activities included scuba diving, powered paragliding, snow skiing, surfing, horseback riding, aerobatic flying, sailing, and driving sports cars and motorcycles.

Her beloved Timber-shepherds, Pratt and Whitney, were her faithful companions for fourteen years, and they produced eight darling puppies. While living in Texas, Sharon enjoyed riding her beautiful black and white paint stallion, Chief, who kept her mother's mares happy, fathering several adorable foals.

Sharon lives and writes on an island in South Florida now. She is an active member of Mystery Writers of America, International Thriller Writers, Sisters in Crime, Florida Publishers and Authors Association, and Florida Writers Association.

Sharon can be contacted at…

www.slmenear.com

facebook.com/slmenear
x.com/%20SL%20Menear
instagram.com/slmenear

www.ingramcontent.com/pod-product-compliance
Ingram Content Group UK Ltd.
Pitfield, Milton Keynes, MK11 3LW, UK
UKHW041823110325
456069UK00002B/237